Illicit Magic

Stella Mayweather Series

USA TODAY Bestselling Author

CAMILLA CHAFER

First published in 2011
This paperback edition published in 2023

ISBN: 978-0-9569086-3-6

Visit the author online at www.camillachafer.com

ALSO BY CAMILLA CHAFER

The Complete Stella Mayweather Series

Illicit Magic
Unruly Magic
Devious Magic
Magic Rising
Arcane Magic
Endless Magic

Deadlines Mystery Trilogy

Deadlines
Dead to the World
Dead Ringers

Dedicated, with love, to M, S & G

CHAPTER ONE

For as long as I can remember, I've been alone. I don't mean in the literal sense. I've had people around me, in the foster homes where I grew up, in school, in the places where I've worked; but I've never had a family. I've never had someone to love and I've never had anyone who seemed even remotely concerned about me, never mind love me back. It's not an easy way to live, but I am alive, so it's certainly possible.

I'm Stella Mayweather, a sometimes office temp, a person people seem wary of which taints my enjoyment of life, no matter how much I say it doesn't bother me. I'm twenty-four and have long golden brown hair that falls in gentle waves from a centre parting that just happens naturally. I've got green eyes and, though my face is slightly sweetheart shaped (in a way that I've never thought characteristically pretty) and my nose slim and Roman, I think myself attractive in a look-twice-to-check sort of way. I'm slightly taller than average at five feet five but I've always wished for an inch or two more. What girl hasn't?

Occasionally I click that other people think I'm good looking in a handsome way and that gives me a little rush of pride even though the description isn't just plain pretty; but then I often chide myself that I'd rather be handsome than an oxymoron. I certainly don't flinch when I see myself in the mirror and I try my best not to be vain.

I like the way I look.

I'm just not sure I like the things that I make happen.

Strange things happen near me, to me. Strange things happen to other people too.

I've had a lot of time to think about this what with my many moments of quality alone time. Over the past few months, I've thought more and more that all the weird things I've considered accidents throughout my life are because of me, rather than just a random collection of events.

I am sure these accidental, sometimes frightening, events are why I don't have friends. People are too cautious of me for that, and when I think about it properly, I, of them. It puts a barrier between the rest of the world and me. In my lonelier moments, I've often thought that it's no way to live.

I can't stay in any job too long because of these strange occurrences; people get scared easily of things and people like me, which they don't understand.

Unfortunately being a serial temp means some kind of reputation always precedes me. Thankfully, it always seems to include my being a hard worker first, if not bizarrely clumsy, second. Clumsy! If only! At least I get to switch jobs a lot and by the time people think I'm weird and start avoiding me, I've usually already moved on.

Who would want people to be scared of them? That's what I was thinking when I checked out my reflection in the bathroom mirror at my latest temp job. It was 5.30pm on the dot; the office was starting to close down for the night and I was ready to walk home right after I dragged a comb through my hair. It needed a wash thanks to a day spent filing dusty folders in boxes ready to archive. It wasn't one of my favourite temping jobs but the boredom and dust factor paid extra. Plus, two weeks in and I was already being slung odd looks so I couldn't wait to be out of there and back in my flat.

I pulled a face in the mirror and rolled my eyes. *No, scaring people doesn't give me the rush of power movie megalomaniacs get.* Being labelled a weirdo meant never having a boyfriend, not even a best friend, and tonight, like so many others, was going to be another dull night in front of the television, on my own.

I gave my reflection a wry smile, smoothed my hair with my hands and slipped the comb into my bag. I left the bathroom, letting the door bang slightly behind me, crossed the landing and merged into the line of people snaking their way downstairs before spreading out to cross the lobby, my boot heels echoing as they hit the tiles.

"'Night, Stella." The burly, bald-headed, security guard, Steve, waved a hand at me and I waved back. He'd taken a shine to me and that little interaction might well have been the highlight of my day. Everyone else had ignored me. Even the unpaid intern girl had cast pitying glances at me until she took a cue from the others and started ignoring me too.

I hefted my bag strap so it rested in between my shoulder blades and braced myself for the outside chill as I stepped through the revolving door and out of the shockingly ugly seventies-constructed building.

I exhaled deeply as the cool air outside the building hit me. I flipped up the collar of my coat, dug my leather gloves out from my pockets and wriggled my fingers inside the cosy jersey lining. It might be spring but it was still cold in London and I kept my head dipped down from the wind as I started my walk home. I could imagine my co-workers going home to their families – children, parents, siblings, flatmates – but the pang of envy I'd once felt had all but gone.

Growing up, I lived with foster families, good ones and bad ones. After a while I learned to cope with the ones who didn't seem to want me, just the cash payment. In the last few years of my teens, I never even bothered unpacking because the social workers seemed to arrive ever more quickly to shunt me to a new place.

I think they were all very glad when I turned eighteen and they didn't have to be responsible for me anymore. I couldn't read their minds but I could see the flickers of fear and knew that they had heard stories about me.

I walked past the bus stop, even though it was my route, because the weather was clear and still just light and the foot bus made for a good workout.

At school, years ago now, I had tried very hard not to wish for anything, not to cause a single accident, and occasionally I had friends. But peer pressure and fear of "the weird girl" plus being shuffled around a lot between homes and changing schools too frequently didn't make for an easy childhood.

So here I was, well into adulthood, living in a not particularly nice flat in a not particularly nice part of London, working temporary jobs for an agency who had my virtues down as "clumsy, but at least turns up, types fast and doesn't steal anything." The latter point, I gathered, was the only thing that ensured I got jobs despite the rumours that I was odd. My semi-feeble salary went, mostly to renting the not particularly nice flat, which was really a euphemism for "grubby, overpriced studio for people out of choices,"

And here, again, not quite soon enough for my liking, was my walk home, after another day of keeping my head down. It was all basic stuff wherever I worked; I filed, made tea, booked people in, made boring phone calls and any other menial task the regular workers felt was too beneath them. In a rare moment of extravagance, I bought a little, red, digital music player so I could listen to music or audio books during the most boring jobs, like my current one archiving files; and mostly felt glad to be left alone to get through the daily nine to five.

Every so often, an incident that couldn't be reasonably explained away happened and then I'd be shuffled off to another post for a few days or weeks.

Striding onward towards home, I thought back to last autumn. I had managed an entire two months on a reasonable weekly rate at an office supply firm which only ended because my pot-bellied, sweaty boss, Albert, had put his hand on my thigh, a little too far up, a little too intentionally and far too forcefully, at the Christmas bash. My concentration was destroyed and a fully loaded bookshelf, previously bolted to the floor, uprooted itself and landed on him, missing me by a hair's breadth. No one could work out how it, the bookshelf, had shaken itself from its bolts. I later heard the odious Albert was in hospital for quite a while.

I would have felt mildly sorry for him, guilty even, because I'd probably *nudged* that bookshelf out of its position – I had been wishing for some way to get his clammy paws off me – but he tried to shirk paying the agency my fee and it had taken them some time to wangle the money out of him. It wasn't my favourite Christmas, out of a whole bunch of mediocre Christmases.

This had all been gleaned from my loose-mouthed manager at the temping agency in Charing Cross while she assessed me in the New Year with her unwavering eyes and contemplated whether she agreed I was as weird as her co-workers thought. Evidently, she didn't mind as she kept sending me work and I kept turning up and she kept getting her commission. That her co-workers had called me a witch was something she was polite enough to keep to herself. I had glimpsed it on an email that sat on her computer when she turned away to pick up a printout with the details of my latest assignment.

It wasn't the first time I'd had the word "witch" hurled at me, but it was starting to rattle me, especially given the spate of recent murders.

So far, my lonely life was working out, sort of, until today. Everything was boringly normal.

Somehow the universe had lost the memo that it was almost summer and through the course of the day, the sky had turned from pale cloudy blue to a dull sludgy grey wetting the air with the afternoon rainfall. The last of daylight had just about slunk away, leaving dusk licking at the fringes of my solitary little world. I wished I didn't have to trudge home but I got on with it one foot after the other, little steps that took me closer to the not particularly nice flat and a microwave dinner that I'd eat on the sofa in front of the TV.

That was my plan until I was halfway home. It was a simple plan, a boring plan, but it was mine.

Until all hell broke loose.

Every step away from the monstrous architecture of my current office block took me further from the safety of bustling buildings and the broad-windowed coffee shops and delis that lived on every corner. Just these few miles alone housed hundreds of thousands of people every day before they dispersed like homing pigeons into the suburbs.

It had taken me only twenty minutes to leave the homeward-bound crowd behind as I plodded further north, every footstep taking me into the quieter surroundings of London's residential streets. With my shoulders hunched up and my eyes on the pavement, I took little notice of people around me as I slipped past them. As usual they were merely on the periphery of my consciousness; faceless people that were barely worth acknowledging as I walked on auto-pilot through these familiar streets. It was safer for them that way. Safer for me too.

The noise that jolted my brain awake from its post-work stupor wasn't anything unusual, but it was... out of place. A single footfall, a heavy one, then there was a shuffle and a stomp of feet. Most impressive was the quiet that surrounded that first stomp. It felt – and I struggled to put the thought together coherently – *the quiet felt wrong.*

I blinked and felt the muscles in my face twitch as I went on alert. I hadn't even noticed that the street noise I'd been ignoring so intently had slipped away entirely. I strained to hear what I was missing. No dogs barked, no doors opened or closed, and the hum of engines seemed to have stopped in time.

I barely slowed my pace but my body and brain were on alert. I tipped my chin upwards, blinking at the wet air and wrinkling my nose to sniff the silent breeze, not sure what I should be looking for but knowing that my senses were telling me to be wary.

Like most city-dwellers, I'd perfected my mental blinkers so I could ignore the constant humdrum of activity that occurred all around me in the capital. So far, my thoughts on my walk home had been as mundane as they could possibly be; *what I needed to add to the grocery list, what show might be on my elderly TV later, should I buy some thicker tights for the cold spring, and why had I worn a skirt when it wasn't quite warm enough yet?* Those fleeting thoughts were safe, familiar, unlike the strange awareness of activity that I felt permeating the air now. I'd been focused on the mundane trivialities of my life and neglected to take note of what was going on around me. I hoped I wouldn't pay for that mistake.

I didn't know what evil smelled like, if it could even have a scent, but I was sure I could feel menace in the air. It was thick and heavy, like leftover cigarette smoke clinging to day-old clothes and it was reaching towards me. Acrid and poisonous, more so than the usual fuel-scented city smog that drifted across the pavement at this time of day, mixed with the hour-old rain... A cold chill dashed down my spine and I shivered.

Slowing just a pace or so, I casually glanced over my shoulder, twitching my head from side to side so I could toss my hair out of my collar like that was all I meant to do. From the corners of my eyes, I scanned the road but I didn't see anything so I kept on my way purposefully, my ears primed for any sound, my muscles on alert though I couldn't fathom why.

They say that you should trust your sixth sense. Mine never teased.

Stomp.

There it was again.

My hearing spiked as I tried to zone in on the direction of that heavy footfall. I didn't have to wait long. Another followed it; then there was the faintest sound of more footsteps falling in to join the first. It was like they had just appeared, footsteps falling from nowhere. But what shook me was that they were all beating down on the pavement exactly in time. Footsteps in London – at the tail end of rush hour as everyone packed up and jostled to get home on crammed buses, the stifling tube or, like me, walking home if the distance was close enough to allow it – was hardly unusual but the staccato *stomp, stomp, stomp* of their regimented treads made my muscles tighten in fear. It was too weird to be coincidence.

I wanted to run.

Instead I stepped up my pace. After a moment the footsteps quickened with me.

I exhaled one long breath that plumed in the air in front of me before disappearing in the wet breeze. Somewhere behind me I heard a grunt, an ugly guttural sound. I couldn't be sure of the distance but it wasn't nearly far enough away for my liking.

If I hadn't been certain before, I was now. I was being followed.

Think, I told myself. *What would some kick-ass girl do? She'd run,* I thought, surprising myself. No question about it. Kick-ass heroines got themselves killed. Practical ones ran. I was nothing if not practical.

I was nearly at the intersection of the main road. Seeing an opportunity to shake off my pursuers I banked quickly to the left, around the side of a twenty-four-hour Booze Bin with big posters in the window announcing cheap wine on a two-for-one deal for Friday nights. I stumbled past the crowd of teens huddled near the doorway, hoods pulled up to hide their pasty faces as they clinked their little bottles of illicit alco-pops. One leaned in to light a cigarette from the barely glowing embers of his friend's and puffed a nasty little cloud of smoke in my face. I glared at him and he shrunk back.

Okay, so maybe I was passively-aggressively kick-ass but at least I could scare a teenybopper successfully.

A quick scan ahead confirmed that, other than that little group, the street was empty of people. I darted forward trying to put as much distance between the footsteps and me as I could. I hadn't power-walked further than fifty feet before I realised that the footsteps had – and my heart sank a little – followed me. I hardly dared spare the time to look behind me as my power-walk turned into a sprint, my leather bag on its long strap banging uncomfortably against my hip as the contents slid around. For the third time today, I cursed this morning's decision to wear a skirt, and, for good measure, threw in regret for my long leather boots that were really no match for a good pair of running shoes.

I jogged forward, not quite in a run, and another turning came up. I threw myself around the corner and as fast as I could, dashed full throttle into the nearest shaded driveway.

Pinching my nose between my gloved fingers, I stifled a sneeze as I shrank back against the overgrown hedge, quickly circling my head to assess my surroundings. I was in the garden of a Victorian house with a big bay window that had a bad case of peeling paint. The ledge, like the rest of the house, looked rotten and decayed in the shadows of the rolling dusk. The lights were off and a curtain hung limply, not quite on every hook and a little too short, to one side like it was broken and forgotten. It didn't quite screen the shadowy room.

It must have been lovely once, before neglect had taken over, and I felt sad that it had been unloved. Being somewhat of a TV property show aficionado, I couldn't help thinking that the add-on eighties porch sagging against the shadow of the street lamp was tantamount to housing abuse. However, I was thankful that I could conceal myself behind the thick overgrown privet. As I huddled in the right angle between the street and the nearest neighbour. I bent forward to rest my hands on my thighs and gasped air into my heaving lungs after the sudden sprint.

It was only scant seconds before I heard the footsteps nearby. They had either seen me come about the corner, or guessed that I had. My heart thumped inside my chest. So much for shaking them off.

The footsteps stopped somewhere in the street but I couldn't gauge how far away even though I could hear them stamp a little as the air took on a glacial chill. The hedge was too dense to see out, or in, and without looking I couldn't tell if they were looking towards my hiding place or away towards the main road. I hoped they would head that way, figuring I would probably seek a busy place and lights just like lone women were always told to do when they were afraid. Lights meant safety. *Crap. I was definitely in the wrong place.*

Sharp, murmured voices passed me on the wind. I couldn't make out what they were saying but there was the sound of confusion and dissent; then a barked order calmed them. I caught the sole word "silence" from a low voice as it hissed past me. The footsteps shuffled and stamped again but no one uttered a word. It was like they were all listening for me. I felt like a fox, terrified and cornered, knowing that the beagles were just behind me, waiting to catch my scent.

Above me I could just see the first quarter of the moon breaking in the sky, casting a dim glow over the city. My jacket was a dark padded cord, good for blending in with both the hedge and low light. My breath was catching like little puffs of cloud in the air so I pulled up my cheap, striped scarf and covered my mouth to keep the plumes from straying to where they could be seen.

Without moving the rest of my body, I strained my head towards my pursuers, the scarf tightening about my neck until I tugged it loose again. I tried to count how many footsteps I could hear as they shuffled, fanned out and regrouped.

With only my pounding heartbeat for company I waited for what seemed like eternity. I tried to count Mississippi's to gauge the time but my mind stumbled over the count and I threw the thought away. I waited for seconds, minutes, hours for them to rush past me, or at least turn and stamp a different way, hoping miserably that they really hadn't seen me dart into this street.

Finally I couldn't hear a thing but the blood rushing in my ears. *Had I made it up? Was I really paranoid enough to think someone would bother following me? Probably. Possibly.* It wasn't the first time I'd been extra cautious, but it was the first time since the news has been full of murder. I shivered and tried to shake away the icy fear.

Edging my way across the privet, the leather of my long boots brushing against each other as I sidestepped, my toes scuffed against the scrub of garden. Fronds of hedge needled my back through my winter coat as I brushed by and fresh drops of dew slid uncomfortably past my scarf and inside my collar.

With my mouth set in a firm, grim line, clamped so tightly shut I was close to grinding my teeth, I poked my head forward, mere millimetres from the hedge but enough to see a gloved hand shoot towards me and grab my coat, the fingers clawing at my shoulder to snatch a handful of material and drag me into the open. A gasp escaped me. *How had they gotten so close without me realising?* Another hand, yellowed at the fingertips and reeking of tobacco, reached for my neck.

A gruff male voice snarled, "Gotcha!"

I shrieked and my whole body went rigid as I closed my eyes tightly. The air went thick and heavy around me, the cold momentarily disappeared and the blood in my veins surged as electricity crackled through my body. For the merest second all the low light and dull sounds of the city disappeared as the power rushing through me overwhelmed and took possession of me.

With the hand at my neck and the fear pumping alongside the electricity, I thought I would die in this moment, but when I opened my eyes again I was on the other side of the street, looking at my attacker grasping at the air where a second ago my neck had been. I saw his fist punch savagely through the air where my jaw should have been. If I had still been there, he would have smashed it for sure.

I felt dizzy and willed myself not to faint. The last of the shriek ebbed in my throat as I realised that I had barely focused on the task but had ended up exactly where I thought I should be when I'd glimpsed that section of empty street. Perhaps my strange gift (I never could decide what I should call it) only worked properly when I was terrified. Moving through space wasn't something I had even been able to control before. And right now, I wasn't afraid to admit that I was absolutely, gut-wrenchingly, terrified.

As I stood there gaping, there was a shout and a cry of anger. A huddle of stocky beings had fanned out behind my attacker and they seemed to multiply by the second. They were searching for me, their prize, such as I apparently was. There must have been a dozen or so, broad shoulders clad in identical black wool coats, zipped to the chin like workmen. Woollen hats were drawn close over their foreheads and rested just above their eyes. I could see nothing more than thin, snarled mouths and square chins. One of them had smeared black paint across his cheeks and I couldn't help thinking that he looked like he was at war.

I had never known such anger and it was all aimed at me.

I shouldn't have watched them for those few seconds, shouldn't have drunk in their darkness, because it took them a fraction less time to spot me. A cry rang out. It echoed through the gang, passing from one to another like a rallying yell until the cacophony of anger and disgust reached me.

Any woman would be afraid of a gang of men chasing her. How many times had I heard the women at work in my various temping jobs recently warning each other to "walk straight home" and "don't take short cuts" or "don't be afraid to knock on a door with a light on if you think you're being followed". They reminded each other with a vague hint of mawkish glee that horrible things could happen and weren't they good about being proactive and warning each other? "Don't be afraid to spring for a taxi," they said, "better safe than sorry, better than ending up dead, or worse". How hollow their words sounded to me. No one seemed to ever think to suggest that maybe, just maybe, someone should be warding killers off, rather than offering advice to their potential victims.

Of course, I was afraid; my whole body was afraid, but not of a beating, or losing my wallet, or of rape – though I didn't want any of those things to happen to me. What I was afraid of was worse because I was sure now that there could only be one thing that had drawn them to me, instead of the millions of other women in the city. The suspicion nagged at me but I didn't have time to fully think it through as their words, like a chorus, hung in the air between us and sent a shiver down my spine. My pursuers confirmed my worst thoughts.

"The witch," they hummed as one, spitting the words onto the wet air to float towards me. "Catch the witch! Burn the witch! *Burn her*!"

The men stepped off the pavement as one and swarmed towards me. The man who had done his best to smash my jaw didn't move, though he was poised to spring; and it was his solid glare that frightened me the most. He was capable of unspeakable things I was sure.

The fear that had been rising in me was absolutely, utterly justified. I didn't need to think about it. I spun on my heel and ran as fast as I could, my shoulder bag whacking me painfully on the hip in the same place it had struck before as I hurtled away from the gang. I would bruise, but it hardly seemed to matter. That was by far the lesser of the evils that threatened me now.

I would be lucky if a bruise from my bag was all I escaped with.

Now I knew them for what they were – witch hunters, murderers, my enemy – my life depended on my escape.

CHAPTER TWO

I was sprinting for all the world like the hounds of hell were on my tail, ruing the day I decided to buy this stupid bag. *Why couldn't I have gotten a neat little rucksack?* Still, the bruises of my own bag's making would surely be preferable to whatever this crazy gang had in mind, which I was sure it wouldn't be pleasant. What could possibly be nice about a single woman being chased down by a dozen men who were drawn solely to her magic? From the second the hand grabbed for my throat, I knew for certain that I was in far more serious danger than a run-of-the-mill kidnapping.

When I opened my eyes and found myself across the street, I could hardly believe that, for once, I had actually done what I meant to do. I'd accidentally moved myself in the past by blinking one minute and then opening my eyes to find myself yards away. For a long time while growing up, I thought I was going loopy. There was the week I caught a cold when I was nineteen and every time I sneezed, I zapped – for lack of a better word – myself somewhere else, somewhere never too far, but far enough that I had to wear day clothes, including shoes, to bed for a week, house keys stuffed in my pocket, lest I sneeze, vanish and pop outside by accident.

After that episode, I certainly didn't need any more persuasion that I was different from everyone else. Very different. If only I knew what the hell it was all about and why it was happening to me. I didn't need to be convinced to run; I was already pounding the pavement.

"The witch," they hummed as one behind my fleeting back. "Catch the witch! Burn the witch! Burrrrrn her!"

I was desperate to put as much space as possible between us as fast as I could. My feet thundered across the pavement in the strangely empty street. I dashed past houses, lights on, the blur of movement showing a montage of people moving past windows, serving dinner, greeting their loved ones, leaning forward to change the TV station. Normal family life that was oblivious to my pursuers and me. I wanted so badly to be inside these safe, warm homes that my heart ached as much from fear as from need.

My lungs, not yet recovered from the previous sprint, were starting to burn. I took the corner to my right, leapt into the road with barely a glance in either direction, and darted between a car and a red bus that was just pulling out. I earned myself a hoot of the horn from the driver, his angry fist shaking as I turned my back and stumbled across the gutter onto the pavement, slipping on the wet kerb. I put my hands out to stop my fall and caught my sleeve on the jagged edge of the vandalised bus shelter, its window smashed the third time in as many weeks. I wrenched my arm free and cursed as the fabric tore. I righted myself and sprinted on.

The bus pulled out. Behind me a voice shrieked and I heard the impact of something large hitting the bus' bumper and bouncing with a dull thud onto the road. It sounded awfully like a person but I didn't dare falter for a second to look backwards to see if the person was all right. There hadn't been any passengers left at the bus stop so I hoped it was the man who had stared at me with such hatred.

I recognised my attackers for what they were. I'd seen the news, the headlines of the newspapers, and heard about the women. The thought of it made me shiver: all were found burned alive, their bodies twisted in agony long before their final moments of death. Their corpses charred and all but unrecognisable, yet bizarrely similar no matter when or where they were found. They had all been bound to wooden stakes which, laced with accelerants, had been torched.

The newspapers were in their heyday. Nothing thrilled a paper better than a string of vile unsolved crimes; the very words "serial killer" sent them into overdrive. They quoted "official sources", which said there was more than one suspect, possibly a gang of killers lurking to abduct women to their fiery deaths.

No wonder the women at work were all concerned for each other. I didn't give myself the indulgence of wondering if they were at all concerned about me. I doubted they would give a damn unless...

I couldn't help the feeling that I was going to be next.

They would probably grimace at work when they

heard about my death. Maybe they would pretend to have been my friends as well as co-workers, purely for the TV time. I pushed on, the fear bubbling in my stomach. *Run!* my brain screamed.

As I took the next left and sprinted forward, racing across the road, I wished I was somewhere more public. I knew feinting right would take me into a smaller, safer residential street where I knew a shortcut across a small children's play park that sat incongruously in a partially fenced roundabout. It would get me home quicker but it would also take me away from lights and, crucially, people. *Witnesses.* There was no time to think. I dashed right and ran full pelt, slowing to slip through the gates, bypassing the swings that were swaying by themselves on creaking chainlinks and slung myself forwards into an alley that divided the houses and led closer to my street.

I couldn't hear any footsteps behind me so I slowed just barely enough to allow me to glance over my shoulder without tripping in the poor light and landing on goodness-knows-what in the alley.

My forehead knitted into a frown as I strained to hear any sound. No one was following me. At last I had a chance to gasp for breath and fill my lungs with air as I reined myself into a fast walk. I could easily have brushed the chase aside as a nasty coincidence or a random attack but that nagging sixth sense fizzling in my nerves warned me to continue to be wary and I kept up the steady jog that would carry me home.

As I came out of the alley, instead of taking the pavement, I slipped through a crack in the fence into a corner garden and then proceeded through front gardens, hopping over small dividing fences until I could hang back in someone else's drive, a few houses diagonally away from mine. The lights were off in this house and there was no car; I vaguely recalled the man who lived here worked away often, so I doubted anyone was going to step out and ask me what I was doing loitering in the shadow of their house.

When something brushed against my leg, I nearly screamed but looking down, saw that it was just a black cat with a single white front paw that had chosen this moment as the perfect time to terrorise me. I stooped to scratch it between the ears as I kept my eyes on my front porch. From my low vantage point, I couldn't see much, but at least it made me temporarily invisible. The cat purred and nuzzled at my wrist, twisting around my ankles and arching its back, so I scratched it there too until it got bored and stalked away through a narrow gap in the fence.

I waited, trying to decide if my house was being observed by anyone other than me but, after a few minutes, I decided it wasn't and that I should go inside or risk standing outside, getting soaked now that the wet air had morphed to grey drizzle. My coat was ripped and my hair started to plaster itself to my forehead and I could feel sweaty damp patches sticking to my skin. *What a catch.*

"Grow some backbone," I muttered to myself, my voice catching in the cold as I examined the sleeve sadly. I'd only owned the jacket since last autumn and had gotten it on sale for a snip. *Damn. Maybe I could fix it later, sew on a new button to cover the rip or give it some kind of nifty patch.* Anything so I wouldn't have to eat into my savings to buy another coat.

I fished the key from the inner pocket of my bag

and palmed it, the jagged edge poking out from between my clenched fingers. It wasn't much of a weapon. Perhaps I should get something else to keep about me, but I couldn't think of anything as legal and effective as a baseball bat, only smaller. It's all very well outlawing weapons but when you are about to be set upon by a group of beefy, potential serial killers, it's small comfort to have a Yale key, a wing and a prayer as your only protection.

I huffed in contempt and darted a glance to the left, then right, before jogging across the road and along the narrow, chequered tile path, made ugly with weeds in their last throes of life. I slid my key into the lock and twisted right once, closing the door quickly behind me, ensuring the Yale lock had snapped shut. Not for the first time I wished the owner would spring for a deadbolt and a more substantial door.

Home was a very euphemistic way of describing the unremarkable terrace where I had been living for the past two years. The owner, my landlady, Mrs Kemp, had the whole ground floor. The small hallway of what had once been a family home had been portioned off so there was the door that led into her flat and then the staircase. It was now boxed in lest any tenant, God forbid, decided to spy on Mrs Kemp and upload pictures to Grannies Uncovered.

Upstairs were two flats – one mine – that had been carved out of the former bedrooms on the first floor. A second staircase led to another flat nestled in the eaves. Mrs Kemp and her long-dead husband bought the house in the sixties, so she told me on the days when she wasn't whining, and raised a family who now lived out of the city and barely visited. ("Good-for-nothings who won't see a penny of my will," was Mrs Kemp's catchphrase. Privately, I thought they were rather sensible.)

The old woman turned the second floor, which her arthritic legs couldn't reach, into an income provider for her dotage. It was a cramped set-up, not particular well kept outside or in, but affordable for Zone 1 and easy to reach the tube or walk to work on the occasions that I found somewhere closeby to temp. That's where the perks ended.

The front door had a large, glazed panel to let in the light but even though it was sandblasted for privacy, I didn't dare linger once I grabbed the mail that had been put on a shelf for me. I bounded up the stairs and, after stopping for a moment to examine if the lock had been tampered with – it hadn't, used the second key to let myself through the door. It would need more than one coat of paint to disguise that it was worthless plywood. Given the lack of consideration regarding security, I was constantly surprised that none of the flats had been burgled. Maybe it was pure luck that the house looked like crap on the outside and repelled burglars.

I thumped the door shut and leaned against it, bracing myself for Mrs Kemp's bang on the ceiling – there it was, predictable as ever. Grateful to be inside my tiny flat, my heart still hammering, the awful fear still swam through every inch of my veins, though I felt a lot happier now that I was enclosed in familiar space. It might not be a castle but at least it was my home. A tear slipped down my cheek in relief and I brushed it away with the back of my hand.

After a succession of ill-fated flat shares and grimy, overpriced bedsits with communal – and even grimier – bathrooms, having my own place at a price I could afford was something for which I was persistently grateful. It was the only reason why I hadn't moved on. I would have to have a good long think about that, now that security might be a problem.

I moved my head forty-five degrees to the side and let my ear press against the sheets of laminated wood. I tried not to breathe. There were no sounds from the other side of the door. Slowly, I rolled my head a little more until my eye was level with the peephole, my forehead gradually becoming indented with the peeling paint job on the thin door. The hall lamp, operated by a sensor, was still on and the hall seemed clear. The two other flat doors were shut but I couldn't hear familiar sounds of footsteps or TVs through our thin, shared walls. My nearer neighbours were not home yet and paranoia was apparently becoming my middle name.

I exhaled, relief replacing fear, and stumbled away from the door, dropping my shoulder bag on the floor next to the sofa, tossing my mail on the little wooden table that I salvaged from a skip one night, and made use of after cleaning it up. I shrugged my coat off and dumped it on top of the envelopes. It landed in an untidy heap and I winced again at the sight of the rip. I tossed my gloves on top and pushed my hair away from my face.

My flat was small, just like my unspectacular wages. Even calling it a flat was spinning out its size as something better than it was. In reality, it was one large room with enough space to squash in a bed-slash-sofa with arms so worn that the colour had all but gone in those spots. Across the room there was a TV that dated from the late eighties – requiring a thump every time the picture went – almost museum-worthy and, like everything else in the flat, in need of replacement.

It was dark inside but I left the lights off as I entered the kitchen. The room was far too optimistically named and resembled a slightly over-sized cupboard (which it probably had been once), with a tiny worktop, a microwave, mini-fridge and sink. There was no oven or washing machine, much less a window. The other cupboard held the bathroom which had just enough space for a toilet, sink and shower cubicle. Though it always smelled damp, I was just thankful that I didn't have to share it with other people and their sketchy interpretations of personal hygiene.

The only light came in through a broad bay window in the main room and it cast shadows over my past-it furniture. The bay looked out over the street and had the unfortunate position of being right next to a bus stop, so the net curtains, sprinkled with mildew at the hems from where the creeping black fungus, which frequently appeared around the windows contacted them in spots, were a necessary evil. I left the curtains open. *Smart move*, I told myself. That way, anyone who happened by the house wouldn't know whether I was in or out.

I flipped on the kettle and rested my lower back against the countertop as I looked out onto the main room. Thankfully, due to my lack of belongings, I never needed much space. I had always travelled light after being shunted from foster home to foster home and never had the inclination to hoard, like some people who desperately try to put down roots. I guess I've just never been materialistic because stuff doesn't matter that much to me.

As such, my few possessions included a cluster of clothes hanging on a rail: a basic combination of smart casual that I could wear to work, two pairs of shoes and a pair of boots (on my feet). A little silver box contained some earrings and bits, and there were a half dozen books stacked by the door that I bought at the charity shop and returned when read because it was cheaper than clocking up a library fine every time I forgot to return them. Aside from two sheets, two duvet sets (one on, one tucked away) and a couple of plates, mugs, bowls and cutlery, I owned nothing else in the world.

The carpet was threadbare and my landlady had never been one for kicking the boiler up to a decent temperature so I kept my boots on to keep my feet warm. I pressed the button on the television set and gave it a thump on top so that the green picture hazed into colour. The news was on so I went back into the kitchenette as the kettle clicked off and paid no attention to the news anchor droning on behind me while I dunked my teabag in the mug and added the boiling water.

As I sat down, my mug in one hand so I could pull the duvet from the back of the sofa over my knees, my head suddenly snapped up and I leaned forward, listening intently to the last of the news broadcast.

"... was found burned on a playing field in Birmingham. Her body was bound to a stake amidst what appeared to be a bonfire and she appeared to have been..." The news anchor swallowed, repulsion etched on his face, then looked straight at the camera, and, in an even voice, enunciated carefully, "burned alive. A source revealed that red paint near the body spelled out 'burn the witches'."

I gulped but couldn't turn away from the smouldering scene captured by the camera. The body was gone, I assumed hidden in a police tent almost out of view, but the bonfire's ashes, her ashes, still sent smoke spiralling up. I wanted to close my eyes so I didn't have to see where this woman died. The news anchor continued with a voice-over. "The crime scene resembled those in Leeds, Manchester, Harrogate, Birmingham, Grimsby and London where several other women have been found burned to death. The women are not thought to have been connected in anyway. Police say they are considering the idea that a serial killer, or killers, are at large and advise women to be vigilant."

I sipped the too hot tea and contemplated what the newsman had said. Of course, it wasn't new. The newspapers had been full of grisly details for the past few weeks. They tossed theories around like the bodies piling up – first one, then two, then several within a few weeks – were the best thing to have happened to them. The current theory was a team of serial killers, roaming the country intent on dispatching women to the next world at random. Every paper was whipped into a frenzy and ruminating on who could possibly do such foul and evil things.

But, women burned as witches all over the country? I shuddered. It was a new one and too horrible to contemplate. We were in the twenty-first century! *There was no such thing as witches,* I thought, not quite convincing myself. The killers had to be crazy, I decided as I sipped my tea and wriggled my toes to get some feeling back.

Thankfully, the news anchor had segued to his colleague who had moved impassively on to another story about fraud in a supermarket chain. As she was concluding the story, she pressed her hand to her ear, listened for a moment and spluttered, "Breaking news. A source has passed us a video purporting to be from the people responsible for the so-called 'witch-burning' murders. We're bringing that tape to you now."

The TV screen flickered again and the picture zigzagged. "Work, damn you," I snapped as I thumped the top impatiently. The screen went black then slowly a face swam into view. I sank back on the edge of the sofa bed.

The man was perfectly non-descript. White face, a little too pale, like he didn't spend much time outdoors, brown eyes, short brown hair and a neatly clipped beard. He wore a black suit and thin blue tie and held a big book in his hands. He seemed utterly relaxed where he sat in a large, leather wing chair against a wall papered in taupe stripes. He could have been a professor or a TV grandfather reading a story. His voice, a rich baritone, was the only remarkable thing about him as he began to speak. "We, the Brotherhood, claim responsibility for killing the witches. For centuries, our forefathers have ignored these wicked beings but the time has come to cleanse our world of these..." Here he looked directly at the camera and waved a pointed finger as he spat out the words, his mouth twisted in disgust, "Monsters. They who try to dazzle us with their magic, who claim to be good women, why, they are nothing more than witches! They are evil incarnate!"

The man swam out of view and new pictures flickered onto the screen. But it wasn't the television reception fading again; it was image after image of silent women writhing amidst flames. Someone had filmed them as they burned. I pushed my hand into my mouth to stifle my screams for them.

"We have hunted the witches in France, Germany, Italy, Bulgaria, Spain, Norway, Russia and England," continued the man, his voice narrating the horrendous scenes. "We will find every witch and we will not rest until every last one of them has burned and their blight driven from this earth. We are the Brotherhood and we have spoken."

The video abruptly ended and the camera panned back to the horrified news anchor. Her mouth opened and closed like a dying fish before she recovered her composure. "We have just seen a video purporting to be from the ... Brotherhood, who claim responsibility for the murder of ... witches ... of women, throughout Europe." She collected herself quickly, ending in an even tone, "We will bring you more news as developments arise."

I reached for the remote and switched the channel over. The next station was just finishing the same clip. And the next station, and the one after that and by then, I had run out of TV stations. *Had all the cable stations just relayed the same message across the country too? Did every viewer have to see those images of the women dying so brutally?*

When a fist pounded on my door, I jumped so high that hot tea slopped over the edges of the mug and splashed on my fingers. I had to bite my tongue to keep from screaming out loud more from fear than from being scalded.

I was tense with fear as I got up. I was sure no one else was in the building other than old Mrs. Kemp and she never came upstairs, so whoever was at the door wasn't someone known to me. I didn't need to look around to know there was no way out of the flat other than the door by which I had entered.

I wished I had an arsenal that I could draw on to protect myself or some kick-ass ninja skills. I wanted to zap my way out of there but I had to remind myself it wasn't an exact art and I would probably materialise somewhere I didn't want to be, like in the arms of a gang who wanted to burn me to death. *Not an option.*

Instead, I slipped towards the kitchen as lightly as I could, trying not to make the floorboards squeak. I snatched a dinner knife from the drawer and with this pathetic little weapon in my hand, I crept towards the door.

CHAPTER THREE

With the handle of the little knife in the palm of my hand, the blade cold against my fingers, I snuck towards the thin, front door and pressed my eye against the peephole.

A woman stood on the other side of the door. I peered at her. Boyish, short hair flicked up at the front but not quite long enough in back to curl over the Mandarin collar of her blue jacket, framed an elegant face. She didn't look like one of my stocky pursuers, and neither of my neighbours had moved recently, so she wasn't a new resident. Still, not recognising her, I regarded her with suspicion. *Besides, how had she gotten in without a key?*

She leaned forward, her shoulders and torso in a perfect line, her head inclined to one side and peered at the peephole. She blinked and her whole body seemed to shimmer out of focus. "Stella?" she called softly.

I paused before answering her. A quick scan along the hallway from my blinkered position behind two inches of plywood seemed to confirm that no one else was there. "Yes?" I whispered.

"I'm here to help you." The woman pursed her lips and nodded once as if that confirmed everything.

"Who are you?"

"Étoile," she answered, emphasising the two syllables, *eh-twall.* Softly, but still cajoling, she whispered, "Will you let me in? I need to talk to you." She had an accent that I couldn't place, clipped with a slight twang. Not English, though certainly an English-speaking country. American.

"No." *Might as well keep it simple*, I decided.

The woman who called herself Étoile sighed. I saw her roll her eyes in a particularly petulant fashion. She straightened her back until she was upright again and shrugged with a roll of her shoulders like she was utterly exasperated. Then she vanished leaving nothing but air and an empty hallway.

"Holy shit!" I breathed.

"Not exactly holy," said an amused voice behind me as I spun around, the pathetic little knife held close to my hip while my body tensed, ready to jab in an instant. I knew it wouldn't do much but it might be enough to give me a few seconds to dash out the door. *Or I could just run now.* I pondered my options. Neither were winners. She'd flatten me. And even if I escaped, I'd be outside. Where they were.

"How did you do that?" I hissed at the woman who, just a moment ago, had been standing in the hall before evaporating and now was just feet away inside my flat. Any normal person wouldn't have believed it, but then, I wasn't a normal person and I didn't know if it was a relief or a new worry that we seemed to have the same peculiar quirk in common.

She, Étoile, was tall, a few inches taller than I, with black hair cut very short. Now that nothing stood between us, I could see she had wide green eyes in a narrow face, slightly jutting cheekbones, and a jaw that was just this side of masculine. She had the creamiest skin I had ever seen. She was dressed in a long blue coat that reached to her knees; tiny blossoms in pink and green in a Chinese pattern adorned it. She had buttoned the coat the full length, right up to the Mandarin collar. Even to my unfashionable eyes, it looked expensive. Underneath, she wore darker blue trousers and smart boots with a square heel in a similar shade. She was beautiful and unusual, the type of woman who made heads turn because she was at once elegant and unique, even if she wasn't pretty, as such. *She didn't look like a serial killer. Always good news, but then, who can tell? Victims almost never could until they'd had it.*

She shrugged as if the answer should have been obvious and a smile flickered on the corners of her mouth. I already knew the answer but I still gasped when, with a flick of her eyebrows, she said, "The same way you do."

I was more surprised when I realised she sounded completely and utterly bored. Zapping, as I thought of it, had always completely freaked me out.

"How do you know what I do?" I inquired, not sure if my question had just acknowledged that sure, what the hell, I could vanish and reappear too. Not that it was something I advertised. Or, for that matter, even knew how I managed to do it.

"We've been watching you." Étoile answered without a lot of interest as she turned away from me, eyes briefly glancing at my knife. She turned the full three hundred and sixty degrees to cast her eyes around my shabby little flat. She wrinkled her nose with obvious displeasure as she dragged the words out. "You actually live here?"

"My real place has the builders in," I replied as sarcastically as I could manage.

"We have to get you out of here."

"Tell me about it." Good to see she was at least on the same wavelength when it came to my dire living conditions.

"No, I mean tonight." Étoile cocked her head to one side as if she were listening to something far away before her head inclined towards the television. She stepped closer to it and her mouth opened a little bit as the newsreader recapped the evening's stories. She uttered a soft moan of sadness. The TV sizzled, snapped off and I sighed. *Great, just when I was getting curious with the news. How would I find out what else was happening now?* Trust my TV to burn out at the least appropriate moment. I'd only just settled on the idea that my pursuers tonight might be the same as the – what had they called themselves? – the Brotherhood and now I wouldn't be able to find out anything more.

Étoile took a step further into my living space and I followed her gaze as she examined the shabbiness, the lack of personality, the lack of... anything. "We need to get you somewhere safe," she said, at last.

"Who's we? I'm not going anywhere." I ignored her assumption that there was more than one person who had a say in what was going on.

"We are your friends and we want to protect you. It's not safe for you here anymore. Not since the Brotherhood are actively hunting our kind down."

Étoile spat the words out with distaste and turned to focus on me again. "We'll take you somewhere we can protect you, and we'll look after you."

"What if I don't want to go? I've known you for, oh, a New York minute, and you want me to swan off with you who knows where? I don't think so." I shook my head in defiance. I was used to doing things my way, being totally self-sufficient and looking out only for myself. *Not like that was getting me anywhere*, nagged a little voice at the edge of my mind.

"I suppose a fiery death sounds better?" Étoile raised an eyebrow and I had the fleeting thought that I wished I could do that. It was just plain cool, the opposite of me. She nodded at the TV and the black and white snow the picture had settled on.

I shook the thought from my head. "Not much."

"Then you need to trust me." Étoile scanned the room again, this time looking for something specific and her eyes alighted on my old sports bag. She grabbed it and tossed it on the sofa bed. "Pack whatever you need. We'll have to leave the rest. I imagine you'll get over it." She tilted her head again as if she were listening for something and not liking whatever she heard or didn't hear, but her voice was urgent. "And, hurry."

"I'm not going anywhere." I squared my shoulders and faced the woman down. I'd had a lifetime of being shunted around with barely any notice from home to home as a child and as an adult I'd suffered through countless temp jobs and grotty flats. *Was it too much to ask me what I wanted to do?*

"I'll force you if I have to, and, trust me, I don't want to. If I lose another witch, I'm toast." I looked questioningly at her and she pulled an apologetic face.

"A poor choice of words, perhaps."

"Lose another witch? Are you calling me a... witch?" I wasn't sure whether I should feel quite so affronted.

Étoile looked at me as if I might as well just flap my jaw and spare us both the idiotic questions. Despite my sympathy for the women on the TV screen, I wasn't too happy about being called a witch. From my knowledge, witches were invariably portrayed as warty things with terrible dress sense and even worse hair. I might not have supermodel looks but I was vain enough not to appreciate such a moniker, or the weight of the word. I might come to regret that.

Étoile nodded at the television again which was starting to spit out some noise. Perhaps it wasn't totally kaput after all. "I was too late for her." I knew she had to be referring to the embers that had been the last image. I gulped.

"Where are we going?" The words were out of my mouth before I realised I had made a decision to trust her.

"We don't have time for questions. I'll answer as we go, but right now, you need to get your stuff together so we can get out of here." Étoile's voice had increased in its urgency and I noted fear in her voice for the first time as she cocked her head. I didn't know what she was listening for but finally, she looked straight at me and hissed, "They're coming." She didn't have to tell me who they were.

I took a deep breath and, hoping I was doing the right thing, took two steps towards her and tossed the knife through the narrow doorway into the kitchen. It hit the edge of the sink and tumbled into the plastic bowl with a muffled clatter.

Étoile didn't move so I stepped around her, unzipped my bag and pulled my few clothes off the rails, shoving them in haphazardly, and tossing the wire hangers on the sofa bed. I pushed in my little box of jewellery so that it nestled down the side of the clothes, too wedged in for the lid to fall open. My spare shoes went on top. My whole life packed into one small, single bag. Pathetic.

Étoile glided towards the hallway door and had her head cocked to one side again. When she looked at me briefly, I couldn't tell if she was impressed that I'd managed to pack in under ten minutes flat or surprised that I really had so little.

"They're nearly here but they're confused. They haven't decided what they are going to do yet," she breathed. Her eyes had an unfocused faraway look and her voice was just loud enough for me to read an undercurrent of fear. She didn't strike me as someone who normally broke into a sweat when under pressure so that note of fear had me concerned. "Have you got everything?" she asked, hurriedly nodding towards the bag.

I scanned the room. I had my clothes, shoes and jewellery bits in the bag. I had taken nothing from the bathroom. "Toothbrush," I said and made a move towards the damp bathroom. It was the best move I could have made.

The fiery missile that exploded through the window and breezed into the room in a gush of wet air, was just a whisper from my face and I felt the rush of heat as it whistled past me to thud onto my sofa bed. Glass fragmented in its wake, shards sucked into my room with the force of the sudden rush of oxygen, and I shrieked in terror, throwing myself towards Étoile who caught me with steady arms. Flames erupted on the bed and the smell of petrol leaked into the air from the crude weapon. I pushed myself free from Étoile and grabbed my duffle bag before it was consumed in the eager flames. I started towards Étoile and she grabbed my hand to tug me away from the inferno as a loud crash sounded at the door.

We wheeled around to see the wood splinter as the head of an axe burst through. Étoile spread her arms behind her to reach for me. Alarm bells sounded in my head as danger approached us from every angle, cutting off both our escape routes. I could hear cries erupt from the street below and anger from the hall. The cruelty carried itself through the air and rained all around us. I knew in that moment that this was what real terror felt like.

Étoile had the foresight to grab my shoulder bag from where I had dumped it when I came in and was edging closer to me, my body between hers and the flames, which were already billowing black smoke. Now we were half facing the door that in just four strokes was almost shattered. A hand reached through and stubby fingers grappled with the flimsy lock.

"We have to go now," Étoile cried, catching my hand and gripping firmly.

Between the Molotov cocktail through the window and the formidable axe smashing through my door, I couldn't have agreed more. Somewhere in the shadows of my mind, I registered the thought that I could smell the hairs in my nose getting singed.

As her hand grasped mine, I spied the little, square tin caddy on top of my TV. "I have to get it," I cried back, stumbling a step away to grasp it with my free hand. I had a few things in it, meagre treasures, the last relics of a life I'd once had but I couldn't let them burn. Smoke stung my nostrils and I coughed against the rising darkness that even the half moon couldn't permeate. I barely had time to wrap my fingers round the hot tin as Étoile grabbed me around the waist.

The door smashed open with a groan, the small frame crowded with first one stocky figure, then two and more behind.

They thought we only had two ways out, both impossibly blocked.

They didn't have a clue.

The air fizzled and burned around us and I cried out as we vanished from the flames.

When I opened my eyes, I was momentarily blinded by having my face pressed against Étoile's silky blue shoulder. I detached myself from her and pushed back my hair. Between the drizzle and smoke, it had begun to stick unpleasantly to my face. I sniffed. The acrid stench of smoke was on me, not quite fully formed but still repellent enough. Bewildered, I blinked back tears and looked around. We were in a tiled cubicle with a toilet behind me, a sink and a hand drier in front, the kind that you dipped your hands in for the blast of air that was so strong it made your skin ripple. There was a long cord with a red blinking light next to the toilet.

"When you said we had to get away, I didn't realise we were escaping to a disabled toilet," I muttered.

Étoile didn't look embarrassed. "It was the best I could do on short notice," she sniffed. She set my shoulder bag on the floor and rummaged in her coat pocket until she found a little mobile phone. She pressed a number, then the call button and held it to her ear, turning slightly away from me as if to prevent me from hearing every word she was saying.

"It's me," she said, her voice low but without that trace of panic she'd had before. "I've got her, but I was only just in time. They're getting faster and stealthier. I could tell they were coming, but not that they were right outside the door! I think they are, well, we discussed that theory already. If I had been a minute later ... Just a minute! Well!" She listened before continuing, sighing. "We're fine. We'll check in straight away. Yes, of course ... See you soon."

Étoile stuck the phone back in her pocket. She crouched in order to see herself in the low mirror, ran long fingers through her hair, fluffing the front slightly and rearranged the collar of her jacket before shrugging, seemingly satisfied with her perfectly lovely and unhurt self. I decided she was probably the type who could survive any disaster while still keeping her lipstick fresh and her heels on.

If only I had fared so well. I tucked the tin caddy I was still clutching into my sports bag and ran the tap. My face had a smear of smoke, made even messier thanks to some stray tears from where my eyes had started to sting. I scrubbed at my cheeks using a wad of toilet paper and the curiously, and slightly revolting, green liquid soap from the dispenser and a trickle of water. I thought my hair might have singed slightly but there was nothing to trim it with so I settled for pulling it into a ponytail and twisting the ends under. The skin between my thumb and forefinger, where I held the tin caddy, was starting to blister and I prodded the puckered red skin carefully. It had begun to sting already. I had my bag and Étoile remembered to grab my shoulder bag, but in the chaos, I hadn't thought to snatch my jacket. *Damn it.* It was cold outside.

At least, it was if we were still in London.

"I left my jacket."

"It was ripped. Weren't you going to get rid of it?"

"I would have mended it." *How did she know it was ripped? Was she watching me when it happened? Fat lot of good she had been then, if she was.*

"Oh," Étoile nodded thoughtfully. "Make do and mend, hmm?"

"That's a nice way of putting it." I eyed the cubicle rather than meet her eyes.

Étoile was quiet for a moment then she said, "I'll get you another one."

"Where are we anyway?"

"Heathrow. Terminal five to be exact."

I hadn't realised I'd been holding my breath so I took a gasp of air. I may have never been to the airport before but at least now I knew where we were. *My Oyster card was probably in my bag. I could get the tube home. Hmm, maybe not.* "What are we doing here?"

Étoile frowned and snickered. "Catching a flight, of course." If she'd added "well, duh," I wouldn't have been surprised.

"I don't have a passport." I'd never needed one.

"All taken care of." Étoile produced a slim clear plastic envelope from the inside of her coat with a little flourish. She opened it and handed me a slim passport. I leafed through it. My name and picture was inside, but it wasn't a British passport.

"Is this a forgery?" I gasped in disbelief. *Didn't*

people go to prison if they were caught with a fake passport? I didn't want to go to prison and spend a lifetime dodging fallen soap.

"No," she sniffed, seemingly insulted. "We have someone who helps us from time to time when we need a rush job."

"I'm not American, either," I pointed out, tapping the blue cover.

"Well, technically, you're only half American but that's good enough for a passport," replied Étoile, as if it should have been obvious. "Anyway, I've only been here a few days and there wasn't time to get a British one as well, but it will hardly matter."

"Why?"

"I don't think you'll be coming back for a vacation anytime soon."

"Am I ever coming back?" I'd deal with the absurdity of throwing my lot in with a woman I'd known for ten minutes, whose first name was the only thing I did actually know about her, later. Scratch that, I knew she was more like me than a regular person. That had to count for something. Plus she hadn't left me to roast. I was feeling positively warm towards her.

"I can predict shorter queues at immigration," said Étoile which apparently was supposed to suffice for an answer. "We should check in. The sooner we are out of this god forsaken country, the better."

I slung my bag across my shoulder, taking care to avoid using my blistered hand and picked up my sports bag; then followed Étoile as she opened the door to the bathroom and stepped outside. I felt gross and hoped I didn't smell but no one glanced our way as we followed the signs for check in. Étoile avoided the queues and walked straight to the empty business class aisle. She took my passport and handed it, with hers, to the uniformed woman behind the desk who checked them, inquired after our luggage and printed our boarding passes, all while barely glancing in our direction. I meekly followed Étoile to the security queue and we silently stuck our bags and shoes in the plastic trays before walking through the metal detectors. There was something slightly absurd about seeing Étoile in her socks.

Once through, we rejoined the throng of people putting shoes back on, fixing belts and buttoning up jackets. I shivered, reminded once again that even indoors it was still cold at this time of year and my jacket was probably burning to a crisp right at this moment. I wondered what I might have had in my pockets. I'd dumped my gloves on top. *Drat.* At least I'd kept my boots on. I wondered what the hell I was doing following this woman around when I should probably make a break for it.

"I don't think that would work out too well for you," said Étoile as if she had plucked the thought from my head and I opened and closed my mouth like a fish. The look clearly wasn't working for me and my shoulders shuddered with the cold. "Let's do something about that," she said and, taking my hand, she pulled me in the direction of the closest shop in the duty free zone, as I looked about me, drinking in the sights. Airports were a new and interesting thing for me, despite the situation. I'd never had the chance to go away anywhere. I spent my holiday time hulking around London's many museums and parks.

Inside the shop, Étoile walked straight to the row of jackets and ran a practiced hand across them, pulling out three. She nodded politely to the sales assistant and told me to try them on. Shaking her head at the first two, she signalled her approval with a small incline of her head at the third. I looked at myself in the long wall mirror. It was grey wool with a full length zip, concealed by a small panel with a dropped waist, a belt that tied in a loose knot and sleeves that flared into gentle bell cuffs. It was well tailored and fit me snugly. It was obviously better quality than anything I had ever worn. I twisted the card attached to the sleeve and winced at the price. It was well out of my league of affordability.

I shrugged it off but Étoile caught it before I could gingerly place it back on the hanger and marched it over to the counter.

"I can't afford it," I hissed in a low voice, as I caught up with her at the till, just as the sales assistant scanned the tag with the wand.

"It's on me seeing as I didn't think to get yours," replied Étoile with a dazzling smile that she re-aimed at the sales assistant with a flick of her head, handing over a black card. "No bag. She'll wear it now."

The sales assistant snipped off the tag, passed me the jacket and wished us a great flight. We'd been in the shop only a few minutes and Étoile had happily stumped up more money than I'd ever paid for a single garment and without a single question. I wondered exactly how she had so much money to just throw away cash at a stranger like that. I guessed she couldn't have been more than a few years older than I.

"I'll pay you back," I promised, pulling the coat back on, now minus its wince-inducing price tag, then zipping it up. I pulled my bag strap over my head again so that it rested across my body like a security blanket. My wallet was, thankfully, inside and I pulled it out. "I have money in my account. Not loads, but enough to give you some back." I pulled out a card. Étoile took it from me and simply snapped it in half.

"What did you do that for?" I tried to calculate what was in my account and then what I would have to do to apply for another card. *Bother.*

"The minute you put that card in an ATM they'll know exactly where we are. They will be following you electronically as well as tracking you by other means. We need them to stay confused until we are well out of the way."

"I could have used it in... where are we going? What do you mean by other means?" I hurried after Étoile as she tossed my card in the bin and moved on.

"You couldn't. They must have no idea where you are. You can never use a bank card traceable to you again, never use your email or your Facebook or anything else that leaves a digital trace. Not even your phone." Étoile took my wallet from my hand and rudely rummaged through it, taking my only other card and snapping that one too. She tossed them in the bin and handed me the near empty wallet. "As for other means, well, they don't like us but they don't mind using our talents when it suits them and when they can get them." She set her mouth in a grim line.

"I don't have a phone." As soon as I said it, I wished I hadn't bothered. Bad enough being a freak, but now I was a freak who didn't even have a phone in the twenty-first century thanks to my social ineptitude. *Great, but hardly my fault* I reminded myself. "What am I supposed to do for money?"

"I told you, I'll take care of everything," Étoile

shrugged like it should have been obvious. She was being very offhand about the whole thing compared to me. "You won't have to worry about a thing."

"I don't want to be kept."

Étoile sighed and leaned closer speak in a low voice. "Stella, you don't have a choice. Right now I'm the only person keeping you alive and you have to do what I say. I know you don't want to. I know you're scared but I will look after you and I'm taking you somewhere safe. Until then, just let me take care of the bills, okay?"

"Where are we going?" I asked feeling a little sullen, like I'd just been told off. I didn't have much choice but to trust her and if I was thinking practically, getting out of the country might be the best thing. She had, after all, rescued me from a firebomb and someone smashing my door with an axe. I was between a rock and a hard place; I couldn't turn Étoile down.

"New York, for the moment. We have... people there and they will tell us what to do next," Étoile told me at last.

"Couldn't you just, you know, zap us over there? Wouldn't that be quicker than flying?"

"I was stronger once, but I can't... zap us that far. We would get horribly wet when we landed in the middle of the Atlantic. Better to fly." It was Étoile's turn to look petulant and I wondered if I'd hit a nerve. She turned away from me for the briefest moment to scan the departures board. "Come on. We've got a little walk to our departure gate and it isn't long before we board. I'll tell you more on the plane."

Thanks to Étoile's business class tickets, we swept

through the departure gate and settled into large, plush seats fairly quickly and again I wondered how this woman, who didn't look much older than I, had the money for two tickets, the ability to get passports (fake ones at that) at short notice as well as the resources to buy me an expensive jacket without flinching. I wondered if she flew regularly, unlike me. *Perhaps she was some kind of entrepreneur,* I decided. *Or a criminal with a heart*, I wondered as I watched her stow my bags in the overhead compartment.

I shuffled in my seat to get comfortable but it wasn't difficult considering how soft it was. Étoile leaned over to buckle me in like a child and grinned. "I hope you don't get airsick."

I shook my head then suddenly realised that actually, I had no idea. It wasn't like I was a seasoned traveller used to hopping on and off planes at a moment's notice. In between the air stewardess' instructions whose arms flapped towards exits that I couldn't see and hopefully wouldn't need, Étoile spoke in a low voice so that the other passengers couldn't hear. She told me there were others "like us", but not all could do things quite the way we could, she said with a wink, making us sound like conspirators. She told me that they – and I hadn't quite fathomed whom "they" were – hadn't been certain where I was for a long time but when they finally found me and thought there might be a threat, they had been keeping a loose eye on me. Apparently, my frequent job changes and home moves had kept them one annoying step behind. It became imperative that I was found, said Étoile, and here she was. She shrugged as if that told a whole story itself.

When rumours of cruel and unusual happenings

to witches had begun to surface over the past few months, they started rounding up the "waifs and strays," as she put it, taking those who couldn't defend themselves somewhere safer, pairing the newer of our kind with the stronger, trying to make sure no one was left alone as a target.

Étoile sighed. "Sometimes we were just too late and now I fear it is not safe for us to go back to England at all for quite some time."

"Did you take them all home with you?"

"No." Étoile frowned as she thought about it. "No. I only had instructions to return with you."

"Why do they want me?" I wasn't even remotely useful. Surely, I didn't have money, or connections; it wasn't like I was a big cheese in any way.

"I don't know." Étoile put her hand over mine and gave it a friendly squeeze. I wasn't sure if she were trying to reassure me, or herself. "Don't worry. They don't tell me everything, but they will make sure you are okay."

"Who are they?"

"Our family." Étoile smiled. "Not biologically, of course, not all of them, but we are a family of sorts. We have our hierarchies and our factions and our jobs and, of course, we look out for our own kind."

I nodded, then realised that Étoile had told me nothing. I pressed her again, "But, who are they?"

"The Witches' Council. They are the ones who govern and monitor our kind."

"Are there enough of us to need a council?"

"Oh yes. Lots and lots of us." Étoile seemed visibly cheered at that.

"Then how come you are the first person I've ever met who's like me?"

She thought for a moment then seemed to decide, "I'm probably not. We don't take adverts out or announce ourselves. People fear us. Just look at what happened in Salem. Some of us are still smarting over that, and those poor people weren't even witches." Étoile paused to order us drinks from the stewardess' cart. I mused over what she told me. Of course, it made sense that if there were others like me – I hesitated to use the word "witch" – they would not want to make themselves known. I'd once seen a documentary about Salem, a pretty New England coastal town, with historical re-enactments of the trials of the twenty-six accused and sentenced to death. They compared it to the town now and how that awful three-hundred-year-old legacy still affected the reputation of the town. The world wasn't exactly known for tolerance of its own race, never mind something other.

I remembered the evening's headlines. I grimaced and then it occurred to me. "Haven't we just been outed?" I asked.

"The Brotherhood?" Étoile waited for me to nod. "For a while, people will just think they are psychopaths. The hysteria won't start for some time yet. Who knows which way the public's opinion will go? Maybe we will be blamed for the credit crunch or terrorism or the freaky weather and people will turn." Étoile shrugged as if it wasn't her concern. "Or maybe they'll want us all to create love potions or put a hex on their neighbours. Frankly, who knows which is worse?"

I stared out of the window as the plane taxied across the runway and picked up speed before we rose with a sudden little lurch skywards. I wondered how many questions I would need to ask before I had even the basic grasp of the situation in which I found myself.

When firmly in the sky, I followed the instruction to unclip my belt and stretched my legs in the wide, plush seats. Air travel, so far, wasn't as bad as I had expected, though my ears were making little pop, pop, pop sounds as we ascended.

"You should rest." Étoile looked me squarely in the face, and I couldn't turn away. Her voice was thick with suggestion as she enunciated carefully, "You are very tired and you need some rest."

I felt my eyelids tugging. It hadn't even occurred to me that I might be tired until Étoile told me that I was. I tried to stifle the yawn, and somewhere in the back of my mind I sensed that I was being sent to sleep, rather than encouraged. Perhaps Étoile just didn't want to explain anymore. I clamped a hand in front of my open mouth and Étoile smiled again. She was awfully pretty, especially when she focused her attention directly at you. *How nice to be so lovely* was my final thought before I drifted solidly out of consciousness.

When I woke again, an airline blanket had been tucked up to my shoulders and the seat belt was clipped back on. Étoile was flicking through the pages of a magazine rather absently. When she noticed me shuffle, she tipped the megawatt smile back at me again. "Hey, sleepyhead. We're landing in less than twenty minutes. You slept the whole flight!" She didn't sound surprised.

"How convenient," I muttered. I shuffled upright from my slump and wiggled my head from side to side, working the cricks out of my neck. The pain had gone from my hand and when I looked, the skin was pink and new without the trace of a burn. *Interesting.* "So, do we, uh, get to see some of New York? Sightsee or something?"

Étoile shook her head. "Sorry, this isn't much of a vacation. Besides, you know, been there, done that."

Sure. She'd probably been everywhere. I meanwhile had barely stepped out of London, and for that matter, not exactly done a whole lot while I lived there. She was the town mouse to my city-living country mouse alright.

She smiled sympathetically and patted my knee. "Besides, we'll want to stay out of sight. We don't know who's looking for you."

"Won't they just check my passport? See where I've gone?"

Étoile shrugged once more. "There will be no records. No one will ever know or remember that you came through Heathrow or JFK, even on this plane."

"How did you do that?"

"Ve haf our vays," she replied in cod German and winked.

"So I lay low?"

"That's pretty much it. Until they decide where we are going next." Étoile didn't seem particularly perturbed by this. Actually, she seemed to be sending calm waves towards me and, though I could feel it, it didn't bother me that I didn't feel particularly bothered.

"Have you any idea at all?" I tried again.

Étoile pursed her lips and looked thoughtful as a little smile danced on her face. "I have hopes but I couldn't say for certain," she said fairly cheerfully. "I know where I'd want you to be, but it's not for me to decide."

"Don't I get any say?" I pressed my ears to stop them popping as we descended further.

"Not really. Sorry."

Étoile stayed right by my side as we disembarked, passed through customs without a hitch and walked past the baggage carousel. When she followed me to the bathroom, I found myself getting cross. "Some privacy, please?"

I wasn't sure if she were being the perfect host or was concerned I might flit the moment her back was turned. She needn't have worried. Without money, phone or, come to think of it, a clue, I had nowhere to go. I sighed as lightly as I could. I didn't want to seem ungrateful, especially as the alternative only a few hours ago was a crispy fried Stella with a side of regret.

"Oh, sure," she said, leaning against the row of sinks and muttering something about following the rules. I used the toilet quickly, smoothed the wrinkles out of my tights and fastened the skirt I'd pulled on over twenty hours earlier for work. I was wondering when I would get chance to change into something a little less battered and gross. After I washed my hands at the sink, Étoile handed me a little bag with the airline logo on it. There was a flannel and a disposable toothbrush inside, so I took the hint and washed my face as well as brushed my teeth before following her back outside and towards the exit route. Fortunately, with our carry-on bags we didn't have to wait at the packed carousel for baggage. Étoile seemed to know exactly where she was going so I followed her, barely noticing our surroundings.

As we exited the baggage claim, we approached a

line of people waiting behind a cordon anchored by moveable weighted and polished pillars. A man in a black suit and sunglasses stepped forward and beckoned us with a little nod. Étoile motioned for me to come on and we followed him outside. Beyond that greeting, they didn't speak, though he grunted something that sounded like a hello at me. Or he could have just swallowed a fly. It was hard to say.

As we reached the road, a huge, black Cadillac with tinted windows swooped down on us. As soon as it pulled up, the man opened the rear door and ushered us inside. He attempted to take my bag but I pushed it ahead of me so that it would sit on the floor at my feet and scowled at him. If I offended him, he didn't show it. Étoile climbed in after me and the man slammed the door shut behind her, then climbed in the front passenger seat without speaking to the driver.

As I put my seatbelt on, Étoile pulled her phone from her pocket and switched it on. It trilled as it powered up and Étoile immediately speed-dialled. "We're in the car and on our way," she said, after which the conversation receded into umms, yes and no. Clearly, she had a lot to answer but didn't want to say much in front of me. I wondered when someone would see fit to fill me in or if I was going to continue to be shunted wherever they felt like with barely an acknowledgment. I didn't want a life like that, anymore than I was thrilled about the life I had been leading. *Had been leading,* I reminded myself. *Who knew what my life was now?* I just didn't want to be a prisoner.

At that thought, Étoile leaned over and patted my knee as if she were comforting a pet and I felt that calm feeling pervade my veins. "They're very excited to meet you," she said to me at last with a small smile as she slipped the phone back into her pocket.

"Great?" I raised my eyebrows in question.

"Yes, it is. They've assembled quite the little welcoming committee."

I nodded at the two men in the front. The driver said nothing to me, his sidekick only fractionally more with the fly-eating grunt and silence thereafter as we sped on. "Perhaps they need to sit in on the welcoming committee seminar," I said under my breath.

"Oh, don't mind them." Étoile dismissed them with a flick of her hand. "They aren't here to be jolly."

If the two men minded being passed over so matter-of-factly, they didn't show it. So I just nodded and looked out the window as we sailed through the traffic in the monster car. I lost count of time as we weaved from the freeway into the city. Buildings crowded us from every angle but I could tell we were moving towards a pricier part of town as the buildings became increasingly nicer featuring glossy, mirror-like windows, awnings and large potted plants stationed like soldiers at the sides of doorways. Presently, we drew up in front of a building with wide glass doors and an actual liveried doorman with a top hat. I suppressed the urge to gawk like a tourist.

Sidekick (as I decided to call our nameless chaperone) hopped out and opened the door for us, offering me his hand as I climbed down which I thought a nice gesture. It was certainly better than letting me do a face plant from a great height. Well, my heart positively swelled. Sidekick grabbed my bag from the footwell before I had the chance to reach back for it and then, keeping it in his grip, paused to help Étoile down with his free hand. She glided gracefully to the pavement as if there had barely been a drop and sashayed into the building without a backward glance, nodding briefly to the doorman as the car pulled away. Her heels clicked on the marble floor as I trailed behind, Sidekick bringing up the rear as we crossed a foyer with a large potted tree and mirrors covering one entire wall. She punched a card into a slot by the lift doors and they glided open as if they had been waiting for us.

"Our private lift takes us straight to the penthouse," she explained as the three of us stepped inside and I shuffled myself to the back. There were no buttons to press as the lift only had two stops. If you got in one floor, it was obvious you were aiming for the other.

I took a moment to glance over my shoulder at my reflection. The quick wash hadn't done much good and the expensive jacket was still no match against Étoile's exotic printed coat. Even Sidekick's black suit looked like it had been made exclusively for him. I felt scruffy and insignificant as I nestled between them.

As if sensing my discomfort, Étoile twisted her head to smile magnificently at me with a row of perfectly white teeth, in a way that I was starting to find not wondrous, but a little disconcerting. I imagined she was rather used to dazzling people into comfort, happiness, acquiescence or whatever else she planned for them when she turned it on. So I scowled like a petulant teenager and she seemed amused as she turned back to the doors with a little shrug of her shoulders.

When the lift doors glided back, Sidekick stepped out first and sped off with my bag before I could protest. I exhaled irritably as Étoile gestured that I was to follow her in the other direction. There was another marble foyer to cross, but this one was somewhat smaller than the building's entrance hall, although just as grand, if not more so. A circular table stood on a pedestal in the centre with a large arrangement of fresh flowers in reds and pinks in a patterned vase. Their perfume drifted towards me in the still air. Heavy gold-striped drapes framed a single window that reached almost to the ceiling and I could see skyscrapers beyond. I couldn't even guess what the table alone must have cost.

I sidestepped to see the corridor that Sidekick had escaped via; it led off one way and I could see several doors before it turned a corner. It was all I could do not to stand and turn and stare like a tourist in a grand house opening. It was the most elegant lobby I had ever seen. It was bigger than the whole top floor of my flat, never mind my own studio. Two sets of double doors led off the lobby and Étoile knocked firmly at one set before opening a door and ushering me inside.

I don't know what I expected but it wasn't the scene in front of me.

There were no black cats or cauldrons, or anything vaguely witchy. Instead, three large cream sofas were positioned around a long, low upholstered coffee table. Occasional tables, with vases of splendid roses in shades of pink and yellow, and pairs of slipper chairs were dotted about the room. It was a room made for coffee mornings, social committees and elegant soirees, not scruffy London orphans. I couldn't feel more out of place.

Against my better judgement, I sniffed, then thinking better of it, and remembering I did have manners, I tipped my chin up a bit and tried not to look like a fish out of water. I'd just have to bluster through, the same as I did when I got a temping assignment that was way beyond my expertise. Only this time I was in the company of witches and couldn't just hide behind a stack of filing. *The hell if I would I let my nerves show, though.*

A man and woman sat on the furthest sofa. The pair were both elegant and well dressed, though not flashy; she in a cream skirt suit, court shoes and a tidy golden bob; he in a charcoal grey three-piece suit with a striped shirt and tie. They looked like they were in their fifties, but a very well-preserved version of that age.

Another man sat on the adjacent sofa, closer to me. Not only was he much younger but dressed considerably more casual in a white t-shirt with a button-down placket, jeans (albeit expensive ones) and leather boots. With his shaggy blonde hair and big blue eyes, he was straight from an advert for healthy living. Though he was younger, there were physical similarities to the older pair. The square jaw was like the older man's and I wondered if perhaps he was their son. He had a playful smile on his face and looked mildly curious, but welcoming. He caught my eye and winked at me. I dipped my eyes and a pink blush crept onto my cheeks. *Embarrassing, much!*

The older man rose to his feet and approached me, his hand outstretched to shake mine in a double-handed clasp and I caught the glimpse of a Rolex. I'd bet good money he hadn't bought it from a street vendor. He had a slightly receding hairline with closely cropped, iron grey hair and a smooth accent as he said, "We're so glad Ms. Winterstorm found you. We were so worried that she was too late." It sounded like an admonishment dressed up in a welcome and I was a little cross for Étoile's sake. She sank gracefully onto the sofa next to the young man and was playing on her phone again, her thumbs busily texting. If she noticed the slight, she didn't give a hint, though her back was ramrod straight, like she wasn't completely at home.

"She had perfect timing," I replied, suddenly feeling a little protective of the woman who had zapped me, quite literally, out of the firing – fire – line.

"So she did," the older man agreed smoothly. His voice had the clipped New York edge that I was familiar with from too much film watching. "My name is Robert Bartholomew and this is my wife, Eleanor. Our son, Marc." Robert nodded towards the younger blonde man who was lounging on the sofa, one leg slung across the other. I thought he would have looked more at home at the beach rather than in this bastion of New York wealth. I nodded at him briefly and he smiled back warmly, melting me just a little. "You, of course, are Stella." I nodded and Robert waved a hand, indicating that I should sit next to their son. So, with a brief glance at him, I did.

Eleanor poured tea into delicate china teacups with a trio of gold bands around the edge, from a set that sat on a tray on the low table. "Tetley," she said, adding hesitantly, as if she weren't sure she got it right, "Just like home?"

"I've barely been away. I don't think I'm quite

ready to be homesick," I said, then held my tongue when I realised how rude that must have sounded. Eleanor stiffened a fraction before continuing to fill the cup. I added quickly, "Thank you. I appreciate you thinking of me. That was kind of you." She relaxed and I gave myself a mental kick as I leant forward to accept the teacup and scooped in two heaped sugars. She poured another cup for Étoile and moved to set it on a low table near her before settling back in her space, ankles crossed neatly. She struck me as delicate but very assured, even if she had assumed the "I'll be mother" role.

"Are you the, uh, council?" I asked the air, not entirely sure whom I should be addressing. I balanced the cup and saucer awkwardly in my hand, unsure whether I should put it down. *What if I spilled on the upholstery, or left a ring mark on the tray?*

"Eleanor and I are members, though this is not the whole council," replied Robert as Eleanor gave a small smile. "We have called a meeting and the council will be here later. As Étoile no doubt told you, they are very much looking forward to meeting you and you will have the opportunity to talk to them."

"What will we be talking about?" I questioned, wondering what kind of chat went on at committee meetings. Maybe we'd talk about the best breed of black cat, or potions or ... well, I couldn't think what witches talked about.

"You, in part," said Robert and I wondered if, perhaps, that should have been a little more obvious. *I had had a strange and long day, I could be forgiven*, I thought. "We will need to decide your future," he finished.

I considered the last twenty-four hours. *My future looked very different now from what I had planned. Hell, I couldn't even have planned the past day.* "And I actually get a say in that?"

Robert smiled companionably. "We can't force you to do anything. You did after all come here willingly," he reminded me, a small smile playing on his lips.

"I didn't have much of a choice. Not that I don't appreciate Étoile turning up in the nick of time," I added hastily, spreading my hands, the teacup wobbling precariously. "I do, but this all seems very much out of my hands."

"If you will do us the courtesy of meeting and listening with the council tonight, you will, of course, be at liberty to do whatever you choose. Naturally, we hope that you will take on board what we have to say and listen carefully to our recommendations before you decide anything," said Robert, and his voice was at once authoritative and open. "It is our wish that you stay safe, above all else."

"Why am I so special?" *God help me,* I sounded whiny and ungrateful.

Eleanor looked at her husband before answering me herself. "Because you are," she replied, inflection on the last word, as if that answered everything. I wondered if Étoile had learned evasive lessons from her.

I pondered Eleanor's answer and wanted to ask more, but I had the feeling that neither Robert, nor his wife, were going to tell me much at this stage. This initial meeting seemed to be about pleasantries, a meet-and-greet and a glance-over, much as I might have gotten at any new temp job, but not a moment to impart knowledge of any great worth. *Well, that could work both ways. Oh well. I had nowhere better to be,* I reminded myself, *I could wait and see what happened.*

Eleanor poured another cup and handed it to Robert. He took it with a nod as he moved towards the mantelpiece and seemed to be staring somewhere over my head as though lost in thought. He sipped and returned the cup to the saucer with a delicate chink. He was clearly in no great hurry either.

"Witches have been a part of the world for centuries," Robert said at last, choosing his words carefully. "I say witches, but, of course, we have been called all sorts of things. Spell-casters, wizards, magicians, warlocks, sorcerers and worse. Witch seems to have stuck in the lexicon. Of course, we have gone to ground for the past few hundred years ever since the ghastly witch hunts that destroyed so many of our kind and others that were accused of being one of us.

"After a few generations, we were relegated to myth and legend, which suited us just fine as we were able to live peacefully once again and regroup. The short version of this sorry tale is this. We're out. There are those out there who have always been aware of us and have taken advantage of the world's turmoil to persecute us once again. We have taken steps to gather whomever we can, to draw them to us and protect them." Robert was getting into his stride, his voice rumbling on and I listened with fascination as he unfolded a history of which I had barely been aware. "Stella, you have a rare gift, an inherited gift. We don't think you can control it yet, and we want to help you and protect you. We want to keep you safe."

It was Robert's last words that chilled me to the

bone. "We don't want to see you burn."

I shivered. The sight on the television – *earlier today? Last night?* I couldn't be sure – seemed to have stuck to my eyeballs. *If anyone wanted to protect me from that, well, great. I was hardly going to knock them back without another thought.*

"Did you save everyone?" I asked.

Robert shook his head and sighed. "There simply wasn't time or enough of us to reach everyone. A lot of the craft has simply gone dormant, or died out. There aren't that many of us with real power, though occasionally some throwback talent crops up and we help where we can.

"Some of the older, more skilled witches went to ground as soon as the attacks came to light in Europe. They will make their way to us, or band together, when they deem it safe. Others are barely aware of their powers and we decided it was safer to leave those who were unlikely to be attacked. Their magic can barely be identified. Some, like you, are on the cusp of realising real power and so it was you we decided to save. We were too late for some."

"Am I one of these throwback... talents?" I asked as Robert and Eleanor quickly eyed each other.

Robert answered. "No, your magic is strong. It could only have come from your parents."

As he was speaking, a thought had been creeping up on me and it was out of my mouth before I could stop it. "You knew where I was?"

Robert inclined his head in a brief nod.

"You've known where I was for... how long?" *Had they known where I was throughout my long, lonely childhood when I so desperately needed people? Solid, dependable people who didn't think I was a freak?* I clenched my jaw.

Robert and Eleanor exchanged another glance and it wasn't reassuring. They had known then. Perhaps they had known where I was for a long time, not just in the few days or weeks that led up to the witch hunt. At least they had the grace to look embarrassed, or I thought they did.

It was Eleanor who answered in her clipped Manhattan accent. "No, we had no idea for quite some time. Not until the last year or so. We couldn't just pluck you out of England on a whim," she said. "You wouldn't have come. Besides, we didn't know what would become of you for certain."

"You managed to get a passport for me when it suited you." I was trying to keep my voice as even and inoffensive as possible. It was tough going.

"That passport is yours. Your name, and your nationality." I was puzzled. *Hadn't Étoile handed me an American passport, when I was English?* As I tried to make up my mind whether it was some kind of fraud, Eleanor took pity on me and solved the puzzle. "Your father is American, as you know. You have every right to be here, though he spent many years in England with your mother."

It was strange to hear these strangers speak about my parents. When I was younger, I often asked many questions about them, but no one seemed to know the answers beyond their names and dates of birth. Letters and numbers on a piece of paper that meant so little and so much. One day they were there, the next they were gone and I was alone. I thought I might have been around five when I last saw them. Too young to form lengthy memories and too young to grasp the answers to my own questions.

"We knew your father well, your mother less so," said Eleanor, quite smoothly. I noticed that her bobbed hair barely moved and its golden colour was subtly highlighted. "Tonight, when the council convenes, you may have the opportunity to ask more questions, if time permits. Some of the other council members were friends with your parents."

Robert was ready to take back centre stage as he deposited his cup on the tray with a light clink. "As Eleanor said, you will have the opportunity to meet some of the council members tonight. We have already decided what may be an appropriate route for you... but we will need to be quite sure that we are doing the right thing for you. As I said though, the final decision is yours but do rest assured that we are trying to do our best for you." I almost missed the look Eleanor flashed at him but Robert didn't and he shook his head at her, with the barest fraction of movement. He paused then added, "To atone, perhaps, for not finding you sooner."

I nodded, agreeing somewhat. *Too right they could atone if they had known I was on my own! Even if they said they didn't know where I was my whole life.* I wasn't sure what to believe. *They were pleasant enough though*, I thought, careful to keep my temper in check. But I couldn't help wondering if what was right for me would travel along the same road that was right for them. It seemed at odds to pick a route, as they seemed to be calling it, that would not somehow be simultaneously profitable for their cause. After all, they'd only just picked me up now when they could have done so years ago apparently.

If I had real power, as Robert said, and others wanted to crush it, it stood to reason that they might want it too. I made a snap decision that it might be best if I kept those thoughts to myself until I had the measure of them. It would do to keep my wits about me and not be seduced by the obvious wealth and implied sincerity, both seemingly designed to put me at ease.

Robert tucked his hands into his trouser pockets, smiled and seemed to have finished his speech. He told me nothing that I didn't already know, other than that my parents were known to them and I wondered if I was about to be hit with a bombshell of information that evening. I rather hoped so.

"Will Étoile be there later?" I asked the room. I still hadn't spoken directly to Marc, and it would be rude to lean across him and whisper to Étoile, but I knew I would feel more comfortable if Étoile was with me. My feelings towards her were based on only a few hours, but I felt I could trust her, given that, I wasn't, well, deep fried.

Robert pondered the idea and after a moment, nodded. "Yes, Étoile is not a member of the council but she will be a friendly face for you."

I looked over my shoulder. Étoile had stopped playing with her phone and sat with her ankles crossed and hands in her lap. She smiled at me and I thought there was a real hint of warmness there. I smiled back and meant it.

"We will let you retire. I'm sure you are exhausted," said Eleanor, every bit the hostess and clearly dismissing us. "Marc, would you take our guests to their rooms?"

Marc was up and at my side in an instant and I stood. I was sandwiched between him and Étoile as we left the room, and she took care to close the heavy doors behind her. We moved across the hallway and

Marc guided us down the hall and around a bend. "Mom has given you rooms across from each other. I'm right down the hall so just call if you need anything." He pointed several closed doors further down. They were all identical so I wasn't sure which one he meant. I would just have to find Étoile if I needed anything. He opened a door to his right and ushered me in first. Étoile leant against the doorframe as I took in the room.

It was a small room, dominated by a big mahogany bed with a cover the colour of bitter chocolate, trimmed in brilliant white ribbons and stacked with pillows. A dressing table sat against the wall at the foot of the bed, near the door. On the other wall there was a closet and a door that was open a fraction so that I could see it led to a small bathroom. Opposite that, the window, framed in matching dark brown curtains with thick tassels, looked out over the city. The curtains alone probably cost more than a month's temping. It had the appearance of a very smart hotel room and the bed looked particularly inviting, even though I slept for several bone-aching hours on the plane. Marc seemed to be waiting for a reaction so I tipped the corners of my mouth into a smile and thanked him.

"Mom likes things to be quite formal," Marc was saying and it took me a moment to realise that he wasn't talking about the bedroom decor, but was instead referring to their council. He probably took the grandeur as standard, I assumed. "She prefers we dress up so she left a dress for you, assuming you mightn't have brought anything formal."

Of course I hadn't, I thought, looking around for my bag.

"Your bag is in the closet," said Marc, following my eyes and guessing what I was looking for. He indicated with his hand, "The dress is in there too. She guessed your size so I hope it fits. Can you be ready for eight?"

I had no idea what time it was – my watch was obviously on the wrong time zone – but there was a clock on the dresser so I nodded and Marc seemed satisfied. He ran a hand through his thick blonde hair and grinned again. "Hopefully it won't be too boring tonight. Signal me if you need rescuing."

I frowned, not sure if he was serious or being funny. I decided to play along either way. "What sort of signal should I give you?"

"Um, nothing too obvious ... maybe ... brush something off your shoulder," suggested Marc, making the same sweeping gesture to show me exactly what he meant. "It won't look out of place and I will get you out of there. The council can be a bit overbearing at the best of times. They're particularly excited about tonight."

I nodded as if I knew exactly what he meant and looked over to Étoile who stood in the doorway, leaning slightly against the doorframe. "I will watch out for any frantic shoulder-brushing," she winked and backed out of the room.

Marc followed her and swept a hand towards the doorway across the hall, but she'd already brushed past and opened the door. She seemed very familiar with the apartment. I wondered how many times she had stayed here. *Maybe she and Marc were a thing?* I couldn't be sure. With a wide smile, Marc turned to shut the door behind him, leaving me alone at last.

Inside the room, I took a moment to glance at my

reflection in the mirror. I looked tired, and ever so slightly grimy. *Great.* There was nothing like a good first impression, as my manager at the temp agency had been so fond of telling me. I guessed I'd blown that first impression already and even if I tried to shrug it off, a little piece of my mind nagged at me for not being at least a bit better presented. It didn't help one iota that Étoile looked like she had just stepped out of the salon, even though she had been on the same rough twenty-four-hour ride as I. I sighed. Crossing over to the closet, I opened it and found my bag inside. I knelt down and checked it was still zipped but I couldn't be certain it hadn't been rifled through, seeing as I hadn't exactly packed neatly.

Easing to my feet, I saw that a black garment bag was the only thing hanging on the rail, I reached forward and unzipped it. A dress, as expected, was inside. I pushed off the garment bag and held it up in my arms. It had a neat plain bodice with a square neckline and no sleeves plus a skirt that puffed out slightly at the waist. The skirt was a damask sort of fabric, with raised swirls of black that looked like it would rest just above the knee. It was elegant and probably, I realised, the most expensive thing I ever touched. Even more than Étoile's gift of the jacket which I realised I hadn't even taken off. A pair of black pumps with a low heel sat on the closet floor. I wriggled out of my shoes and inserted a foot. Of course, they fit. Eleanor was the type of woman who could size you up at a glance and probably left nothing to chance anyway. I put the dress back on the rail and shut the closet door, feeling a little ashamed that I was even thinking about its cost; *but then,* I reminded myself, *I was surrounded by the most enormous wealth while I was used to so little.*

A low rumble emanated from my stomach and I patted it, trying to remember when I had last eaten. The only meal I could recall had been before the plane and my stomach was working its way up to reminding me of that with a series of no uncertain grumbles. I would have to wash first then look for a kitchen. It occurred to me Eleanor might not want me poking around in her home and she didn't look like the home cooking type either. I would have to swallow my pride and just find someone to ask instead, or go hungry. I hoped they weren't into fancy hors d'oeuvre with miniscule portions instead of real food.

I shrugged off my new jacket and hung it over the back of a chair. Smoothing the coat's shoulders, I was reminded again that I was still wearing the same clothes I'd worn to work and then on the plane. *Yuck.* I hoped I didn't smell but I wasn't going to have a sniff to find out. *At least no one had wrinkled their nose at me.*

I shrugged off my top, feeling grimier by the minute and unzipped my skirt, shaking it to the floor so I could step out if it. I pulled my bag out of the closet, leaving my clothes in a little pile inside. I rummaged through the bag and pulled out clean jeans, another top and a fresh set of underwear and socks, thankful that I'd been to the laundry recently and that they hadn't been near the smoke long enough to be tainted.

After setting my clean clothes out on the bed, I went into the bathroom. Although it was small, it was well stocked with anything a guest might need. There were bottles of shampoo, conditioner and shower gel in the shower cubicle. An unused toothbrush and toothpaste set sat on glass shelf above the basin. Soft towels hung on a heated rail.

I turned on the shower and wriggled out of my underthings, dropping them in a little heap on the tiled floor, before I dived under the hot water, holding my head under until my hair was soaking wet and trailing down my back. I scrubbed my hair and shampooed until my head was full of suds; then worked on my body to remove every last bit of grime. I took the time to revel in the luxury of it as I compared it to my usual dribble of a shower and, for those few minutes, lost myself in thoroughly enjoying the water pounding on my skin. I was almost reluctant to get out and towel myself dry but I forced myself anyway. I wrapped one thick towel around me, tucking the ends in at the front and wrapped a smaller towel around my head to keep my hair from leaking down my back, then brushed my teeth thoroughly and gargled.

Though I could have only been in the bathroom a few minutes, someone had been in my room while I showered. A tray sat on the dressing table, with an actual silver cover over the plate. Still towelled up, I lifted the lid and my stomach grumbled again. It had been hours since I had last eaten. *Maybe even more than a day*, I thought as I gave up trying to calculate how long I'd been here and how long the flight had taken. With the time difference, I wasn't even sure I had worked out which day it was.

The tray held a salad and grilled chicken with a creamy dressing, and a warm bread roll with a little pat of butter in its own miniature dish. Then there was a chocolate soufflé, slightly bubbling, in a white, fluted ramekin and a tall glass of orange juice crammed with ice cubes. I didn't bother to dress. I had barely pulled out the velvet-buttoned stool from under the table and sat down before I fell on the food with an appetite that would have embarrassed me, had I been in public. I was just too hungry to care.

Fifteen minutes later and I let the last of the chocolate soufflé melt in my mouth, my eyes half closed in the simple pleasure of it. *Delicious.* I had read in a magazine, on a work break a few weeks earlier, that fear could make the next meal taste like nothing else on earth. Apparently there was a "shock and eat" trend that was the latest thing in London – people actually paid to be frightened to pieces then fed a slap-up meal. I reckoned this meal would be delicious any day of the week, even without any tomfoolery beforehand.

My eyelids drooped and I realised nature was pulling me in a different direction now that my appetite had been sated. I pulled on the clean underwear I set on the Bed, hoping that whoever had brought the tray had ignored them, and the t-shirt, leaving the jeans lying on the bed. I crawled, rather ungainly, over them and pulled back the sheets to slide under.

The thought that home – London, my life – didn't exist anymore was on the tip of my mind as my eyelids pulled lower, but I was asleep as soon as my head hit the unfamiliar pillow. Edging out of consciousness thankfully stopped the rising panic overtaking me from fully forming at the one-hundred-and-eighty degree about-face my life had suddenly taken.

CHAPTER FOUR

I knew before I opened my eyes that I was not alone. I cracked one eye open, just enough that my pupil was still masked by my eyelashes, and to allow me to see before anyone else could discern that I was awake.

I was right to be cautious, I told myself, I was in a strange apartment, in a strange country with people I hadn't known existed less than forty eight hours before. To be perfectly honest with myself, I should have snuck out hours ago. Not that I had anywhere to go, *now that my flat was toast*, I reminded myself with a huff of resignation. Actually, I should probably be feeling really, really grateful but even that didn't stop me from being careful.

I scanned the room through my lashes. My room invader was Étoile and she was perched at the end of my bed examining her nails and fanning her fingers to check the polish.

"Hey," I said, opening both eyes now and stretching before propping myself up on my elbows. I was glad I remembered to put on a t-shirt. Saving me was one thing; getting an eyeful was quite another.

"Hey you," Étoile replied, cocking her head with a congenial smile. She gave her hand another shake; her nails were electric blue. "I've been sent to tell you that the council will be arriving shortly. Did you rest well?"

"Yes, thank you." I'd slept solidly and looked around for the clock to give me a clue about the time. The curtains were unclosed and it still looked light outside, but that could have been a trick of the glittering skyscrapers beyond the window.

"Is the dress okay?"

"It's lovely," I said, glancing at the closet, adding, "and the shoes fit."

"Good." Étoile was already dressed in a long, inky blue dress which was made out of a thin jersey that clung to her in a very flattering way. Even as she sat slouching, she didn't have a hint of a muffin top. *So unfair.* Her dress had a high cowl neck, no sleeves and seemed to be missing most of the back. I couldn't work out how she kept it on her shoulders. She had big chandelier earrings in a hammered silver that were far longer than her hair. They swayed when she moved her head. Her nails were a shade lighter than the dress. She looked beautiful. She wasn't kidding about dressing up.

"I'll come back in ten minutes. Will that be long enough for you to dress?" Étoile patted my leg through the covers and I felt a supreme sense of calm wash over me. "The council are assembling now."

I nodded. It shouldn't take me long to scramble into the dress and shoes. And as for makeup, well, thank goodness I'd been blessed with clear skin because I didn't have much in my bag.

Étoile smiled, pleased, and sashayed out of the room. I don't think Étoile walked that way for my benefit, I think she just was a true sashay-er.

I shoved back the bedding and swung my legs out, flexing my toes to bring life back into them. I stood, stretched my arms towards the ceiling, making my shoulders creak in protest, and went over to the closet to take out the dress. I laid it on the bed and put the shoes on the floor below. I rummaged through my duffle bag, pondering briefly if I was supposed to unpack. *Was this supposed to be my home now?* From the way the Bartholomews had spoken earlier about deciding my future, I guessed not. So, unpacking could wait. My hands, rooting around blindly, found the little bag of makeup I kept for special occasions, not that I had many of them, and I pulled it out. The last time I had gotten made up was on a date seven months ago and it hadn't ended well. I sighed. *At least I could make myself presentable now.*

Leaning forward so I could see myself in the mirror, I slicked on some lip gloss and a single coat of mascara, then tugged the brush through my hair. It had dried while I slept and I needed to coax the knots out. I was clean and presentable, at least. I tried not to sigh at Étoile's singular elegance, knowing that no matter how pretty and expensive the dress lying on the bed was, it was still a borrowed one and I could never achieve Étoile's unselfconscious loveliness.

I reminded my reflection that jealousy was not a virtue and besides, Étoile could not help the way she looked any more than I could. I tried to think a nice thought about myself, something I had read in a magazine about boosting your self-esteem. I finally settled on the thought that I had really nice legs, not too muscular, just nicely defined. *That would do.* I smiled. That was another trick from the magazine. Just the act of smiling was enough to make you want to smile. *Great for diffusing tough situations, like wishing you were a hot, skinny witch,* I thought while trying out a smile that didn't seem quite as much like a smirk.

I pulled off my tee, laid it over the back of the chair and rifled through my bag for a black bra, snapped it on, then slipped into the dress. I could just about zip the back up, but I'd have to ask – *who? Étoile?* – to zip up the last inch. I smoothed the skirt over my hips and assessed my reflection in the mirror. It fit perfectly, skimming over my breasts and cinching in my waist before flaring slightly over my hips and finishing at my knees. It was understated but quite eye-catching. A smile spread over my face. It was good to see that I scrubbed up nicely. I had a pair of nude tights rolled in my bag. They were worn, used for the odd occasions I wore a skirt suit to work, but at least they weren't snagged.

I sat down to roll them on then slid my feet into the shoes. I don't wear heels much but I once had a foster mother who made all the girls practice that time-honoured tradition of marching up and down the hall in heels while balancing a book on their heads. For once, I was grateful for all those missed evenings of television watching. At least now I wouldn't fall flat on my face in front of a room of people who had been gathered to scrutinise me. I rummaged through my jewellery, extracting a pair of plain silver ball studs and poked them through the little flesh holes in my lobes before giving myself a second appraisal in the mirror.

A knock on the door tore my attention away from

my – admittedly, rather nice – reflection. I opened it to find Étoile with Marc standing a step behind her. He wore a black suit like a second skin with a white shirt and striped tie – quite the upscale preppy look. He was handsome and he knew it. I would bet the pair of them were as used to dressing up as I was not. Marc's eyes swept me from head to toe and back again. He pursed his lips and gave me a low appraising whistle. I grinned, my cheeks reddening, not sure if I was grateful for his approval or a little embarrassed.

I stepped outside before I could think about changing my mind and pulled the door closed behind me. Hands brushed my back and I felt my cheeks flush again as the zip was given a little tug, then Marc slipped his arm through mine and, in our quiet trio, we followed the hallway back to the lobby.

With Étoile in front of us, I felt more like I was being guided than marched. Everything they were doing seemed to be measured just right so as to not frighten me off. From sending Étoile to save me, to having she and Marc escort me – two perfectly nice looking, well dressed people close to my own age, (which had to be the idea) – to the offer of assistance, protection and, last but not least, the dress. If they wanted me to feel comfortable, they hadn't stepped out of line yet but I couldn't help but feel uneasy. I wondered if they planned the whole series of events from two days ago to this evening and immediately felt guilty. After all, they had done nothing but help me and provide for me, while asking for nothing…*Yet,* said my nagging brain.

As we passed through the hall, the doors were all shut, including those that flanked the lobby. I couldn't hear a thing, we could have been alone and I wondered just how vast the apartment was. Marc, unlinking his arm from mine, stepped ahead of Étoile to open the set of doors adjacent to the one where I had been received earlier.

If I expected that our already being in the apartment would make us one of the first to arrive at the party, I was wrong.

The room was another lesson in wealth and taste. Wider and broader than the previous room, it had floor to ceiling windows that looked out across the dusky New York skyline over what could only be the treetops of Central Park. The windows were closed to the large terrace beyond. I could only guess at the wealth that must have been accrued to afford a place like this. *Prime real estate*, a voice in my head whispered like an American TV host, *megabucks*.

A large chandelier was suspended in the centre of the ceiling and tiny jewels sparkled against the electric light. Below, around two dozen people, dressed to the nines in suits and cocktail dresses, milled around the room in quiet chatter. In the centre of all of them were Robert and Eleanor, exuding silent power over their collective.

When all heads turned to me, I realised Étoile and Marc had already stepped into the room, leaving me framed in the doorway rather like a bride at the church doors. I felt myself being eyeballed from every angle and forced myself to stand tall, head up, shoulders and back straight. I thrust my chin forward a little and kept my hands very still at my sides. I would not wilt as I was scrutinised. I could attribute my poise to the stickler-for-etiquette foster mother and I sent a tacit thank you to her, wherever she was now.

Seconds passed before Robert emerged, extending his hand to me, upright and elegant in a suit that was just a shade under black. "Welcome again, Stella. Welcome to our gathering." Though his face was the picture of welcome, it was all I could do not to shiver. Indeed, Robert was giving every indication that he was thoroughly delighted to see me and glad to have me in his home but I sensed an insincerity that I wasn't about to dismiss.

Robert inclined his head and kissed me on the cheek with the barest sweep of his thin lips and turned to face the assembled crowd. With one hand on my elbow, he propelled us forward. I couldn't put my finger on what it was, but there was something about Robert that made me feel... not frightened, but anxious. It wasn't anything discernible like his demeanour, or his actions, but there was a current of caution in my veins and I wasn't going to ignore it even if I did feel horribly ungrateful.

"Stella, dear." Eleanor echoed her husband's greeting with her own barely-there air kiss that landed in space, just a few millimetres from my cheek. She cast her eyes over me and nodded with appreciation. "You look lovely." She was dressed in a dark green cocktail dress that finished under the knee. Her only jewellery was a gold necklace, the centre piece of which was a large red stone. I thought it might have been a ruby and marvelled again at their wealth.

"Thank you, Mrs. Bar ..., uh, Eleanor," I stammered, unsure if there were some sort of protocol. Around us, conversation expired and I felt that the people were waiting, poised for instruction.

"We would like to introduce you to some of our

people before the council convenes," said Robert from my left side. He nodded at Eleanor before turning away, his hand still on my elbow as he manoeuvred me towards the people on his left, two women and a man who stood together. We shook hands and they introduced themselves as Mary, Bridget and Steven. The two women, both brunettes and somewhere in their middle forties, wore cocktail dresses too; the man, a little older, with hair fully grey at the temples and salt and pepper all over, was in a black suit with a black and gold striped tie. He was somewhat ample in girth and I thought he was just a step away from a bee's colours. He appeared to be a good deal older than the others and I put him somewhere in his late sixties.

"Steven is our Second," Robert told me, emphasising the number with pride in his voice.

"I'm not sure what that means," I replied, realising it must be some kind of title.

"It means, Steven is our...," Robert paused to think of the right word, "I suppose you could say, he is our vice chairman. My second-in-command, if you will."

"It's a pleasure to meet you. We've been waiting for you for some time," said Steven, his voice smooth as silk and his hand warmly grasping mine. I wondered just how long they had been waiting. I didn't think they were referring to the short time in between them arriving this evening and my appearance now.

"I'm honoured to be here," I said in my very best telephone voice, guessing it would be a good thing to say. Apparently, it was the right thing because all four beamed at me like I had just told them they were shortlisted for Time magazine's most powerful coven.

"I hope we'll get to talk to you more later," said one of the women, Bridget, I think and I nodded before Robert spun me away. For the next fifteen minutes, Robert made a point of introducing me to everyone in the room. I had two dozen eyes in close quarters wash over me in. My head was swimming with names, positions of authority, or not, pleasant welcomes and genial sound bites and my palms began to itch with perspiration.

I craned my head over one guest's shoulder as she droned on about nothing in particular and was grateful to catch Marc's eye. He was standing alone by the windows. I remembered that he'd jokingly given me an escape route. I scrambled through my brain to remember what it was, then, slowly, and very deliberately, I brushed some imaginary lint from my shoulder. Marc was at my side in seconds, his arm around my waist, politely wheeling me away under the ruse of getting drinks.

"Not having the most amazing time ever?" he asked, with the faintest hit of a sarcastic smile.

"I'm starting to have a hard time remembering who's who," I admitted. Marc had taken me over to a sideboard set up as a little bar. I had seen something like it on a rerun of the Antiques Roadshow being appraised for a huge sum. A row of glasses stood on a tray with carafes of wine behind them.

Marc reached forward and hesitated. "Red or white?"

"White, thank you." Marc poured the wine and passed me a glass. He took one for himself too and we turned back to the crowd.

"So your dad is head honcho?"

"Yes." Marc nodded, his face passive. "Has been for a couple of years."

"And your, uh, mother? Your mom?" I remembered the American vernacular and tentatively tried it out.

"Not so much into the clout, which is almost funny." He raised his glass to his mother across the room and she gave him a tight, little smile.

I didn't have chance to ask him what he meant as Étoile sidled up to my other side, a half-empty glass in her hand. The rim had the faintest trace of her lipstick. "They're about to begin," she murmured, nodding towards Robert and laying a hand on my arm. I felt much easier having the two of them flank me.

I looked over to Robert and, sure enough, he was clapping for attention, his hands raised to his head, and drawing the small crowd to him. He waited patiently until all eyes were on him. "We're here tonight to welcome Stella to our family, our country and our council." Eyes flickered briefly towards me and back again. "While Stella's arrival is tinged with sadness for many of our brethren, we are, of course, delighted to host the last of the English witches."

I raised my eyebrows and whispered, "The last?"

Étoile looked embarrassed and nibbled her bottom lip while she worked out what to say. After a moment, she whispered back, "You were the only one we could rescue. The Brotherhood got most."

"Got?" I asked, then spat out the most unpalatable question. "As in dead?"

"Uh-huh. There are more, but the ones that were magic to the bone were more obvious and easier to locate, like you. The ones who acquired their magic found hiding preferable and they've gone to ground." Étoile was careful with her emphasis so that I could understand there were two different types of witch, like it wasn't hard enough to get to grips with one type.

"So, I'm not really the last then?" I hardly dared sound hopeful, but I wanted to be. The last of anything sounded pretty rotten. I bet the last dodo and dinosaur once thought that too.

"Oh no, you're the last." Étoile almost sounded blasé about it. "The ones who acquire magic don't always c..." She trailed off after a harsh look from Marc. I had been sure she was about to finish with "count" but couldn't fathom what she meant. *Magic was magic, surely?* Maybe I was being naive. *Who knew what rules these people lived by.*

I didn't have the chance to ask her anymore because Robert was beckoning me. I deposited my glass back on the table and went towards him, with a backwards glance at Étoile. She seemed to have fallen into a sulk and Marc had twisted his torso slightly away as though he were ignoring her.

Robert motioned me to his right and put his arm around my shoulders in a way that was supposed to be friendly and fatherly, I guessed. It would have been impolite to wriggle out from under his arm so I stayed stock still and tried not to mind. "We are responsible for Stella's care and wellbeing," he told the gathering, gesturing at them with his wine glass. "We are responsible for her orientation into our world and we are here to decide Stella's future."

"And what does Stella want?" asked a male voice. A little sigh escaped my lungs; I could have kissed the guy. *At least someone remembered that I should have some say in my future. What with it being about me and all.*

"Uh, ah, yes, of course," Robert flustered as he flashed a dark look at the questioner who was just beyond my line of sight, even when I tried to move my head to see. "Stella?"

Eyes fixated on me again. Okay, not so great and I hoped I wasn't reddening from tip to toe. But not knowing the options the council were discussing, I knew what I wanted most of all. "I want to stay alive," I said simply, which, when I thought about it afterwards, was ironic really, considering what happened less than thirty seconds later.

Étoile had edged up to the front of the audience so I ducked out from under Robert's arm and went to stand beside her, where everyone could still see me but where I wasn't quite the centre of attention anymore.

As I took my place next to her, the window behind me shattered. Glass exploded in every direction as a missile rocketed its way in and sailed through the space I'd just occupied, missing Robert by mere inches. The missile lodged itself in a fizzing mess in the wall. Like an idiot, I waited for the explosion but it didn't come. Instead, something viscous, thicker than air but not as heavy as smoke, slithered from the bomb and all hell broke loose as those who had been caught by the glass cried out in pain and shock. Some of the gathering had fallen to the floor, bleeding, and the uninjured leapt forward to form a barrier around them as the sinister essence undulated nearer. I could hear a low murmur of chanting rise above the moans.

Marc and Étoile lurched into action, grabbing me and, with their arms entwined across my back, thrust me out of the way and into the lobby. We nearly collided with two suited men, our drivers from earlier, as they ran into the room. Voices rang after us, cries of astonishment and anger.

I heard a man's outraged voice say, "We can't retaliate with our magic until the shields are removed," but his words were met with angry disapproval followed by the steady of hum of voices in chorus, chanting words I didn't recognise.

I cowered in Étoile's arms as she hugged me tightly, one hand stroking my back in a curiously comforting way, which alleviated my panic. "They're spell casting," she whispered, her voice tickling my cheek as she explained, "some are reinforcing our protection. Some are trying to find the culprit. Mostly, they are keeping the magic from that bomb at bay."

Marc stood in front of us, his face etched with fury, his fists balled as smoke curled out of the room but he didn't make a move forward.

"What the hell was that?" I whispered, not sure if I should raise my voice.

"That, dear Stella, was very nearly your head," said Étoile, in an equally horrified voice. For the first time, she appeared visibly shaken.

Steven, Robert's Second, who had been standing with Bridget and Mary, came out of the door and signalled to us. I had half a mind to shoot for my room, but Étoile and Marc framed me, urging me forward.

"It's quite all right now," said the man. His head was bleeding and his suit was ripped at the shoulder. I could see a large shard of glass embedded in his upper arm. "Our magic has been reinstated and will hold." He looked shaken and white as he swayed in front of us. I helped Marc manoeuvre him into a chair. Étoile grabbed a cloth from somewhere and was pressing it to his shoulder as she gripped the shard.

"Don't do that. He could have sliced an artery," I hissed.

Marc was holding my shoulders with both hands. "Étoile knows what she's doing," he whispered but I missed what he said next because Steven shrieked as she pulled the shard from his shoulder, dropped it to the floor and pressed her hand over the wound.

"We should call an ambulance, shouldn't we?" My voice was almost a wail as I felt my heart beat faster with renewed panic.

Étoile shook her head and lifted her hand. Steven's shoulder was bloody but the wound had healed. There wasn't even a trace of a scar.

"Thank you. I always knew you were an excellent healer among your many talents." Steven said as he tugged a pocket square from his breast pocket. He dabbed his forehead with it. "Now run along. More will need your help."

Étoile nodded and hurried back into the devastated room. Bridget had staggered out and was leaning against the hallway holding a cloth to her face. Her dress sleeve was torn and her arm bleeding where she had been struck by glass. I guided her to the chair adjacent to Steven and she slumped into it, whimpering slightly. "The Brotherhood have found us," she heaved.

"How did they breach our defences?" growled Marc, swinging his head around as if he were looking for the perpetrator. His fists were curled, ready to fight.

Steven shook his head and took a deep breath. "I

don't know. We didn't think they had even made it to the States."

Marc put his arm about me and his lips were millimetres from my ear as he whispered. "This is one of the most fortified places in the country for people like us. It's protected by magic, powerful magic that we thought unbreakable. That someone, something, could breach it is unthinkable."

I nodded, trying to understand but knowing at least that this was something big and bad.

"We need to finish this meeting and disperse," continued Steven, shaking his head at Marc as he prepared to speak again. "We can't be sure that it is safe here for any of us anymore. I hear the incantation has ended. Will you please come back in so we can finish?"

I looked to Marc and, despite his obvious anxiety, he nodded and started towards the room.

"Stella," Steven's voice was low as I passed him. He caught me by the elbow and I froze as he pulled me closer to him so he could whisper in my ear, "Find me later. I have something for you."

I nodded and helped him to his feet, allowing him to lean against me as we went back into the room. The glass window had been repaired, and the shattered glass and debris that littered the floor had disappeared. Whatever it was that punctured its way through the room to land in the wall had also gone. If it weren't for the injured moans and the trails of smoke, I would have wondered if I hadn't imagined it all.

Robert stood with a woman, *Mary,* I thought. She had her hands pressed to the crater in the wall but when she turned to the crowd, she shook her head.

"There is no trace," she said with surprise in her voice. Her eyes were narrow and puzzled as if she couldn't quite work out why she had to say such a ridiculous statement.

With my back against the wall, I scanned the room trying to register everything. Faces were red, hair dishevelled and the air was thick. In the minutes that we had hidden in the lobby, I could tell, even in my own inexperienced way, that powerful magic had corrected the preceding events. I felt it echo in the air around me like a fog. I had never felt magic like this before; I had never felt anything but my own magic until the moment when Étoile had rescued me. Here, it trailed past me, whispering through my hair and coolly washing over me, chilling me to my core. Then I felt it withdraw like it was being snapped backwards. It was the strangest thing I had ever experienced and I shuddered. Everyone else seemed to be ignoring it.

"She's trying to find a signature," said Marc in a low voice, as he sidled up to me and nodded at Mary who still had her hands pressed to the shattered wall, "like a crime scene investigator would for a bomb. Magic has a signature too."

I nodded, trying to appear like I understood. The magic I had just felt had seemed alive – *perhaps that was what a signature felt like.*

"But she didn't find one?" I asked.

Marc shook his head and explained, "That's bad. Very bad. It means we don't have a clue who attacked us and whoever it is, must be extraordinarily strong to get through the defences here."

Étoile found us again. Her dress was stained with a large splotch across the skirt. I thought it looked like blood. Her hair and makeup, however, had not changed one bit. I vaguely wondered how she could appear so perfect amongst the strife. "They've wound new wards around the apartment," she told us, including me as much as Marc. "We should be safe for the short term, but Steven's right. We can't stay here much longer. I expect they'll make a decision about where we are going very soon." She seemed nonplussed, as if she already knew what the decision would be, but she didn't seem at all convincing when she added, almost as an afterthought, "Don't worry. You will be safe."

"We have been infiltrated," began Robert, his voice solemn as he addressed the untidy clan. Some of the guests had remained seated on the floor as others pressed what I thought were healing hands to wounds. Everyone looked dusty and tired after the skirmish. "Our safety has been breached. Stella, at first light you will be transported to another of our sanctuaries. It's a safe house of sorts and you will be able to live there out of harm's way for a while at least. Étoile and Marc will take you there and stay with you. You are under Étoile's protection."

Étoile and Marc nodded in agreement. Clearly, they knew something I did not but I would ask them later. I wasn't enthused. *What good was a safe house if apparently the headquarters could take a blast with no notice? And why was only Étoile my protector, and not Marc?* I would have to ask later.

"We're only sorry that we were not able to host you longer," concluded Robert, moving towards me after delivering verbal orders to several members of the party. It sounded like he was telling them all to go to ground as soon as possible. "We'll retire for the night. Thank you for coming."

And just like that, we were dismissed.

Before I had chance to protest, Étoile piloted me out of the room, her hand firm on my elbow, which I was seriously thinking about covering up seeing how it was being used as some sort of quasi steering wheel for my body. I was so floored by the brevity of the pronouncement that I didn't know what to think. Étoile put her arm around me again and was patting me rather absently while I drew in a breath.

"Stella?" I turned around to see Steven follow us outside the room. He signalled to follow him to one side, away from the entrance doors towards which people were amassing. He flapped a hand at Étoile and Marc so they lingered a few feet away. When we were at the hallway that led to the bedrooms, he extracted a slim blue card box from under the overcoat that hung across his arm, which he held out to me. Cautiously, I took it.

"In my other life," he started, "I'm a lawyer. I worked for your parents and when they were declared dead, I wrapped up their estate. I kept these for you in the hope that one day we would find you and I would personally be able to give these to you. It's mostly paperwork but there are some other bits and pieces that I thought you might like. There are some instructions too. Oh, nothing of immediate importance after all this time." He shrugged nonchalantly, giving me a small smile and I thought what a nice person he seemed to be. "It's yours now."

"Thank you," I replied, surprised. A little flutter of pleasure hit my stomach as I tried to think what on earth he could have kept of my parents. "It was kind of you to keep these things for me."

Steven nodded and his face creased into a smile. I

couldn't help thinking he suddenly looked much older than when I'd first met him in his bee-like finery. He looked over his shoulder quickly and turned back to me, leaning in, his voice etched with age. "Your parents were good friends of mine. Perhaps one day, when there's more time, I'll have the chance to tell you more about them. Keep the box safe."

As he inclined his head in a rather formal little bow, I caught sight, over his shoulder, of Eleanor looking at our exchange curiously. She quickly turned away and said something to a guest who seemed to be sobbing into a handkerchief, her hand pausing on the woman's arm.

"Good luck, Stella, until we meet again." Steven said as he took my hand and kissed it and I rather expected him to click his heels.

"And you," I said, my voice wobbling a bit. Steven nodded and traversed the hallway, tipping his head to Eleanor and closing the door behind him. From the living room, I heard the heated explosion of voices and Robert's rising above them to the tune of Eleanor's heels clicking across the lobby.

"I have to make some calls," murmured Étoile, who had glided across to me as soon as Steven had taken his leave. Marc was right behind her as she continued, "To make sure they're expecting us though I imagine Seren has already told them. My sister," she added for my benefit when I frowned at the name.

"Stella, can you be ready for seven tomorrow morning?" asked Marc.

"Yes, of course."

"I'll take Stella to her room," said Marc as Étoile set off along the hallway and was in her room in a flash, shutting the door before we had taken our first step along the same route.

"Where are we going?" I asked Marc when we reached the door to the guest bedroom serving as mine for this night. "Tomorrow, I mean."

"We have lots of places around the country but I suspect that we'll be going to a place we have along the coast. Like my dad said, it's a safe house, of sorts. Our kind go there to practice, to be taught, to learn." Marc thought for a moment as if he hadn't quite made up his mind. "It's a good place to be."

"Do I get any say in this at all?" I meant to be a bit more polite, but the words came out in a hiss. I shouldn't be angry at him, he had looked out for me all evening and I thought I saw a kindred spirit in him, despite the differences in our backgrounds. "This is my life and I got along fine until you all got involved in it."

"And if the Brotherhood weren't bent on killing us all, you'd probably still be fine," replied Marc. "We can't send you back out there to be picked off by one of them."

"So, it's a case of do what you say or die?"

"Not what I say," Marc emphasised and I wondered if his was quite a lowly role. Certainly Étoile seemed to have been spoken to with more reverence than he, which struck me as odd since he was the prodigal son. "What the council says. Look, Stella, I know it might suck right now but honestly, it's the best decision they could have made. The place we're going to is pretty good; there are others of your kind there. You'll learn how to defend yourself and when you can do that, well, maybe things will be safer for you. It's not forever."

I slumped against the door frame, the box in both

my hands, and sighed. "You've no idea how difficult it is to be taken away from everything you know."

"And was that everything so great? From the little Étoile told me, it didn't sound like you were having such a great time." *Ouch.* I wondered if Étoile had been watching me for any longer than that day, my last day of feeling relatively normal. I wondered what she said. I hoped she hadn't mentioned the squalid state of my flat, especially not to people who were rich beyond my wildest imaginings. Looking around, I was seriously going to have to pinch myself. I felt like Oliver Twist in Buckingham Palace.

"No, but it was my life, my decisions." I struggled to tell Marc what I was feeling about being wrenched away but I could tell it was no use. My immediate future had been decided by a bunch of people I didn't know. Plus, as Marc had already implied, *where else could I go?* Like he said, I might be killed, and after the attempt in London, strike that, two attempts now, my immediate future was looking dire. *Being a transatlantic attempted murder victim really didn't have any romantic ring to it*, I thought and shivered.

"Don't look so glum. Étoile will be there. And so will I." Marc flashed me a smile filled with perfect, white teeth.

"At least I'll know someone," I muttered.

"There you are, looking on the bright side already." Marc knocked me playfully on the shoulder with his fist and I couldn't resist smiling back at him.

"It could be worse."

"So much worse," he agreed.

"Good job I didn't unpack."

"See? It's like it was meant to be. We'll leave early tomorrow, hope you get some rest. Don't worry; the wards will hold for tonight."

"Thanks. And Marc?"

"Yes?"

"I do appreciate what you guys have done for me. Saving me from the crazies in London, making sure my head didn't land in a wall here, you know, minus the rest of me." I shrugged like I was saying, small things, no biggie!

"No problem." Marc's face was inches from mine and getting closer as we whispered in the hallway. I couldn't help thinking how lovely he looked with the shaggy blonde hair and his piercing blue eyes. He was the kind of guy who would never have looked twice at me at home, yet here we were, on the interesting side of weird, having a conversation as though we were friends. Marc brushed a lock of my hair behind my ear. When I didn't push him away but instead, rested my cheek in the warmth of his palm, Marc dipped his head and brushed his lips across mine, and for an instant, I wondered what the hell was going on, before pressing my lips back against his. His arms circled me and the kiss deepened but I didn't know whether it was eddies of desire or the fear and adrenaline of still being alive that whirled in the pit of my stomach. I pressed against him and was abruptly aware of the card box I held, digging into my middle.

Drat and double drat.

We pulled apart slowly, and after a pause, where the floor seemed massively interesting to us both, Marc tipped my chin upwards with his hand and kissed me again, a delicate light kiss this time.

"Good night," he said, his voice breathless.

"Good night, Marc." It was all I could do to turn the handle, fall through the doorway and push it closed, leaning my back against the door as if I couldn't possibly stand by myself.

The box was still clasped in one hand, so I set it on the bed as I contorted my arms behind my back to get the zip undone. I wriggled out of the dress and hung it back in the closet. I thought I had worn it for less than two hours and it was thankfully blood free. *Perhaps they could still dry clean and return it,* I thought for a moment, before shaking my head, deciding that *the Bartholomews were most certainly not those sort of people.* I wondered if I would ever have to consider the likelihood of getting my outfit blood-spattered in the future. I smiled to myself as I imagined asking a sales assistant for something blood repellent and in black. That would make shopping awkward.

I shuffled off the heels and lined them up on the closet floor where I found them, pulling on the t-shirt I had worn earlier. Out of instinct, I stayed away from the window, even though the curtains were already drawn.

Sitting cross-legged on the bed, the covers pulled over my knees and curiosity currently closer to killing me than magical flying bombs, I pried off the lid of the box Steven had given me.

The box seemed to contain papers mostly. I rifled through them. Papers and envelopes and a small cloth pouch. I dropped them all back in before starting at the top more slowly. The first documents I lifted were birth certificates. My mother's, my father's, mine. They named me Estrella Isadore. It had been so long since I'd heard my full name that I had almost forgotten my mother's name was my middle one.

Here was their marriage certificate too. They had married in New York. I hadn't known that and I wondered about them living in the city I had arrived in only a few hours ago. I traced my finger across the names that I recognised and then set them aside. It had never occurred to me that my parents were not both English. I just hadn't known them long enough to know anything of significance. Most of what I knew about them was second hand.

Death certificates, but English this time and issued in England. "Unknown" was the unsatisfying cause of death verdict. Their bodies hadn't been found but after five years they had been declared dead, said a one-page report stapled at the back of my father's certificate. I put them on top of the other papers. There was a small photo album covered in a mid-blue fabric that felt like suede. I opened it. The first image was a man and woman together, holding hands and smiling. Jonathon and Isadore was written underneath on a white label in a neat print.

My parents.

I so rarely heard their names that I had forgotten them as people with actual identities. With a twinge again, I thought of my mother's name melded with my own. The next few images were of the same couple, sometimes one or the other, sometimes both of them, the occasional snap of them with a group of people I didn't recognise, but some faces were repeated. Several times, another couple appeared. On the tenth page was my parent's wedding picture. The couple I had noted before were pictured with them. My mother was in a lace wedding dress that pooled at her feet and my father was laughing. The other man looked directly at the camera with a broad smile; the woman on his arm was gazing at my parents. Her face didn't carry any expression.

I put the picture on the pile I already looked through. The next few pages seemed to be a honeymoon on a coast somewhere rugged. Gradually, the pictures showed the woman pregnant, the man hugging her, smiling at her, not the camera, and then a baby who grew into a toddler as I turned the pages. I was looking at my parents and me. It was like nipping into some other family's photo pages. I didn't feel overwhelmed with emotion, just a little surge of joy looking at this happy besotted couple.

Abruptly, the photo album stopped, leaving a number of blank pages. There were some scraps of paper shoved into the back page and I tweezed them out with my forefinger and thumb. Cinema stubs, a tube ticket, concert tickets. Little snippets of their lives. I wondered which one of them liked David Bowie and who had wanted to see "St Elmo's Fire" twice? I went through the album once more, then set it aside on top of the birth certificates.

Some other bits of paper that didn't seem particularly important. A deed to a property, *a house* I thought, without knowing why and some bank and solicitor letters saying that there was no longer a mortgage and it was owned outright. I mentally filed the address away. I would ask someone later. Some bank books, partially used and a will from the same solicitors, signed by my parents. I scanned it. They had left everything to me, as any parent would. I recognised Steven's name as executor. There was an envelope addressed to me in a neat hand that I set aside to read later.

A few more pieces of official looking paper then a little velvet pouch. I pried the string apart and tipped the contents into my hand. A brilliantly coloured bird of paradise brooch, *made from enamel*, I thought, and a few other pieces of costume jewellery. I turned them over in my hands. I recognised some of the pieces from the photo album. My mother had worn the brooch on her wedding day, a bright spray against her simple white dress and again in my first birthday picture. They weren't costly pieces, but they were my mother's and I had never had anything of hers before. I slipped them back into the pouch. There wasn't much else so I carefully slotted everything back into the box and put the lid on top, kicking back the covers so that I could scramble out of bed and put the box on the dressing table.

After so much emotional deprivation, it was like my brain had gone into emotional overload and I wasn't sure where I should file all this new information in my mind. Sleeping on it would probably be a very good idea. I switched off the lamp on the side table and crawled back into bed, pulling the coverlet up to my neck and curling up like a baby. After a moment, I got up again and retrieved the box and set it on the nightstand next to me, at the same level as my eye line, now my head was on the pillow.

It was when I was on the periphery of sleep, at that halfway house between wakefulness and slumber, that the feeling that had been niggling at me finally developed into a fully formed idea and forced me back into awake mode.

Why hadn't anyone else realised?

The Brotherhood could never have attacked us tonight. Even my brain, rudimentary with the knowledge of magic, was turning cogs fast enough to realise that something was amiss. *The air was too thick with the magic of attack as well as defence. Only something magical could have so stealthily crept up on this committee of powerful witches and attacked us so bluntly without warning. Us,* I thought, *hmmm.*

"It doesn't make any sense," I whispered to the ceiling as I rolled onto my back. Why would the Brotherhood, who hates witches – us, me – use magic? They were old school. They were snatch, grab and burn, not spells and unearthly powers. They had proven that in the way they killed.

There had to be something or someone else. Someone else who wanted to maim and destroy this collective.

The gnawing feeling had changed. Now that I had my finger on the problem, I could only feel fear that I'd been seconds away from being killed tonight. Two attempts in as many days but perhaps not the same attackers. *Did someone here want me dead too? And if so, who the hell was it if it wasn't the Brotherhood?* My brain swam with ideas. I didn't feel any safer with the idea that I might have two foes.

I was wide awake now and I pulled my knees up so my arms were round them.

It should have been the excitement of Marc's stolen kiss that kept me half awake until dawn, but it wasn't, though that was a welcome distraction. Instead, there was the persistent niggle that something wasn't right.

I was glad my brain was forcing me to stay awake and think because in the early hours of the morning someone turned my door handle, pushed my door open an inch and paused. No one spoke and I was too scared to ask as I scrambled for a pillow and hurled it at the door. After it shut with a thud, I threw back the covers and took the few paces to the door as fast as I could. I turned the lock and dashed back into bed quicker than someone could say, "There's a monster under there."

I didn't dare doze again. Instead, I waited, hunched upright in bed with my arms clasped around my knees, shivering, until the first dawn broke.

CHAPTER FIVE

When I woke up in the morning, after a fitful couple of hours, someone had already pulled back the curtains to let the first streaks of sunlight sweep across my face. There was a tray on the dresser with cereal, a little jug of milk and a glass of orange juice. I looked for the blue box and saw that it was still on the nightstand exactly where I left it.

It disturbed me a little that whoever had come in, like the night before when I showered, had been quiet enough so as not to wake me and that I never even knew they were there. The bedroom door opening in the night flashed through my mind and I shuddered. *Had that person come back too?* I couldn't be sure.

I reached for my wristwatch on the nightstand and checked the time. Someone had been close enough to me to adjust the hands and it read six thirty, a time I'd never been fond of, no matter where I was. Except today I wasn't struggling from sleep in order to trudge to work. I was in bed in a luxurious apartment thousands of miles from home and, as far as I knew, had nothing even remotely familiar on my day's agenda. It wasn't a particularly comforting thought.

It took all my energy to slide out from the warm covers and stumble into the bathroom to use the toilet, shower and brush my teeth. Ten minutes later, I was dressed in jeans, a t-shirt and v-neck sweater in the palest lilac which was the best I could do for travelling clothes without knowing where I was travelling to or how. *Was Étoile planning on zapping us somewhere?*

I flittered around in the centre of the room for a moment or two, wondering if I was supposed to tell someone that I was awake. Then my eyes caught the breakfast tray again; my stomach gave a little grumble and I sat down to eat. I spooned a mouthful of cereal and brought it up to my lips just as a knock on the door interrupted my solitude. I called, "Come in."

Étoile peeped her head around. Of course, she looked immaculate in a deep navy turtle-neck sweater, which only accentuated how pale she was and how high her cheekbones were. She smiled. "We have to go now. The sooner the better."

"How are we going?" I asked, my spoon hovering in the air. I put it down before I spilled milk across my sweater.

Étoile frowned as if I'd just asked something really dumb. "By car, of course. Marc will drive."

"Oh." I swallowed the last of my orange juice. "Good. When will we get there?"

"A few hours or so," answered Étoile. I could see that she had a small bag packed and it stood in the hallway, just beyond the door. "Can you be ready in five minutes?"

"Yes, of course." Étoile ducked out but left the door ajar. I ate the rest of my cereal so fast that I could only hope I wouldn't get indigestion. I faffed around for a few seconds trying to arrange the tray before throwing a napkin – starched white, of course – over the bowl.

I pulled my bag onto the bed and tossed the few things I'd taken out back in, then wrapped the blue box in a sweater, placing it on top before zipping up the bag. I tugged on my trainers and bent to tie them, then pulled on the grey jacket, remembering to pick up my smaller shoulder bag with my wallet full of useless coins and notes. I wondered if the day would come when I wouldn't be able to pack all my stuff in minutes, when I wouldn't be at the mercy of other people sending me here and there. I chided myself silently. *If it weren't for Étoile, I'd be dead now. If it weren't for the council, I wouldn't have a home or protection.* I should be grateful for everything that they were doing for me, not whimpering about how hard my life was. *As if it had ever been easy! And really, what was I missing anyway?* Marc had been right. Not a lot.

I pulled my hair back in a tight ponytail with a band and checked it was smooth in the mirror, nodding at myself in approval. Sure, the ends were still slightly singed but I'd have to deal with that another time. "Man up, Stella," I whispered at my reflection and the irony wasn't lost on me; that was something I certainly could not do, however hard I tried.

Étoile was waiting outside my door. She had pulled the retractable handle out of her bag and was leaning on it.

"Is that all you've got?" I asked. Étoile was

looking splendid again, of course, in expensive jeans that hugged her long legs and the clingy navy sweater. I wondered if she used some sort of magic to keep herself so neat. I wondered if I could learn that.

"I already have things there." Étoile linked her arm to mine as though we had been friends forever and wheeled her case behind us with her free hand. Marc was waiting for us in the lobby but his parents weren't anywhere to be seen. I looked around and surprise must have been etched on my face because Marc said, "Mom and Dad said to tell you goodbye and apologised that your stay was cut short. They're attending to business at the moment and can't be spared."

I wanted to ask if it was the kind of business that involved asking if anyone other than the Brotherhood was a threat but instead, kept my mouth shut and nodded. "Are we leaving now?" My voice sounded plaintive and small in the big room.

"Yes," replied Marc, as he swung a black rucksack over his shoulder. "There's extra wards protecting the building and they cast a protection spell on the car. Spells don't last long while things are moving, but it should be enough to get us out of the city without being observed."

We followed him out the door to the private lift that served the penthouse. As we travelled down, I wondered how much I could ask about where we were going and what they would tell me. *If they would tell me anything at all.* It wasn't my modus operandi to follow other people around blindly. I stifled a laugh in my throat and Étoile twitched an eyebrow at me. *What could I say?* I thought as I turned the slightly hysterical little laugh into a cough. It wasn't in my

M.O. to hop on planes, or, for that matter, even hang out with people. Nothing was normal anymore. Étoile let go of her bag long enough to place a cool hand over my wrist and her touch alone sent a wave of calm over me, driving the brief hysteria back along with the rising lump in my throat. Marc, lost in his own thoughts, didn't seem to notice.

The doors slid open to the underground car park and we followed Marc to the huge black Cadillacs, but to my surprise, when Marc pressed his key fob, the lights of a silver Prius parked next to them flashed.

"Much less ostentatious," Marc explained, opening the door and motioning that I should get in on the correct passenger side, which wasn't the side I had stepped towards. He took my bag and tossed it in the trunk with his, then took Étoile's as she climbed into the back and slid over so she was behind the driver's seat. As I plugged my seat belt in, Marc took the driver's seat beside me and turned the ignition.

"I know I've already asked," I said, as the engine sprang to life, "but where exactly are we going? I know it's a sort of safe house?"

"It's a safe house that we use," confirmed Marc, as he checked the rear view mirror and reversed. "It's owned by a friend of the council and we use it as a, sort of, training ground. Our veterans help the novices learn how to control their powers, both wisely and effectively."

"Is this friend a witch?"

Marc looked at Étoile in the rear view mirror. From the corner of my eye, I saw her give a little shake of her head. Marc looked over at me briefly and said, "Not exactly, but she's not against us either. She's neutral."

"Have you been there before?" I asked wondering who "she" might be.

"Étoile was there for a while until she was sent to England a few days ago and I come and go."

"It's very nice and there are a few of us there," said Étoile, leaning forward between the seats. "I'm sure you'll like it. You'll learn a lot. Plus you'll meet my sister, Seren, and your friend, Kitty."

Marc flinched at the name as he threw the car into drive.

I twisted in my seat to look at Étoile. "I don't have a friend called Kitty."

"You will," said Étoile, with absolute confidence.

Marc drove across the car park, past a series of expensive vehicles, and manoeuvred the car up the exit ramp. He waved to the uniformed attendant standing in the guard box at the top of the ramp and waited for the barrier to rise before turning onto the street and accelerating. He drove carefully so as not to attract any attention towards us and soon we were on the bridge. I almost wished I had been here as a tourist so that I could spend some time marvelling at the bridge's construction and the city retreating behind us. I wondered if I would ever come back.

Marc closed his hand over mine and gently squeezed it before regrasping the steering wheel. I was grateful for the human touch and a warmth spread through me as I remembered last night's kiss. Marc winked at me and I dipped my eyes so I could suppress a smile.

"Do you... did you both train there? At this school?"

"No." It was Étoile's turn to speak. "Our parents instructed us, but lately, after... well, Seren and I needed to re-learn some things and it's convenient for us to be based at the house."

"What can you do?" I asked. "I know you can move yourself the same way I can."

"That," agreed Étoile. "I can see the future too, just glimpses. Seren is an empath. She is very intuitive to the feelings of others, as well as animals. She shimmers too. Those are our main strengths but we have other skills too."

"What about you, Marc?"

Marc's hands gripped the wheel and he stared ahead for a moment before answering. "I don't know yet."

"I don't understand."

"Marc is a slow learner," said Étoile with a snicker.

Marc drew in a breath. "For some of us, magic doesn't come straight away. It's in me; it's inherited, but I don't know what I can do with it." He shook his head and continued as though he were used to explaining it. "It's an anomaly but it happens."

I wondered what his parents, the council leaders, thought about their son being an anomaly amongst all the power that their clan brandished. I suspected they weren't thrilled – *it would be like two maths professors having a kid with dyscalculia*, I thought. But I suspected that it was harder for Marc not knowing what power he did possess nor how to access it when everyone around him was teeming with it. Even I could sneeze and... "shimmer" and I didn't know what the hell I was doing.

"I'm sorry."

"Don't be. It'll work itself out." Marc's voice was stiff and decisive. *As far as conversations went, we'd pretty much killed that one.*

Étoile had her phone out again and was busily tapping keys while Marc concentrated on the road. I leant my head against the headrest and watched the world whiz past my window as I contemplated Étoile's Blackberry addiction. *It must be nice having so many people to constantly contact,* I thought. Though it was early morning, after a while, I could feel my head loll. I twisted my head from side to side but the jetlag and the past night was finally catching up on me as the burr of the engine lulled me to sleep.

By the time I woke again and blinked at the clock on the dash, Marc had been driving for hours. The scenery whipped past in a blur of roadside businesses that gave way to trees and open farmland. When we finally left the highway and turned into town, I was pretty sick of sitting in the car and desperate to get out and stretch my legs. We drove a little further until Marc slowed and turned through a pair of open gates.

Manicured lawns hugged the drive with borders of neatly clipped mature shrubs and a spattering of coloured flowers. It looked for all the world like a large family house, inconspicuous in its normalcy. I wasn't sure what I was expecting, but it wasn't this. Marc parked the car in front and I stepped out before he could walk around and open my door. I inhaled deeply and was tickled to find the air slightly salty, like seawater. I wondered if the ocean was closeby. I hoped so. I had never had much cause to go to the beach but the idea of one nearby seemed pretty nice to me. *And so completely normal.*

The house was a two-story, white clapboard with an oversized porch. One end of the house jutted out at a right angle to the main part. Several cars were parked off to the left and there was enough room on the drive that none would have to move for the others to pass. The front door, painted in a soft sage green, was framed with four windows on each side and I could see that the house stretched backwards. It was large and welcoming.

Someone had clearly been waiting for us because the door popped open just as Marc unloaded our bags. An elderly lady in a floral dress with a white half-apron covering her skirt stood in the shade of the porch in obvious anticipation. She smiled broadly and I couldn't help but smile back.

"Don't just stand there, dears. I've baked scones and made iced tea for you all after that long drive." She beckoned us to follow as she retreated inside.

Sure enough, the aroma of baking drifted towards us. We grabbed our bags from where Marc had set them on the driveway and entered the house; Étoile pausing to stoop and kiss the old lady on the cheek.

"Go on into the kitchen. I'll just tell everyone that you're here," said the old lady as I passed her. When I looked back to the door, she was already gone and Marc was pushing it closed.

"Who was that?" I asked.

"Not so much who, as what," muttered Marc softly, before saying more loudly. "We call her Aunt Meg. She owns the place."

"Come on through to the kitchen. Aunt Meg is a whiz at baking." Étoile signalled to me to stow my bags in the hallway next to hers and I followed her past doorways that led off to rooms full of furniture – but empty of people – and into the kitchen. As promised, the long, scrubbed pine, farmhouse table was spread with a large glass jug of iced tea, icy rivelets dribbling down the sides, and a cluster of glasses next to it. A cake plate with a short stubby stand and fluted edges had a mound of fresh English fruit scones and I sighed with pleasure. There was a stack of china plates and pots with butter and jam. Knives rested on folded cotton napkins. My stomach gave another little rumble so I kneaded it with my knuckles.

"Have a seat, have a seat, my dears. Stella, we're so glad to have you here." Aunt Meg took my hand in hers, covered it with another cool hand and shook it. I shivered at her wintry touch but remembered my manners and said I was pleased to meet her and thanks for having me.

"Not at all," murmured Aunt Meg, indicating to sit while she poured iced tea for us. She sat at the head of the table and smiled beatifically at us as she passed out the plates. "What a long drive you've had. I've made up your beds. Stella, you will have our yellow room. It's not really very yellow but there are an awful lot of rooms here, so that's what we call it. Étoile, you are next to Seren as per usual. Marc, you have the blue room. I know you like the green room but that has been commandeered by a new recruit. Do have some jam, Stella. I made it from the fruit from these gardens."

I helped myself to the jam and slathered it over my split scone, biting into it. It was still warm from the oven and the apple jam was gently scented with something, *cinnamon*, I thought. Étoile was already reaching for a second.

"I'm sorry a welcoming committee hasn't turned out to greet you but we've all been rather busy. Rest assured, everyone is very keen to meet you and they will drift along sooner or later." Meg cocked her head to one side and leaned back a little to look along the passageway before turning back to us. "Ah, here's one now. Evan!"

I brushed the crumbs from my mouth and took a sip from my iced tea. When I looked up, it was all I could do not to gasp.

The man filling the doorway was at least six foot two with broad shoulders that tapered to a neat waist and long, jeaned legs. Toned arms extended from under a grey t-shirt and his hands didn't look like strangers to work. As my eyes travelled up from his chest, I noted a tanned, square jaw that hadn't seen a razor in a day or two, a slim nose and brown eyes so dark I could barely distinguish iris from pupil. His hair was cut short and so dark it could almost have been black. He wasn't beautiful in the traditional sense but he was captivating, the type of man people automatically turn their heads to have another look at. I couldn't drag my eyes away and my heart did a little flip.

A fleeting image of being wrapped up in his arms, his lips crushing mine, overtook my mind. He caught my eye and held my gaze. I was glad he couldn't see inside my mind, but I blushed furiously. His face looked thunderous. And now, come to think of it, Marc didn't exactly look happy either.

"This is her?" he asked no one in particular, his eyes still fixed on me, his expression fading from thunder to completely impassive.

"Stella," I spluttered, my cheeks still red as the image in my head seemed to topple over and send us sprawling, limbs entwined. *Was I supposed to shake his hand now? Good God.* "Hi."

Étoile looked from me to Evan and coughed lightly, her hand covering a smile and I just had enough time to wonder what she had seen before she said, "Evan will be teaching you."

"I will not,' announced Evan, his mouth set in a firm line. "She leaks. Find someone else."

"David could teach her," snapped Marc, scowling at Evan. The muscles in his arm had tensed though he was still sitting and I could see the veins bulge. *What was with him?*

"David is teaching Christy, Clara and Jared," said Aunt Meg placidly. "Evan will be teaching her. That's why he's here."

The ensuing silence was deafening. Marc scowled at Evan, Evan looked spitefully at me and I gripped my glass as if it were a life rope in a storm. Étoile finished up her second scone and looked around gleefully as if we were the height of entertainment. Meanwhile, my mind was getting increasingly lurid and I could hardly look Evan in the eye for fear that he would know that I'd just had a very exciting mental picture of us doing something that really should not have popped into my head while I was having a scone with civilised company.

"If you don't want to teach me, fine," I gasped, daring to look at Evan from under my lashes. Marc had leant back in his seat, arms crossed; Meg and Étoile were still looking at the man expectantly. Étoile coughed, but not before I heard her snicker again.

His jaw shifted and he breathed out. "I'll teach you," he said at last, making it sound like the least pleasant chore he could be assigned.

"Okay."

"Fine." Evan stepped back out of the doorway

and strode back the way he came.

"Whew!" said Étoile. "That was weird. Like he was ever not going to teach you."

"He's an ass," muttered Marc, swallowing the last of his iced tea and banging the glass back down on the table. "I'm sorry you're stuck with him."

"Evan Hunter is a very good teacher," Aunt Meg chided as she gathered up the plates and swatted Étoile's hand from the cake stand with a napkin before she could reach for another scone. I noticed Aunt Meg hadn't eaten or drunk anything and hoped she didn't think I was greedy for gobbling mine as fast as I could.

"What did he mean – I leaked?" I asked, thinking that sounded, well, *gross*.

"Your magic," said Étoile. "He can feel it. So can I. You aren't containing it, so it leaks. Not your fault."

"Étoile, would you show Stella her room? Seren is outside somewhere waiting for you," said Meg, effectively killing that conversation stream dead.

"Of course, and thank you for your delicious scones." Étoile didn't seem to be at all upset that the third scone had evaded her. She stage whispered to me, "Aunt Meg likes to feed. If you're not careful, she will make you awfully fat."

She grabbed my hand to skitter out of the kitchen as the elderly housekeeper shooed us out with a laugh. We walked back towards the door but peeled off right to the stairway and I followed Étoile as she scampered up. On the way, I peered into the downstairs rooms looking for Evan but he had vanished and I tried to shake the thought of him from my mind. Upstairs, the landing was long and bright, flooded with light from the picture window and punctuated by many doors. The walls played host to a series of landscape pictures. “How many bedrooms are here?” I asked, trying to make conversation while I got the lay of the land.

“About ten upstairs, I think, including the two in the attic,” said Étoile. “And a couple downstairs and there’s a little cottage on the grounds too for when the house is very full. It’s a very old house. Aunt Meg’s family built it at least a century ago and they have added to it over the years.”

“She doesn’t have any family?”

Étoile shook her head as she counted doors, her fingers trailing on the chair rail. “One, two, three... here we are, yellow room.” She pushed open the door and grinned at me. “Got it right, come on in. So, Aunt Meg’s husband died aeons ago and then her daughter. She had grandchildren but they’re gone now too. Oh no, not dead. Seattle, I think. So, you know, close! I think that’s why she likes us here, coming and going and filling the house up. Plus she is paid generously to put up with us.”

“She’s not a witch?”

“No, she’s a...” Étoile stopped herself. She pursed her lips and took a breath, then said, “No, not a witch but we love her anyway.”

She had avoided the question in the car too and I wondered what Aunt Meg was that was so bad no one wanted to say. I was going to ask her what she meant but when I stepped inside the room, the thought slipped away. The yellow room was, indeed, not very yellow. There was wallpaper with pale yellow stripes and tiny roses and a big iron bed with a white coverlet sprigged with pastel flowers, set in between two windows with white shutters. One had a window seat with scattered cushions and a folded blanket. There was a white dresser and a closet set into the wall and a door opened just a crack that led to the en suite. The room was bright, airy and quite the prettiest room I had ever seen. My flat – my former flat, I corrected myself – was positively grotty in comparison.

"I love it," I said, grinning at Étoile.

"Great. Meg knew you would, she always knows. I am next to you and Seren the other side of me. Marc is downstairs. Kitty is opposite and you'll meet her later. Evan is at the end of the hall."

Evan flickered into my mind and I imagined myself alone in a room with him and blushed again. I could not handle having a crush, especially such a lurid one, on my apparent teacher. Étoile winked lasciviously at me.

"He is rather yummy, isn't he?"

"Evan? Sure, I guess." I shrugged, trying to look nonplussed.

"Sure. Whatever. Not sure any of us exist on his radar. Not that any of us have tried," she added as an afterthought. "I am going to head outside to find my sister. Can you find your way back out again? There's a door to the yard off the kitchen. You can go where you like here. Just stay in the grounds, please."

I nodded.

Étoile started to leave, then paused and put her arms around me, giving me a little squeeze. "Welcome home," she said and kissed me on the cheek before disappearing into the hallway.

I looked after her, momentarily blindsided by the little show of affection, then pushed the door. It closed with a little click. My bag was just inside the door so I took it to the closet and decided to empty it, seeing as it looked like I was staying. I hadn't protested anyway. I hung my clothes on the hangers and folded a few tees into the drawers. Even out of the bag, they looked pitifully few. I put the blue box into the top drawer and my bits of jewellery in the dish on top. It was shaped like a little bird with a fanned tail and my oddments glittered against the enamel.

I took a moment to brush my ponytail and smooth the sides of my hair before poking around the room, finding, to my delight, that the en suite had been left with fresh towels folded over the tub and a basket of toiletries. There was even a toothbrush still in its card wrapper, which was just as well because I hadn't brought one with me.

I sat on the bed for a moment and bounced once, twice, laughing at myself before hopping up to look out the window. Beyond were gardens, mostly lawn, then a path leading off to my right which meandered towards steps that dropped down into another garden level. I could just see a further level that rolled down to a beach, wooden steps carved into the rock and a curl of blue water beyond. I hoped I'd get to explore sometime soon. *Maybe even now? Étoile had said I could go anywhere.*

I was out of my room before I could talk myself out of poking around someone else's property.

The first room I came across, after scampering down the stairs, was the living room, directly opposite the stairs and across the entrance hall. It was comfy with wide sofas and a big TV in the corner. I scanned the DVDs lined up on the shelf above it. "Buffy the Vampire Slayer," "Twilight," "An American

Werewolf in London," "Supernatural," "Carrie." Some wit had folded a piece of card and put it on the shelf in front of them; "documentaries" was the label in a flowing script. I stifled the urge to laugh and then thought a bit. Perhaps there was something more to the label than a joke. Despite the warmth, I shivered and turned away.

The living room was comfortable with three big sofas in blue ticking and two armchairs. A stack of thick floor cushions lay behind them. Clearly, the room was designed for seating many people and I wondered how many the house could hold. On one wall was a fireplace with a stack of logs in a basket and next to that, the large flatscreen television and a DVD player with the remotes stacked neatly on top. On the other wall was a wide window overlooking the front garden; the opposite window had French doors that viewed a small patio with an iron table and chairs worked in a fancy pattern that made it look like lace.

I headed back out to the hallway and retraced my former steps past two closed doors, which I assumed were the ground floor bedrooms (I wondered which one was Marc's) and towards the kitchen. The old lady, Aunt Meg, wasn't there so I went out the open door, across the patio, following the path into the garden.

A small group sat in a circle under the shade of a large tree. Marc had trailed behind me and he nudged me as I debated which way to go. "Settling in?"

"Yes, thank you. My room is incredibly pretty."

"The girls thought you would like it. They've been looking forward to you coming. They're a bit starved for company here."

"So anyone new will do, huh?" I jested but Marc

frowned, deep lines setting between his brows. I rolled my eyes. "Joking."

"Under the tree there is David." Marc indicated to the thin young man gesticulating at the group of three who sat in front of him. A long welt ran from his eyebrow, across his cheek and finished under his chin. It was new and angry. Marc lowered his voice. "He was attacked three weeks ago. He got out just in time and managed to get here. He tried leading a regular life but I think he's happier to be here now."

"And the others?"

"Jared is new like you." Marc pointed to the boy who sat in front of David. He didn't look more than seventeen. "He pretty much can't control anything he does. Seren's had to put spells on Jared to stop him breaking stuff. He's already broken three chairs just by looking at them the wrong way. Aunt Meg was getting pretty pissed."

"Can you do that? Just put a spell on someone?"

"You're not supposed to." Marc frowned and looked thoughtful. "But Seren did discuss it with Jared first and he was pretty embarrassed so he agreed. He can lift the spell anytime he likes; Seren made sure of that. He's not being forced."

"What if someone put a spell on you and you didn't know?" I asked.

"No one should use a spell against another so that they do what the spell caster wants, or can't... There are severe consequences for that," Marc finished. He dug at the ground with the toe of his sneaker. With his hands thrust in his pockets and his shaggy hair spilling over his forehead, he could have been discussing a photo shoot, not the perils of illicit magic. He pondered what he said for a moment, then shook his head and continued, nodding at the two girls in the circle. "Christy has been here for a few months and she's pretty smart. Clara is her sister and struggling a bit but she's keen and that counts for a lot. They're all finding their feet here."

"Did the council know about them?"

"About Jared, yes, and they decided he needed some intensive training, well, away from the regular world. Christy and Clara just turned up one day. They say they didn't even know why, just that they felt they should be here and the wards that guard this place just let them walk right in."

I nodded, trying to show that I understood in some way. Marc led me away from the group and around the side of the house.

"So this place is guarded by magic?" I asked like a total newb. It was quite at odds with the image I wanted to project. I was independent, stubborn and self-sufficient. *So much for that!* Here I was completely reliant on other people.

Marc nodded. "It keeps everyone here safe. Sort of like an early warning signal." But he didn't say exactly what it was keeping us safe from.

"I came in fine though. I didn't have to say a password or anything." I blushed when Marc laughed.

"Magic recognises magic," he explained simply.

Étoile sat on a bench with another striking woman. "That's Seren, her sister," he said as the pair rose to greet me. Seren rested her hands lightly on my upper arms as she leaned in to kiss me briefly on both cheeks. It seemed they were both a tactile pair and I warmed to her instantly. She had the same slightly pointy, high-cheekboned face as Étoile but with a softer edge, framed with wavy hair that dusted her collarbone. She was a striking dresser too, but where Étoile seemed to favour darker colours, her sister wore a strapless maxi dress in a shade of sherbet orange.

"Étoile has been telling me about you," Seren said. "It seems you had a very exciting exit from your country."

"I wish it had been a little less exciting," I confessed. "Fire bombs and chases don't do much for my nerves."

"If it makes you feel better, the fire service were able to put out your fire and your landlady was very pleased with her insurance claim. She's thinking of retiring to the coast," said Étoile.

"A little bit," I admitted. "But how do you know?"

"We keep tabs. Besides, I thought you would want to know so you wouldn't worry if she had survived or not."

"I think the old battleaxe could survive anything. I didn't like her but I'm glad she wasn't hurt."

"Hello!" A new voice called from behind us and I noticed Marc stiffen slightly. I turned round to see a woman about my age bound towards us. She stretched out her hand to shake mine in a friendly manner before seeming to surrender and embraced me in a hug instead. "You must be Stella? I'm Kitty Williams." She nodded at Marc and her smile seemed to fall from her face just a fraction. He gave her a curt nod back.

"Hi, Kitty," I said.

Kitty, like her name, was as cute as the proverbial button. That is, if buttons exuded sex appeal too. She was small, no more than five two, but tanned and toned with a curvy hourglass shape clad in shorts and a spaghetti-strap top. Bundles of bouncing curls clipped back with girlish bows fell to her shoulders.

"Stella, promise me that you won't let Étoile and Seren monopolise you. Every other girl has a sister here and I have no one, so, I'm not afraid to say, I'm a little desperate for us to be friends. Say it will be so?" she cajoled.

I couldn't help but smile at her enthusiasm. "It will be so."

Étoile and Seren had tipped their heads to one side as if listening to something and then inclined their heads slightly to smile at us. "We have seen," said Étoile with Seren finishing, "and it will be so." It was endearing rather than weird and I wondered if they made a habit of finishing each other's sentences.

"Well, now the psychics have said so," said Kitty, linking her arm through mine. "It will be so and very glad I am, too. Shall I give you the tour?"

"How much do they see?" I whispered as Kitty shooed Marc away, propelling me beside her before I had a chance to agree. When I looked over my shoulder, Marc gave me a little wave and shook his head.

"Did Étoile not think to mention it? Probably not! They are quite powerful, both Étoile and Seren, and it all gets amplified the closer they are to each other. They can see the future, just glimpses, of course, but enough to see what will happen."

"Does everything happen the way they see it?"

"Everything is subject to change," said Kitty and it took me a moment to recognise that she was mimicking Étoile's clipped voice before reverting to her own. "They see things the way they are meant to be at that moment in time. Of course, if something changes, some action or intention, then the future shifts too. They see more the closer they are together and it's a very powerful tool. Right now, they saw us being friends, so unless you turn out to be completely revolting in the next few minutes, I think we can safely assume that we will be."

"And they can move themselves too. You know ... teleport?" I asked, looking for the right word.

"Yes, though not that far now. They used to be able to shimmer right around the world in the blink of an eye but they are a bit more limited these days."

"Why's that?"

"There used to be three of them which made them very powerful as witches and sisters, but with just the two ... although they are strong, it's a weaker circuit," Kitty explained.

"Is the other sister here?"

"Oh, no." Kitty looked shocked. "No, no." Then she clamped shut and wouldn't broach the subject again, making me wonder if anyone could tell me more than partial truths.

After a few minutes, I changed tack. "What can you do?" I asked.

"I can do things with the weather," Kitty said after a moment and then giggled. "I'm like a weather station, I guess. No one has any idea if that is any use or not. I can manipulate things by confusing the air. I am, however, good at spells."

"As in chanting and rhymes?"

"Oh no, I can't rhyme. I don't know why legend has it that witches have to rhyme to cast a spell; can you imagine what a bother that would be? What if I wanted to rhyme something with the word 'orange'?"

Kitty laughed. "David is teaching me spell-casting while Evan figures out what the weather bit means. It must mean something, otherwise I wouldn't be able to do it, though Aunt Meg says she's never had a better crop of fruit than since I've been here, so at least I've come in handy for that."

My garden tour took no more than half an hour with Kitty pointing out the fruit orchard and a set of white painted, wooden steps that led down to a beach on the other side of the garden. "It's not private, as such," said Kitty, "but there are no other houses on this stretch of shore and no one else really comes here so we think of it as ours."

From there, she took me back towards the house pointing out seating areas here and there and then back inside where I was shown where to find glasses and snacks in the kitchen. "Aunt Meg doesn't like us to be on ceremony here. Mi casa es su casa and all that." She showed me the half bathroom downstairs and where to find stationery and spare keys in the hall drawer in case I wanted to go out, though Kitty mentioned there wasn't much to do in the town beyond a bar, a small library and a few shops and businesses. I didn't mention Étoile had told me to not leave the property – *that just wasn't cool.*

In my room, she showed me where to find spare towels and bed linens and pointed out that she was just across the hall if I wanted anything else. Her name was being called downstairs and she smiled apologetically at me before hopping away to answer it.

Alone again in my room, I collapsed on the window seat and after kicking off my shoes, rested my head on the window. I could just glimpse the sea from my perch and the sight of the waves lapping at the beach was mesmerising. I played with the catch and was surprised that the sash window slid up easily, as if it had been oiled recently, letting in the salty breeze so I could inhale it. I arranged the cushions behind my back and drew up my legs as I looked out at the infinite sea. I thought about all the events of the past couple of days and my new housemates. I wasn't sure what to make of it all. Everything was so far out of my comfort zone.

A knock at my door interrupted my reverie and I called, "Come in."

Marc ducked his head around the door. "I came to see if you were okay."

"I'm good, thank you."

Marc walked across the room and slid onto the seat with me as I drew back to give him room. He picked up my legs and put them across his lap. Taking one foot, he began to rub it absently.

"So, you've met the whole crowd," he said, kneading my sole as I rested my head against the wall, eyes partially shut to enjoy his familiarity. I wondered which part of me was totally okay with letting him caress my feet. The part of me enjoying it suggested I shut up.

"Yes."

"They're an oddball group, but nice and it'll be good for you to learn here. David's an excellent teacher, Evan is ... well regarded."

"What do Étoile and Seren do here?" I asked, my heart giving a strange little leap at Evan's name. He hadn't seemed to think much of me and I wasn't sure if I should feel insulted. It wasn't like I chose to be here. I was surprised to find myself feeling hurt.

"They don't seem like students."

"They're not. They pretty much live here and it's a good base for them to come and go while they take on their missions. They're away as often as they are here. We don't have many witches of their calibre to spare so they help teach occasionally."

I frowned. "I thought Étoile said there were lots and lots of witches?"

"Yes," Marc agreed, "but not many with their power. We're a dying breed."

I thought about that for a minute. "And what do you do, Marc?" I asked at last.

He pushed his thumbs into the ball of my foot and sighed. "I don't know."

"What do you mean?"

"I mean just that. I don't know. I could do stuff when I was little and then, one day, it just went away. I couldn't do anything anymore. No one knows why."

"Isn't that a little strange?" I hadn't meant magically – I knew from Étoile's teasing that he hadn't any magic of his own yet – but I'd let him roll with it.

Marc exhaled through his nose and rested his head back against the wall. "My parents don't really talk about it but I know they think it's odd. I think they're even a little embarrassed; but my father is certain one day it will ping back on just as quickly as it disappeared." He talked about his magic like it was a faulty light switch. I wondered how long it had taken him to sound so offhand about the missing part of his being.

"Do you want it to come back?"

"It's not easy," Marc replied and I knew he had probably spent a long time thinking about it. "When you're around people who can do all the weird and wonderful things that you should, in theory, be able to do too, it's a little galling that you're pretty much a regular guy who has to walk to get places and wait to find out what happens."

"I imagine there are a lot of people who would like to swap places with you right now."

Marc smiled. His thumbs massaged the balls of my feet and I could feel the warmth of his hands. "I hadn't thought of it that way; that my being ordinary was something to be envied."

"So what do you do instead?"

"I run around after people, making sure everyone has what they need, coordinate people, general logistics, that sort of thing."

Marc reached for me and I swivelled on the window seat so that I was sitting in between his legs as he drew me backwards to rest my head on his chest, wrapping his arms around me. He rested his chin lightly on my head and I wondered if he was smelling my hair. *Thank goodness it was clean.* He breathed deeply and my lungs rose and fell in line with his.

"I'm sorry you've had to go through such a shitty time," he said, breaking the brief silence between us.

I tried to look on the bright side, the same way Marc had with his lack of magic. "Well, I wasn't having the greatest time anyway," I said, trying to show him that I really didn't mind. That it was okay to have my whole life uprooted, tipped on its head, shook around a bit and then replanted a continent away. "Getting the box of stuff from my parents was pretty wonderful. It's about one thousand times more than I've ever had of theirs."

"You don't remember them at all?"

"Fleeting memories here and there, like snapshots, but I don't know if they are real memories or just stuff I saw on television or got from my foster parents. So, no, I don't remember them at all. I was very little when they disappeared and I was found."

"That's sad."

"Yes," I agreed. "It is. I wish I had known them and all about this world but they must have had their reasons to hide me before they disappeared."

"You think they'll come back?"

"No." It was depressing to admit it but I had never thought they would come back.. I'd always been certain of that. "I'm sure they are dead. Otherwise they would have found me by now. They were declared dead years ago. Steven gave me the paperwork."

"What do you think happened to them?"

I had speculated about that for a long time during many lonely nights in my childhood. If my parents had died in an accident, they wouldn't have felt the need to hide me with strangers. Besides, someone would have found car wreckage or bodies, or something to indicate what had happened. Something had to have been after them, perhaps the same people who had chased me only weeks ago, and that something would have been irreversible. I breathed and my voice, after so many years of speculation was steady. "I think someone, or something, killed them both."

"Life sucks."

"Not as much as death." *There wasn't much turning back from that.*

Marc wrapped his arms closer around me and I

snuggled into his warmth, feeling for all the world that I could drift off into a pleasant nap, feeling safe and cosseted in his arms while the sea breeze tickled us. The last few days had really wiped me out and I was looking forward to getting my energy levels back to normal.

It was with a jolt that a knock stirred me. Apparently, we both dozed because the sun had dimmed a little and it was turning cold. Marc must have pulled a blanket over us because our legs were covered with a pink and grey checked wool cover. The knock sounded again and I blurrily called out, "Come in" as I rubbed my eyes with the backs of my knuckles to wake myself up.

It was Evan who opened the door and scanned the room; when he eyed me, he scowled. "Meg sent me to tell you dinner was ready." He sounded none too happy about it and glared at Marc who was rolling his shoulders in small circles but otherwise not moving. "I didn't realise you weren't alone," he said somewhat stiffly.

"I'll be down in a minute," I promised. "I won't keep you all waiting."

"I doubt anyone will wait." Evan muttered, shutting the door with a bang.

"Is he always so charming?" I asked, shuffling myself away from Marc and standing up, my sleepy legs not quite so enthusiastic. I wondered if I should feel embarrassed that I had curled up and dozed off with him; it seemed a rather intimate thing to do with a guy I had known all of two days.

"Always," scoffed Marc and I wondered if they had some sort of history.

I stretched and went to pull on a cardigan. The sea

air was cool and since I didn't know what temperature they liked to keep the house, I didn't want to end up shivering at the dining table. Marc pulled the sash closed and folded the blanket on top of the cushions.

"I can't believe I fell asleep," he muttered, and I could feel him watching me.

"Me either. It's been a funny few days and my sleep is all over the place."

"You'll get used to the different time zone soon. And they do say sea air is good for you." He opened my door and gestured to leave. "Shall we?"

I followed Marc downstairs and he pointed out which room was his as we passed the closed door off the hallway. Then I followed him into the kitchen where everyone was seated around the big table. Big dishes of lasagne steamed in front of the assembled guests. There was a glass bowl filled with salad leaves in several shades of green and another plate piled with slices of garlic bread. Pitchers of orange juice and water sat at each end of the table and I could smell coffee too.

Marc and I took the two remaining seats, next to each other and he held my chair while I sat, before sliding into his chair and taking a plate from Meg who was serving. She ladled a huge helping onto my plate and I inhaled the delicious fresh meat sauce and bubbling, cheese topping. I checked to see if everyone else was eating the garlic bread before I took a slice, because I didn't want to be the one that everyone avoided later. That would make life as the new girl awkward; not that I wasn't used to that. *Perhaps it was time to turn a new leaf,* I hoped and the idea of making friends gave me a little surge of warmth.

Having filled everyone's plates, Meg was busily

filling glasses and handing out mugs of steaming coffee.

"How do you like the house, Stella?" she asked, setting a cup at my right hand and pointing to the sugar bowl.

I swallowed my mouthful of lasagne. "It's beautiful."

Meg beamed. "Why, thank you. My family have owned it for going on one-hundred-and-fifty years now. Thankfully, it's a lot more modern now due to the more recent additions." She poured coffee into Marc's cup until the pot was almost drained then walked back across the kitchen to put it by the sink. For an old lady, she walked lightly with uncharacteristic grace. "It's too big for just me though, so, once again, I'm very happy to have you all here."

Her words were met with hearty endorsement and I joined in as the glasses were held aloft in toast to Meg and clinked together. She flapped her hands at us to stop, but I could tell she was a little thrilled. The joviality quickly subsided as the food was devoured. I vacuumed up my helping and accepted a small second, not too worried whether I was coming across as piggish. I was hungry, tired, and mentally over stimulated with all the changes in my life. I felt good and ready to fall asleep for a very long time rather than resuming the series of catnaps I'd been relegated to. I refused the ice cream dessert and Kitty proposed watching a film which led to a long discussion over choices.

"Practical Magic," suggested Christy but her sister, Clara, shivered and replied, "Don't you remember the time that Gran accidentally brought that dead guy back to life? Too close for comfort." *I was so not going to ask about that.*

"Something less realistic then," said Meg, her mouth twitching into the barest smile.

"Mission Impossible?" suggested Jared.

"I've watched it five times and I still don't get it. How did Ethan piece it all together?" I asked before clamping my mouth shut. I'd forgotten myself; maybe they didn't want the newbie's input.

"Ugh, me too," sighed Kitty, putting my fears to rest. "And don't get me started on two and three."

"The singing Buffy episode? I have the score so we can sing along," said Clara and I guessed the boxset on the shelf must have been hers. Her enthusiasm was quashed quickly with a chorus of groans.

Eventually, a new comedy release was not so much agreed upon, as not entirely rejected by the table, with Evan shrugging his shoulders in a "don't care" way. He had barely said anything throughout the meal but I'd seen him shoot a glance in my direction when he thought I wasn't looking.

"Can I help you clear away?" I asked Meg.

"Thank you, dear. If you'll just stack the plates in the dishwasher, well, that will do nicely."

I was glad to have a job to do to save me feeling out of place and Kitty quickly joined me in clearing the table as Meg foiled the leftovers.

"So, you and Marc?" said Kitty when there was just the two of us left. She wasn't as chipper as she had been earlier and I wondered if she had had a long day too. "What's going on between you?"

"Marc and me?" I replied sounding like an echo. *Maybe Evan had said something about us being curled up together in my room?* I opened the dishwasher and stooped to stack it. "There's nothing between us. We only met a few days ago."

"Oh, I thought you two might have been ... dating or something."

"No. He's nice and I like him. He's attractive but we're not dating." I rolled a scenario through my mind. I liked him and trusted him and he would make a good boyfriend, I decided. Not that I was looking for one. I blushed as I remembered the kiss. *The very nice kiss.*

"I see." Kitty gave herself a shake and went to retrieve the glassware from the table. "Do you want to, you know, date him?"

"I don't know." I was getting a little uncomfortable with being grilled about a man I barely knew by a woman I'd just met, even though I'd already had Kitty pegged as forthright. "I haven't really thought about it. I don't even know if he's dating anyone."

"He isn't." Kitty's voice was quiet and I looked up at her from where I was stacking the last plate. *Ahh. Maybe Kitty had a thing for Marc.*

"Anyway, I'm not really that into dating," I said quickly to fill the silence. That was technically true anyway. My last date had been months ago and I'd soon decided I'd rather not bother if that was what was on offer.

"Have you known each other for a long time?"

"Forever practically. We grew up together, went to the same school. My family knows his, yada, yada."

Étoile ducked her head around the door. She had a small plastic folder she held to her chest. "If you're finished, Stella, I need to go over a couple of things with you. I'll be quick. I'm sure you want to chill out with the movie too, get to know everyone a little better."

Kitty waved me away. I wiped my hands on a kitchen cloth and sat at the table with Étoile. She opened the folder and spread a few things out. "I know you have a British driver's licence but you can't use it long term here, so here's your American one." She pushed it towards me – my picture was already on it.

"How did you get this?"

Étoile shrugged. "That's not important. We closed your bank account and transferred the money into a new account for you. There's your card and statement."

I looked at it and raised my eyebrows. The figure on the opening balance was far higher than what I had in my current checking and savings combined. *Like, ridiculously high.* "There must have been a mistake."

"No mistake. Steven transferred cash from your parents' estate. He said there was a letter in the stuff he gave you explaining everything."

I recalled the letter. I hadn't read it yet and made up my mind to open it later.

"They can't have left me this much."

"They did and Steven has looked after their assets so it's all yours."

I traced my name in the little letters on the card. "I thought I wasn't supposed to have anything traceable."

"From your old life, yes, but this is new and the things we set up ... well, you won't have a problem. You can start your life afresh."

"Friends in high places?"

"Something like that." Étoile was offhand. "You already have your passport so I think that's it."

"What do I tell people? I don't have an American accent."

"The truth should suffice if you stick to the facts. You had an American dad, he died early and you grew up in England and now you're trying out life here." It sounded so neat and succinct the way Étoile explained and I nodded. Étoile slipped the cards and paper back into the folder and pushed it over to me. "Now we're done with that little business, we've got film night to look forward to. I didn't vote for it, so if it's terrible, you can't blame me. Come on."

The sofas were fully occupied when we joined the rest of the household, so we pulled floor cushions and nestled on the floor. I stretched out my legs and leaned against the arm of Kitty's armchair and she patted me on the head like a favoured pet while David fiddled with the DVD player and the opening credits loomed on the screen.

Whether my companions were lost in the film or in their own thoughts, I couldn't tell but it did give me the opportunity to look over them. When I looked at Evan, careful to barely adjust my head, I found him already observing me and I held his gaze a long moment before he returned to the book he had opened. He seemed to have been searching my face, though I couldn't decipher what for, but I noticed he didn't turn the page for some time even though he seemed lost in concentration.

When I looked away, I saw Marc was watching me too, so I gave him a little smile and refocused my eyes on the screen, though my thoughts were on Evan. I couldn't help wondering what he might have to teach me, and why I had been lumped with him when he seemed so openly hostile to me.

I knew one thing though.

I was desperate to learn. As much as I appreciated everything that was being done for me, I wanted my life and I wasn't prepared to just be kept indefinitely. The only way I was going to get some semblance of my life back – it was clear to me now – was to be able to control my magic.

CHAPTER SIX

If I thought I would get any time to acclimate myself to my new home I was wrong. My first lessons started with a rude awakening from several thumps on my door as Kitty called to me, giving me a scant few minutes to drag on jeans and a strappy top before scampering down the stairs. I had just enough time to grab a muffin and the last of the coffee and stuff them down my throat just as Evan appeared in the kitchen doorway.

"We'll head into the library," he muttered, signalling that I was to follow, without greeting anyone else.

Behind his retreating back, Kitty pulled a face and I stifled a giggle as I scrambled after him.

I'd passed the library several times since my brief tour but never paused to look inside so I was surprised to find it not at all stuffy. Instead, the room was large and airy, every wall covered with white shelves holding hundreds of books. Some were old and well-thumbed with creased spines, others newer purchases; all of them covering a myriad of subjects. There were some easy chairs and side tables with lamps spread around. It was a lovely room.

"I hadn't thought magic would be all about book learning," I said, scanning the spines for familiar titles.

"It isn't. In fact, ignore the books entirely." Evan waved a hand dismissively at the groaning shelves. "Unless you want to pick up something to read later in your free time."

"So, how do I learn?" I frowned.

"It's not like a class, Stella. I don't give you a textbook that we work through. You'll learn as we go along and we'll adapt as appropriate. Show me what you can do."

"What do you mean?"

"You must be able to do something." Evan paused and waited for me to jump in; then, exasperated, prompted me with a flick of his hand and raised eyebrows, "Something magic?"

"I can move myself," I replied cautiously.

"How?"

"I don't know! I'm in one place, and then I just ... vanish and end up somewhere else."

"Show me."

I took a deep breath and thought about being somewhere else. I closed my eyes and waited. I waited for the tingling and crackling in the air and the powerful burst of energy that signified me flitting out of the world. After a minute, when the feeling didn't come, I opened my eyes and looked around. I was still in the library and Evan was looking perplexed. I felt like I had just lied on my résumé and been called on it in an interview. I heaved a sigh of disappointment. This was not going to be easy.

"One of two things happened there," said Evan and I looked at him hopefully. "You either went and came back so fast that I didn't notice or, nothing happened."

I rolled my eyes petulantly. His sarcasm was so funny. *Not.*

"Try again."

I tried again... and again, for the next thirty minutes. I tried with my eyes open and with my eyes closed. I tried holding my breath and I tried breathing deeply. I tried until I gave myself a headache. Evan stood in front of me, his arms folded across his chest, the entire time.

"Okay. Let's leave that a while."

"I've never really focused on doing it before. It just seemed to happen," I practically tripped over my tongue to explain, feeling a little like I had just failed a test. *Maybe I wouldn't get my witch hat now?* I guessed I would get over that.

"Tell me about the times you've moved before." Evan signalled to a chair and we sat facing each other. I rested my chin on my hands and my elbows on my knees as I thought about it.

"I think it happened more often when I was younger. My foster parents were always saying that I was a really fast runner when they couldn't work out how I had gotten past them, but I think I must have just moved myself. When I was a teenager, if I ended up some place different, I just thought I hadn't remembered. You know, like walking along thinking about something else and you look up and think, hey, how did I get here?" I looked to Evan to see if he understood and he nodded so I continued. "When I was older, it really only happened when I panicked and that's when I knew I was different and it wasn't just because I wasn't paying attention. There was a fire once and I should have been trapped, but I moved myself outside. And one time with my boss, well, a bookcase tipped over and I should have been under it too but I wasn't. Then, last week, when I was being chased?" I gulped and fought the panic that clamoured in my ribcage. "He had me by the throat and I just vanished."

Evan chewed on that and then asked, "The bookcase just tipped over, huh?"

I frowned. "Well, I was thinking that it would be great if it did tip over and... it did."

"So you might be able to move things too?"

"I..." *Well, yeah,* I thought, wondering why the idea made me feel so glum. I knew it had been me but the idea of being able to do that kind of stuff at will? It excited and frightened me all at the same time.

"It's called telekinesis. Instead of moving yourself, teleportation if you like, telekinesis means you can move objects with your mind."

I thought about it. There had been a lot of unexplained things happening around me that couldn't be put down to coincidence. It wasn't out of the realm of possibility. "Well, maybe, but I've never really tried. I guess it might be that." I looked up at him to see how he was taking it. A normal person would be laughing at me by now. Evan's thoughtful face was refreshing. He didn't think I was nuts.

Evan looked around and I followed his eyes as they ran over the laden bookcases. He grinned for a moment and I was caught so off guard by the lovely line of his mouth that I almost missed him say, "Perhaps we shouldn't be in smashing distance of a bookshelf right now."

I smirked at him and barely stopped myself from rolling my eyes. It was an unpleasant habit and hardly one to bring out the best in people.

"We'll try it out some other time. So lately, you've only moved when you've panicked?"

I nodded.

"Well that's something," Evan decided, his voice strong. He nodded and I thought some of the hostility seemed to have gone from his face.

"And Étoile held on to me once and moved me." I recalled her grabbing me and moving me from my flat to the airport. "She did it at will."

"She's been taught from birth."

"Lucky."

"You've really not been taught anything? At all?" Evan was searching my face like there was some sort of clue waiting there for him to discover.

"Not a thing."

"Unlucky."

"I guess."

"It would have been easier for you to have been taught as soon as you had shown any magical inclination."

"Can't argue with that," I agreed. It would have been nice to grow up with others who shared my predilections. Maybe my childhood would have been a lot less lonely.

"Lesson is over for today."

"But I haven't done anything?" My voice inflected like I was asking him a question.

"You have shown me what you can't do and told me what you can do. That's enough. Take a break. David will come find you when he wants you."

"What does David want me for?"

"He'll teach you some learned magic. Book magic, if you like."

"I didn't think magic was like learning from books." I tried not to mimic, but threw the words back at Evan all the same.

"The kind of magic I'm teaching you, no, but David's kind is different."

"Magic isn't just," I grappled for a word and settled, dully, on "magic?"

Evan shook his head. "Magic comes in many different shapes and forms. For many, it's illusion. The 'make a boat disappear, pull a rabbit out of a hat' kind of magic. That's not really even magic; it just looks like it. Humans like to call it magic anyway." He held up a finger. "Then there's learned magic. That's comes from people with an inclination towards the magical but who have to learn to use it. They learn spells and incantations. They can mix up potions to cure ailments and influence people. Sometimes they have a core magic too; it runs a bit in their blood and that's why they have a strong calling to magic. Then there's us." Evan raised another finger, paused, and raised another.

"What are we?" I whispered.

"We're absolute magic. It's in our blood and bones. It's in every fibre of our being. It is what we are. You and I are different but the magic affects our bodies and our brains in a similar way so we can manipulate the universe to do our bidding."

"Can everyone do the same things?"

"No, of course not. Like regular humans aren't all great at sports or riding horses, or sailing boats." Evan rested back in his chair and swung one long leg across the other. "Some can teleport, some have telekinesis, some are psychic, some can influence people or the weather or the air. Magic is different for all of us."

"Is anyone both?"

"Yes, but usually the strengths lean way or the other."

"Usually?"

"If someone has weaker magic, say the core magic within them, they could use learned magic to supplement their skills, making them stronger still."

"Is that why David will be teaching me too?"

"We all thought it would be a good idea to expose you to some of the learned magic while you practised controlling your own magic. David will be able to teach you the basics, things that can heal and protect you. Even if you never use it, you'll at least have some understanding of that aspect of magic."

"Okay."

"Plus David has a great potion for a cold remedy, not that we get sick a lot."

"A cold remedy?" It seemed a little absurd.

"He uses lemon and honey."

"I hate to burst David's bubble but Lemsip has already been invented."

"Bet it doesn't come with a spell to ward off infections though."

"Will it turn me into a frog?" I asked facetiously.

"He'll teach you that another time. I don't recommend it."

"What are you?" I asked, recalling that he had just said that we were different. I couldn't see any difference, but maybe I didn't know what I was looking for.

He looked me in the eyes and I felt my stomach do little flips as the silence hung in the air between us. I was about to prompt him when a knock at the door and a male voice announced David's arrival.

I went to answer it but when I turned back to say goodbye to Evan, he had gone and I didn't have a clue how he could have left the room without me seeing. *Show off.*

David's lesson took place in the kitchen and also included Kitty, the sisters Christy and Clara, and the accident-prone teenage boy, Jared. First, he had them demonstrate some of the things they learned. There was a little potion that could make the room fill with smoke (Meg didn't like that one, as she protested that night at dinner to a rueful David), powders that could heal a wound and another that could make a barrier around a person, like an invisible wall.

Just when I was beginning to wonder if his lessons were not going much further than household products and science experiments, David made it rain. In the kitchen. Then he produced a rainbow that splintered into glorious stars, which danced across the ceiling. I didn't know what the point of it was, but it was pretty and I gazed at the display in awestruck wonder.

After the demonstration (that had served to intrigue me), David moved on to spells.

"Will I have to rhyme?" I asked as we sat around the table, pencils and paper in front of us. Kitty winked at me. She realised I knew the answer to that one.

"Of course not. This isn't English literature," David sniffed and I wondered just how many times he had been asked that same question. "Spells are just words. Simple. It's the magic in you that transforms them into power and action. They need to be heartfelt and they need to be indicative of what it is that you want to do.

"Sometimes a spell is accompanied by a potion to give it more power. The potions are like baking a cake. You mix together the right stuff, and the right thing happens. You get a cake. Forget an ingredient and it just won't work. The cake won't rise properly or it won't taste right." He looked at each of us to see if we understood his analogy and we nodded in turn. "Good. Here's your task."

David spelled out to us – puns aside – what he wanted us to do and instructed us to make a simple spell that would illuminate our surroundings. I guessed it would come in handy if a fuse blew, at least.

Christy and Clara were naturals, racing to raise their hands at almost the exact same time before I even put pencil to paper. Kitty rolled her eyes and I guessed this happened almost every lesson. While they proudly said their spells and lit up the space around them with a strange glow, I leaned into Kitty.

"Why are you here?"

"Same as you. Need to learn about this stuff until I can manage my magic properly."

"How come you haven't learned all this stuff already?"

"Magic skipped a generation with me. By the time my family realised what I could do, the grandparents, who everyone thought were just crazy had passed. There was no one to teach me," she whispered.

Jared was next to perform his spell. I hoped he couldn't see David wince as the last line came to a close, then sigh with relief as nothing broke. Three orbs of light hovered in front of Jared's head and he dismissed them with a click of his fingers.

"Kitty?"

Kitty shrugged her shoulders and focused. Even with my limited knowledge, I realised she had redirected sunlight with her mind, rather than create a light from incanted magic. *Still, she said she could manipulate the weather, perhaps the sunlight counted as part of that.*

"Not quite. Stella?"

I thought for a moment and ignored the doodles I had scrawled on my paper, then said, while trying not to feel completely ridiculous, "I want to see what I cannot see. I want the light to find itself from my bright mind." And I was rewarded with a faint orb of light, which made up for feeling like a complete idiot.

David smiled with pleasure. "And not even written down. A good first attempt, Stella."

When we broke for lunch, I was glad to sit next to Étoile, eating grilled cheese sandwiches as the conversation reached a heavy hubbub. Evan was the only one missing and I wondered where he was, before wondering why I was wondering.

"How do you like your lessons?" Étoile asked, conversationally.

"So-so," I replied, noncommittally. It was my first day, after all, and I needed to think it through.

Étoile placed her manicured hand over mine and I felt a surge of contentment. "It will get easier."

I nodded. If she said it would, it would.

The next two hours were apparently earmarked as free time, which allowed me to lounge in my room before taking a walk. Instead of staying in the gardens, I passed through them to the steps that led down to the beach. On the bottom step, I held onto the railing so I could slide off my shoes with one hand. I tied the laces together and hung them over my shoulder.

I walked across the sand, pale golden and a little gritty, and down by the shore so I could wiggle my toes in the soft swirls of surf rolling in. The water stretched to infinity beyond me; to the left it curled around a promontory and I lost sight of the sand. The hillside swept up further down. I could see birds swooping into the trees some distance away, their calls echoing on the wind.

To my right, the sand stretched on for a few miles. The hillside was lower here and grassy, rather than tree-lined. I wondered why no one had built out here. Surely this land, with its far-reaching views, would be a prime development zone. There wasn't much to explore so after a while of gazing out to sea, wondering how many thousands of miles away my former home was, and if I was even looking in the right direction, I turned back and went to sit on the steps.

When Étoile landed next to me in a flash of electricity, I leapt from my perch and had to stoop to pick up my shoes, which had fallen to the sand.

"Sorry," she said, but the sentiment didn't quite carry to her face. "I'm sent to bring you in."

"Should you be using magic outdoors?" I grimaced in case she thought I was chastising her since I had no place to do that.

"Generally speaking, no, but who's to see here?" Without taking offence, Étoile swept her arms to the uninhabited land to the left and right of us.

"How come this is the only house out here?"

Étoile shrugged. "I wouldn't know." She reached for my hands and held them in her own. "Ready?"

I nodded. The air crackled and I just remembered to draw a breath as the gritty sand was replaced by the feeling of soft carpet. She winked at me like we had shared some little secret before walking out of the library.

Evan had been working on a laptop but pulled the lid closed when we appeared.

"Same again?" I asked, not exactly thrilled at the prospect of failure again. I wasn't even buoyed by Étoile's teleportation. *That had been her, not me,* I reminded myself.

"Let's try telekinesis this time. Take a seat." Evan tucked his laptop into his bag, then stood and walked the few paces to the bookshelves. He plucked a book off the middle shelf and tossed it on the table in front of us where it landed with a thud. I took a seat and bent to pull on my shoes and tie up the laces as I waited.

"You're going to try and move it," he said, nodding at the book, after contemplating me for a moment. I tried not to shrivel into a ball under his scrutiny.

"I don't think I can."

"I think you can."

"I really don't think I can."

"Try and see. Look at the book."

I sighed. There was clearly no point in arguing. I looked at the book. It was a slim hardback and appeared to be a novel, though I couldn't make out the print upside down. "How do I do this?"

"You have to tap into the magic inside you." Evan

placed a hand over his heart and tapped his fingers. "You have to believe that you can do it."

"I still don't understand."

"You don't have to, Stella. Just try. Focus on the book. Feel it, feel your mind reach for it."

I stared at it for long minutes that stretched on. I felt like the weight of the task was pressing down on me. It was hardly the carefree, blink-of-an-eye magic that Étoile had demonstrated to me several times. I wondered if I would ever have such control or if I was just a one-stunt dud. A depressing thought. *Maybe they wouldn't want me if I couldn't stump up the goods. Where would that leave me?* I sighed. I seemed to be spending a lot of time sighing lately. It wasn't healthy.

"What are you thinking about, Stella? It doesn't seem like the task." Evan sounded frustrated. *Like I wasn't!*

I surprised myself by answering coherently. "I'm wondering if I'm a dud."

It was Evan's turn to surprise me and his face cracked into an effortless smile as he chuckled over my concerns. His eyes wrinkled at the edges with laughter lines and his mouth was broad with perfectly pink lips. He really did have a lovely face when he smiled. *What was I thinking?*

He said slowly, "You are, categorically, not a dud. You just need to learn."

"Not a dud," I repeated like a moron. My eyes settled on the book again and I felt myself fix on it with a strange sort of longing as I tuned in to the rise and fall of my lungs. Hell, I wanted the damn thing to move and, at last, it did, wriggling just a few short millimetres to the left.

I looked up at Evan with the most enormous

smile on my face and then bewilderment as I realised the natural light had dimmed. I must have focused on the book for much longer than I thought. But I had done it.

"So, not a dud." Evan smiled at me, an easy smile this time, but not one of a proud teacher. He seemed to be assessing me and I returned his gaze without a quiver. A shudder ran through me and I was the first to turn away even though I would have been quite content to continue appraising him. *On the sly, anyway.*

"We'll start again tomorrow."

And just like that, Evan was gone, before I even remembered that I still wanted to ask the question of what he was.

~

The week progressed in the same way. I took a lesson with Evan first, my frustration rising as the time passed without event; then a lesson with David which was more enjoyable because I could make little things happen. Following the little orb of light I created from my first spell, there was a protection spell and other little things that were enjoyable to do. Then it was lunch and free time. Once I went back to the beach and walked out my frustration of simply not knowing anything - the council, what I had to learn, my future - they were all enigmas to me. Another time, I snoozed on my bed. A couple of times I unwrapped the headphones of my MP3 player and listened to music as I curled on the window seat, my head leant against the pane.

The evenings were spent in a cycle of the same things; cards in the kitchen after dinner or watching a movie in the living room. Sometimes I let Kitty braid my hair and we talked about girly things that were as far removed from our life of magic as could be.

Some evenings I spent in the library, curled up with Marc talking about books we'd read and our lives. It was pleasant and relaxing and I could feel myself growing attached to both of them in a way that I had never felt attached to anyone before.

Maybe it was because we weren't part of a ready-made group like Étoile and Seren, or Christy and Clara who kept largely to themselves. Kitty and Marc seemed so open and lively that I enjoyed being around them no end. I still noticed that Kitty and Marc were scrupulously polite around each other and thought that one day I would have to ask what their deal was.

Even David and Jared seemed to have teamed up, somewhat incongruously. Once, during one of our evenings crowded around a film, I snuck glances at Evan like I could figure him out if I got just one more look. Sometimes I felt his eyes on me too but only once or twice did our eyes meet, making me colour under his gaze.

By the end of the second week, I was fed up and my nerves were frayed. I hadn't teleported even an inch – not even accidentally – and the objects Evan set before me stayed just where they were, despite the minor triumph I'd had on my first day.

So I was grumpy and fed up when it was suggested that afternoon that we go out to a local bar for dinner. If I could have worked out who came up with the original suggestion, I would have gladly hugged them for giving me something fun to look forward too.

Evan had even waved me away that morning, brushing off the thought of a Friday afternoon lesson in favour of reading in the big sitting room, rather than putting up with another fruitless lesson with yours truly, not that he said that in so many words.

By early evening, we had all gravitated towards the living room and I found myself perched on the furthest sofa from the door, half turned away from Evan, with Étoile between us and Kitty crouched on the floor, painting her toenails a bronze shade. My feelings of frustration seemed to be having company. Everyone had the dull expressions of the overworked and underplayed.

Even David, normally so enthusiastic and chilled, was flagging and had snapped at everyone in today's lesson. He kept rubbing the long scar across his face like it was bothering him and I wondered why he didn't just ask Étoile to heal him. Clara and Christy were still ignoring him after the lesson in which he had been brusque and short. Marc had been flicking through the DVDs without much interest while Jared undertook some kind of monologue at him that seemed to include a lot of enthusiastic waving of his hands and the occasional nod from Marc.

According to Kitty, who was chattering as she swept the brush over her toes, the bar had a real live band playing that night and served the best steak in town. I wondered if she had ever been there, before my arrival, of course, and guessed she must have; but I didn't ask as the idea would have laid upon eagerly by our little group of civilization-starved people.

"What should I wear?" I asked Kitty quietly. She had tucked away her nail polish in a little bag and grasped my hands to pull me upstairs in a playful way that made me laugh. She was bubbling over with enthusiasm at the idea of going out.

As she pulled me along behind her, I glanced over my shoulder and caught not Marc's eyes but Evan's. He had remained on the sofa, his big arm resting on the side, a thumb marking the page of his book. He smiled at me and my heart did that stupid flutter thing. A smile crept onto my face before Kitty swept me away again, bounding up the stairs two at a time, so fast I could barely keep up.

"Jeans," she pronounced, flicking through the hangers in my closet, a pout forming on her Cupid's mouth. "And more jeans. And, ooh, t-shirts. Sexy." The last word came out with a little snort.

"It's not like I've had much time for shopping," I replied with a shrug. Truth be told, my wardrobe was not exactly exciting to me either. Thanks to my parents, I had a nice stash of cash that had been squirreled away for years accruing interest but I'd had no time to spend any. *Plus*, as I reminded myself, *the money should be spent on something useful and there might come a day when I really needed it.* I wasn't a particularly frivolous person and had never really indulged myself. I bought serviceable all-weather clothes, not going out stuff.

"Wait here. You can wear something of mine." Kitty darted out of the room and across the landing to hers. I could hear her footsteps padding none too delicately around her room and then back again. She held up three hangers. There was a slinky, blue jersey with a v-neck, a strappy, green top with a crystal motif and a white Grecian top with one sleeve and a gathered bodice. "Try them on," Kitty urged and she looked so excited about the idea of dressing me that I could hardly say no.

I slipped out of my shirt so I stood in my jeans

and bra and shrugged on the blue, catching sight of the plunging neckline in the mirror and whipping it off, just as fast. "Not me," I pronounced, shaking my head at the strappy, green top next. I pulled on the white top and Kitty reached forward to arrange the hem.

"You could wear it with your skinny jeans and those cute flats of yours and it will look pretty, but not dressy." She spun me around so I was in front of the long mirror. Behind me, she tugged my hair out of its ponytail and ran her fingers through it so it fanned over my shoulders in waves. She had trimmed the singed ends for me and it looked healthy again. "We could curl it just a little, so it looks natural, you know. Or maybe put in a couple of plaits, hippy style." Kitty twisted my hair in her hands so it curled slightly. "I can do your makeup. What do you think?"

"I think where were you when I was a teenager and needed someone to sort me out?" I laughed but I couldn't take my eyes off myself. I looked tall and strong and the top made me want to stand a little straighter. I had firm breasts and a slim waist and arms that were toned but not frighteningly muscular and hair (a true golden brown) that framed cream skin. I looked pretty, I relished with pride and wondered if I was about to shed a tear. *Get a grip*. It was like I had never seen myself look halfway decent before.

"Well, now," said Kitty, slipping her arm about my waist and giving me a squeeze. "You would think you'd never put on something pretty before."

"I haven't," I admitted. "I'm a jeans and tee girl. I wore regular, dowdy, boring things to my regular, dowdy, boring jobs. I don't... I didn't... go out much."

It surprised me a bit how ready I was to talk about my life in the past tense and I was chagrined to admit just how uninteresting it had been. Maybe that would change. I hoped it would. Everyone deserved a fresh start, *especially when someone was trying to kill them.* I shook the thought from my head. I didn't want to be reminded of that now.

"Life is one hundred percent different for you," replied Kitty, her hands on my shoulders as she spoke to my reflection. "Why don't you let yourself be a few percent different too? Try out something different."

"Will you take me shopping?" I asked, surprising myself.

"Thought you'd never ask. Tomorrow?" Kitty was clapping her hands together and I laughed.

"I don't think I'll be able to get out of lessons. Evan is a task master."

"We could get him incredibly drunk tonight," Kitty suggested, "then maybe he'll just sleep through and forget all about classes."

I gasped in feigned outrage and went to wriggle out of Kitty's white top, tying a bathrobe about me instead as I pulled off my jeans and tossed them in the basket. "I can't believe you would suggest such a thing. Besides," I shrugged as I knotted the belt. "I do need the lessons." *And I kind of liked being around Evan* but I didn't say that out loud.

Kitty cocked an eyebrow. "We could just mention it's Saturday tomorrow and we all deserve the time off." She turned to fiddle with something on my dresser and added after a moment, "He is rather nice to look at."

I rolled my eyes. She could be so sly. "It's not that. Well, it is that a bit. He is good looking. Very." I was in danger of getting sidetracked and shrugged off the thought. "Most of all, I like what he's teaching me. I've never had anyone teach me before. I've never been able to control anything; I still can't make myself do what I want to do, but I've noticed that I haven't caused accidents, so I am more focused. If I'm cross, I don't accidentally hurt someone. You have no idea what a relief that is."

"I can guess. It's not been easy for any of us, but most have had family around to teach us from birth the right way to use our gifts. Well, not that my family was great, but at least they had something of a clue and they did get me help when I needed it."

"Do you really see it as a gift?"

"If by 'it' you mean the various things we can do, the telepathy, the telekinesis, the zapping and everything else, then yes, it is an absolute gift and even when it's been tough, I wouldn't be who I am without it, without this world of ours."

"You're happy?" I didn't know if I was asking a question or making a statement.

"Just like any other regular girl." Kitty gathered up the rejected tops and took the white one from me to hang on a hanger on my closet handle. "I have to go get changed too. Remember skinny jeans, cream flats. Totally cute. I'll come back and do your hair in twenty, 'kay?"

"Thank you, Kitty."

"My pleasure."

I calculated that I would have enough time to shower and wash my hair in those few minutes if I hurried, and hurry I did, scrubbing and sluicing water and shampoo through my hair until I felt squeaky clean. I towelled off and rubbed cream into my skin from the little flowered bottle that had been left in the basket by the sink. I put on new underwear and a bra without straps, seeing as the one-shouldered look would be difficult to pull off with a regular bra, and slipped on the skinny jeans Kitty had pointed out, then shimmied on her white top. The flats were at the bottom of the closet and I slipped them on as I looked at myself again in the mirror and indulged myself with a twirl.

Who would have thought that not only was the lonely girl from London actually getting ready for a night out, but that she looked pretty damn good too? I smiled and the mirror me smiled back.

Kitty knocked before slipping inside. She was wielding a hot hair wand and a square metal box with a handle, which she set on my dresser and popped open to reveal tubes and pots and square trays of colour. Apparently makeup was serious business for Kitty.

"I'll dry your hair first." Kitty directed me to sit on the chair, which she put in front of the mirror and stood behind me with the hairdryer as she brushed and steamed my hair dry. When it was straight, she teased soft waves into it that fell around my face in an oh-so-casual way. I would have to ask her how to do stuff like that. She fiddled in her case. "You're lucky you have great skin so we'll just put a little shadow and a slick of mascara, the barest lip gloss, just a touch of extra colour on your cheeks. Nothing too much, just a little extra."

"Thank you so much."

"Oh, pah. You know I like doing this stuff." Kitty waved my thanks away as she closed my eyes with her finger and swept on the shadow in neat strokes, directing me to look up so she could brush on the mascara. She deposited the wand back in the tube and laid it carefully in its place before plucking out a soft tube of pale pink gloss. "I'll just squeeze a little on your lips then you need to rub it around, okay?" She mimicked mashing her lips together and I copied her to move the gloss around.

"Actually, I wanted to do hair and makeup, maybe do some styling, as a job but this magic stuff took priority." She didn't seem too upset about her strange change of a career, if I could call it that.

Kitty stood back to admire her handiwork. She grinned. "Well, it's not like the canvas was a bad one to start with but you do look pretty good to me. You're going to knock someone's socks off tonight."

"I don't think I could knock anyone's socks off," I replied, wondering if she meant Marc, whom I'd surprised myself by not thinking about all day. He had spent the last couple of days with his phone almost glued to his ear but never shared what he was doing. He seemed cagey when I'd asked.

"Sure you can," said Kitty sliding onto the bench by the dresser and checking out her own perfect makeup with a long, considered look. She twisted to face me. "You really have no idea how pretty you are, do you?"

"I think you are the nicest person," I grinned. "And a great confidence booster."

Kitty snorted. She stood and tiptoed in a circle. "Enough about you, how do I look?"

"Sensational." And, of course, she did. She had changed into white shorts, cut to just above the knee, with a tan leather belt and a pale brown vest. She'd swung a long gold chain round her neck and knotted it near the end. She wore white Chucks and looked the picture of preppy chic. "But we should get going."

"After you," Kitty turned the handle and pulled the door towards her as I darted out. If only I'd looked first, I wouldn't have ended up barrelling into Evan and stumbling backwards, because there was no way a body bound with muscles like his was going to give way.

My cheeks burned as I ricocheted back into my room. "I'm sorry, I didn't look."

"No damage," he shrugged, like he barely noticed. "After you."

Kitty danced out behind me. I smiled apologetically at Evan as Kitty grabbed my hand and tugged me after her, not giving him an inch to pass.

Half our little party were waiting already. Marc was leaning against the hallway, wearing his usual jeans and an open-necked shirt. Étoile was standing straight like a slightly bored, albeit very well dressed, statue. She was wearing a floor-length dress in a cotton print with a tan belt cinching it in at the waist. Seren was wearing the same dress in a different colour. Both smiled at me and rolled their eyes slightly at Kitty's illimitable enthusiasm.

Evan stepped down next and slipped past us to walk to the kitchen and back again, Jared and David in tow. Within minutes, the hallway was positively crowded and we shuffled out with a wave from Meg who mentioned something about going for an evening stroll. I didn't miss the look Étoile and Seren exchanged at that.

Kitty hooked her arm through mine. "The bar isn't far so we'll just walk over."

"Do you guys go there often?" I realised this was

my first time off the property since my arrival. No wonder I was feeling antsy.

"Now and again, when we're in town." She stifled a laugh and leaned in to whisper. "The locals think we're a yoga retreat. That could be believable, but what do you think Evan does here? He's not exactly the Rising Sun type of guy is he?"

I snuck a glance over my shoulder and looked at Evan, deep in conversation with David. I had to agree with Kitty. I couldn't imagine him lycra-clad, bending and stretching. *Oh ... maybe I could. Hmm.* I turned my face away quickly when he looked up.

The bar, like Kitty said, wasn't far and it took us less than twenty minutes to walk there. It was a wooden building with double doors to the front and "Rusty's" in big painted letters on a sign over the top.

The few patrons barely glanced in our direction as we entered the bar. Thankfully, it was still early and largely empty so we could spread out across one of the larger tables while the band tuned up on the small stage at the other side of the bar.

There was a menu that Étoile picked up, seeming almost amused by the choice of fast food, which was basic but relatively cheap. At least, I thought it was with my limited fiscal knowledge. Seren found a waitress with a cocktail menu, which she regarded with the same curiosity as her sister before smiling at the waitress and ordering, rather unexpectedly (to me at least) a beer.

The waitress stayed for the rest of us to add our orders. I was one of two to get ID'd, after it was established that Jared could stay but not drink. I was grateful I'd stuffed my driver's licence in my pocket before we left along with some dollar bills. I'd been practising telling the notes apart, like a tourist.

"You can't be too careful," the waitress said, comparing my picture to my face. She had a soft rounded face and hair straight from the eighties. "We can get fined big time and a few of those would finish us off, so I check out all you pretty young things now."

"I'm just glad I don't look as worn out as my friends here," I quipped and was rewarded with a shower of beer mats hurled from every direction. I tossed them on the table in good humour and when Evan caught my eye, he was laughing too. This catching eyes thing was starting to get far too regular. Marc, however, couldn't have looked more sour and scowled at me. *What the hell had I done to him?* I turned away and lost myself in the chatter of ordering food.

Less than an hour later, our plates pushed aside and the baskets of fries nearly devoured, second round of drinks on the table, and the band were in full swing. They played a mix of covers and a few of their own songs, which, though not well written, were played and received enthusiastically. They seemed to be pretty popular in the neighbourhood. I had drained my second wine by the time they took their encore bows in front of the rapturous little crowd and left the stage to take up a corner at the bar to receive their adulation in state.

The jukebox kicked in with a country song that the older regulars clearly knew, judging by the sing-a-long going on in one corner.

"Are you having fun?" Evan slid into the empty chair next to me. Christy and Clara had been on the dance floor, bouncing to the music as soon as they finished eating, leaving the seats around me free.

"Yes, I think I am."

"You think or you are?"

I thought for a moment. "I am," I decided.

"Good. It's nice to be out."

"You don't go out much?"

"I'm no recluse," Evan laughed, "I do go out but I'm a little short of time right now. So, I go out when I can. Let my hair down." He ran a hand through his short crop to demonstrate and I smiled.

"What do you do for down time otherwise? When you're not out, or being busy?"

"I read a lot. And listen to music. I have my laptop here with me so sometimes I watch DVDs in my room."

"What do you like reading?"

"Mysteries mostly, a little crime or a comedy. I like stuff that makes me think or laugh."

"Sounds like a good combination."

"It is." Evan took a sip of his beer. "What have you been doing in your down time?"

"Actually, nothing much. I didn't bring a lot here with me and I haven't really found time to get a library ticket," I joked. "So, I've been watching TV with the others when it's on in the evening and sometimes I just daydream a bit when I want to be quiet. I have an MP3 player and sometimes I walk on the beach."

"Want to borrow a book?"

"Yes, please."

"I'll get some for you tomorrow."

"I would appreciate it. Funny ones though, please. There's enough tragedy in the world without me having to read it for entertainment." I thought this was the first time we had had a conversation that didn't revolve around magic; *perhaps he was warming to me. Interesting.*

"Consider it done." He took another sip. "You've been tapping your feet the past half hour. Do you like to dance?"

"Actually I do."

"Do you want to dance now?"

I tipped my head to one side and listened to what was playing. Johnny Cash was booming out and I knew the song so I nodded and Evan surprised me by taking my hand in his own large one and leading me to the dance floor by the stage. As we got there, Cash clicked off and a slow, Iron and Wine song started up. Evan wasn't remotely phased and though I had half a mind to go sit down again, my cheeks beet red, that would have looked silly. Besides, I liked dancing and I couldn't object to being on a dance floor with the type of guy who made girls' hearts melt. *Wow. Talk about over thinking things.*

Evan put his hand about my waist and, though we were stiff for the first few bars, as soon as I forgot about the rest of the room and lost myself in the rhythm, I felt comfortable with him. Evan was a nice dancer. Though clearly taller than anyone in the room and muscular – I could feel his shoulders ripple under my palms as he moved – he held the beat and moved without any awkwardness. I wondered if he had always been this way or if he had once been a gangly, uncoordinated youth who had learned to be graceful.

Heat emanated from him as the second song – another slow one – clicked on. I rested my head against his chest, purely for a moment but Evan circled his arms around me a little tighter and held me there, swaying with me in time to the music. I didn't want to move so I left my head like that and sighed. I felt a little burst of happiness at being held by Evan and tried to swallow it down. My head swam with the thoughts I'd had the first time I met him. *Oh, hell.*

"Tired?" he whispered, his breath tickling my hair.

"No. Warm." *I wasn't sure I could trust myself to say anything else.*

"Me too."

"I'm a radiator all right."

"I was thinking like a hot water bottle."

"You want to put your cold feet on me?"

"No! I was thinking you're kind of small and I could tuck you up and ..." Evan trailed off and I stifled a giggle. He exhaled and I could feel the reassuring thud-thud of his heart in his chest against my ear. "I don't have cold feet," he murmured and for a moment I wondered what he was talking about.

"I'll take your word for it."

"I hate to interrupt," said Étoile from behind my back as Evan loosened his arms slightly, *almost regretfully,* I thought. "But we're going to head back. Are you coming or are you going to stand here and hug?"

"We're dancing," I replied.

"You have to move to dance." Étoile was amused. "You are hugging."

Evan's arms relaxed and I stepped away from him, feeling my cheeks flush as I let my arms drop to my sides. *What had gotten into us?*

"Besides," Étoile continued in her off hand way. "The jukebox seems to be stuck on slow stuff. Marc kicked it, several times actually, but apparently that didn't fix anything." She raised an eyebrow and looked squarely at Evan who shrugged and faced her down.

"I guess I'll head back too," I said, waving at Kitty who was lingering by the door.

"We'll all go," agreed Evan following me, before sidling to the front and holding the door open for us.

Kitty had already skipped ahead to where Marc was waiting outside, leaning against the railings, his hands thrust into his pockets. He turned and followed her without a look at me. Étoile was herding the girls and Jared like a mother hen, all feather-light until one of them strayed and she had to nip them back into order.

I stepped off the porch after them and shivered. The evening had turned cold and the heat of the bar rushed back inside the closed doors. The jukebox had clicked over to something more up tempo and the heavy beat drifted through the doors.

"Did you bring a jacket?" Evan asked, stepping onto the ground beside me. I rather thought he was counting heads as much as he was checking I was fine.

I shook my head. "Didn't think to."

"Here. Take mine." Evan draped his jacket over my shoulders before I could refuse, but once it was on, I was grateful to escape the nip in the air.

He surprised me by saying, "Tell me about London."

"Not much to tell. Big city, Queen, lots of people."

"I meant about your life there."

"I grew up in foster care for pretty much as long as I can remember. Mostly nice people but I wasn't theirs and I wasn't the easiest kid to look after." I didn't elaborate about the long string of "accidents."

I'd mentioned some to Evan already. "After I left school, I worked in a series of temp jobs. I had a little place that I rented, nothing great."

"You leave a lot of friends behind?" We started to amble after the others, but didn't try and shorten the distance between.

I paused. "No." *Hell, I hadn't left anybody behind.* I didn't know if that was depressing or lucky. I wondered if my temp manager was wondering where I was.

"You had to leave pretty quickly, I hear."

I wondered how much Evan knew, if the Bartholomews or Étoile had briefed him, but I answered his not-quite-a-question anyway, with a flick of my hand. "Étoile just swept in one night and swept me out. Pretty much in the nick of time, as they say. I was being chased. They were probably going to kill me." I shrugged, *nonchalantly* I thought, *like it hadn't mattered that I was terrified at being chased by a gang of thugs who wanted to hunt me down and burn me alive at the stake.*

"You've had to deal with a lot of shit."

"Yep."

"I wouldn't wish it on anyone."

"Really?" I looked up at him.

"Don't get me wrong," Evan draped his arm casually round my shoulder and rubbed my arm through his jacket as if it were a completely natural thing to do. I leaned into his warmth, but held my hands, slightly awkwardly, in front of me. My comfort at being so close to him was starting to make me question myself; I wondered if I was enjoying his touch a little too much. There could have been rules against this sort of thing for all I knew. "I like who I am and I like the people I'm with, for the most part, but I wouldn't wish fear and pain on anyone. It just seems to be part of the supernatural world."

"I see what you mean," I said, though I wasn't feeling terrific about the last bit of that. "I like the people we are too, and no, I wouldn't wish it on anyone either."

We didn't speak again but a few minutes later we turned onto the driveway. The porch light was on and the door had been left ajar. We must have dawdled to have lagged so far behind the rest of our group. Stepping onto the porch, I slipped off Evan's jacket and handed it back to him with a thanks.

"Any time," he replied.

"See you tomorrow."

"Bright and early." He wasn't making a move to leave, I noted. I couldn't help stare into his eyes, my heart speeding up a fraction as I realised with a rush that I didn't want this to end. I wanted Evan near me, maybe even closer than when he held me while we danced. I wondered if he could hear the little thuds my heart was booming.

"Kitty hoped to get you horribly drunk so we could all have a lie-in," I blurted. *Sheesh. What a doofus!* And to think I'd been doing so well. I stared at my shoes.

Once again, Evan surprised me by laughing and his face was easy and worry-free. "I wondered why she kept refilling my glass. Have a lie-in. You deserve one."

It was my turn to be surprised. "Really?"

"Stella, I know this past couple of weeks seems like a whole lot of nothing but you have been learning, even if you don't realise it."

"And I was thinking you loathed me."

"Definitely not." Evan leaned forward and I caught my breath as I turned my chin up to look at him. He looked so far into my eyes I felt like I was melting into pools of... yum. I didn't know what I expected. No, I did. I knew exactly what I was waiting for but instead, he kissed me lightly on the cheek and went inside. I was rooted to the spot for a moment and, by the time I followed him in, he was gone, so I scampered up the stairs. Kitty was coming out of my room with her makeup box and tongs and she waggled her fingers in a goodnight gesture as she faked a yawn. I knew I should have asked if Marc had gone to bed, but I didn't. He stormed off and hadn't bothered to say goodnight; but then, I'd dawdled with Evan and, well ... I'd just have to see him tomorrow.

I brushed my teeth quickly and changed into my pyjamas. I had just pulled back the covers when there was a faint knock at the door. I tugged it open but there was no one there, and no one on the landing. Just as I wondered if I was imagining it, the little pile of books at my feet caught my eye and I stooped down to pick them up. Four well-thumbed mysteries, their covers creased with age, and sitting on top was an iPod with headphones wrapped around it.

I smiled and kicked the door shut, setting the bundle on my table next to the posy of flowers I'd picked a couple of days ago from the garden. The roses had bloomed, soft white petals clustered loosely about each other. An idea pinged into my head.

I plucked one of the white roses from the vase and sat on my bed, twisting the stem between my fingertips. *White roses meant friendship, right?*

Focusing on the flower and where I wanted it to be, I lulled myself into concentration and sent it vanishing into the ether before I even really thought about what I was doing.

From down the hall, I was sure I heard Evan laugh and that took my mind away from the thought that something had been watching us, out there in the half-light of nightfall.

CHAPTER SEVEN

After the frustrations of those first two weeks, I was glad to have the weekend largely to myself. I slept in to mid-morning both days. Deciding that it was thoroughly antisocial to hide in my room, I took one of the mysteries and Evan's music player into the sitting room and curled up in an armchair.

The sunlight streamed through the windows and kept me warm as I found myself either engrossed in the story or eagerly checking the music player's digital display to find out what band I was listening to. I liked Evan's music a lot and I made a mental note to see if he would like to borrow my music player in return. *It was like a supernatural swap shop*, I thought, with a giggle.

Meg was noticeably absent that weekend along with Étoile and Seren. Étoile had ducked her head in before they left to say she was leaving for a few days and that she hoped I would be happy to stay with the group. I was.

Marc left shortly after them and they all ended up

staying away all week, though I didn't know if they were together. Marc didn't call but I could hardly complain; I had no claim on him, though I wondered what he was doing that kept him away so long. I was glad that I had chance to familiarise myself before he left. At least I didn't feel so alone. Kitty was pleased to have my company, David and Jared too; while Christy and Clara kept much to themselves as usual and Evan spent a lot of time out of the house, though he never said where.

Ever reliable, Meg fussed over all of us when we saw her. I thought she was lonely and wondered where her family was and made sure to be extra helpful when she asked, and even when she didn't.

The next week was less frustrating. Now that I knew I could not only teleport an object but also send it to where I wanted it to be, and Evan knew it too, my confidence had a brief burst of ego. He set up little tasks for me to practice. Move something, a peg or a pencil, from one side of the table to another. Sometimes I could do it, sometimes I couldn't but the control was getting easier to harness. Later, Evan tried harder stuff like committing an object to memory and then trying to locate it in the house. I even tried to move myself again but ended up a frustrated mess.

I flopped back in the chair. We were in the library again and it seemed a given that this would be where we'd study every day. I knew Evan worked in here on his laptop between lessons and I gathered it was something to do with his business. He hadn't volunteered what it was that he did so I hadn't asked. I'd been feeling a little off about the dancing and chaste cheek kiss and wasn't sure if I was supposed to bring it up or ignore it. Maybe it meant nothing at all to Evan and I was deluding myself into thinking there was something more between us than teacher and student.

"I give up." It was my final lesson of the week and it wasn't going well. I was tired and a headache was beginning to gnaw at my temples.

"You can't give up."

"Apparently I can't start either." I sniffed. Evan was still a taskmaster but we'd settled into an easier routine and he didn't seem entirely unhappy about teaching me anymore at all. I liked being around him but he hadn't touched me again, except for an accidental brush of his hand against mine that sent my heart leaping.

"We'll just have to work out why. We know you can do these things, we just need to know how you can activate them."

"You make it sound so simple."

'It will be simple when you work it out."

"Why do I need to do this stuff anyway?" I felt like flouncing around. "Why can't it just come naturally?"

"It would have come naturally and you'd be in control by now if you had had guidance while you were growing up."

"So, maybe it'll take a few months or a few years; who's counting?"

"The timing counts."

"Why?"

"Because..." Evan sighed, but it was one loaded with expression as he picked his words. "Because there's going to be a war, Stella, and we're probably going to end up right in the middle of it."

"I don't want to be in a war!" My voice pitched upwards and my heart clamoured inside my ribcage.

"Who does? It's not our choosing. If people won't leave us alone, if magic gets thrust into the open when people aren't ready for it, there will end up being a war. It won't be guns and tanks but death and mayhem and we'll be targets, even from our own governments. The world will never be the same again."

I slumped further down in my chair. "But we're not going to harm anyone!"

"You won't. I won't. Who's to say others won't?" Evan shrugged. "Or they'll just think we will, because we can. That's probably an argument the Brotherhood would advocate."

I shuddered. I tried not to think about them at all. "Why would anyone else want a war?"

"The same reason regular people want wars. Power, greed, domination. Just because there's a world of magic on top of the regular world doesn't mean we all want to spin love potions and keep cats."

"That's depressing." I wondered if Evan kept a cat. Or had ever spun a love potion? *Who would he use it on? What the hell was I thinking about?*

"Let's call it quits for today. We'll start again next week."

"I thought you wanted to get me all armoured up?"

"We've done enough for this week."

"Okay." I wasn't going to argue.

"You can practice in your own spare time," suggested Evan.

"O-kay." *Slave driver.* I stepped up and smoothed the wrinkles out of my jeans as I remembered to delve into my pocket. I handed the little rectangular device to Evan.

"What's this?"

"It's my music player. I've been listening to yours all week. It helps me sleep. I can't quite get used to the quiet. I thought you might like to try mine." I shrugged. No big deal. "There's some different stuff."

Evan turned it over in his hand and ran a thumb over the controls, his face expressionless. "Thanks," he said at last.

So I nodded at him and left the room the conventional way.

I slept better than ever that night. I swapped Evan's headphones for mine when I switched music players and I put the buds in my ears and fell asleep to Fiona Apple. As usual, the buds worked themselves out of my ears by morning and I woke tangled in wires. I noticed the battery was low so I wrapped the headphone wires around the player and set it on the nightstand. I'd have to find a charger.

When I finally got up, showered and walked downstairs, Seren and Étoile had returned and they invited me to sit with them. Seren was crocheting some bright yarn on a tiny needle and Étoile was winding the wool. As one, they sat up straighter and sighed happy sighs.

"What?" I asked. I was getting used to their little quirks.

"I've just realised who this blanket will be for," Seren answered, her eyes dreamy as she rested her hands in her lap for a moment. The blanket was but a few multicoloured squares but Seren's quick hands were adding to its size speedily.

"Who?"

"It's a mystery," Étoile laughed and wouldn't be pressed.

"To everyone but you two," said Marc, coming up quietly behind me and then sitting on the arm of the chair. He put a hand on my shoulder and I reached up to pat it.

"When did you get back?" I asked him, but nodding at Étoile and Seren to show that I was including them in the question too.

"Last night for us," said Étoile.

"And this morning for me," said Marc. "I was in New York. My parents had a meeting that I had to attend."

"We were at the Washington branch," added Seren, like she was talking about a chain store.

"Should I ask about what?"

Étoile pursed her lips and thought. "Our elders are coming up with plans to get us more organised. The Washington group want a register. Imagine!"

"Is that so bad?"

"Can you imagine the Brotherhood getting their hands on a register of witches?" Marc shook his head. "Not so great. There's more against than for, at the moment, but there's a good chance some will acquiesce to it."

Seren shook her head in disappointment. "Politics!"

"I hate it." Étoile threw the unfinished yarn down in her lap. "All the bickering is so unproductive. We don't have a single solution that someone else hasn't shouted down. Everyone is divided over what to do."

This was the first I'd heard of the situation with the Witches' Council. I hadn't realised things were so precarious and I wanted to know more. I kept quiet lest they decided to curb their tongues in front of me.

"How did it go in New York, Marc?" Seren asked.

"Much the same." Marc shook his head wearily. "Dad could barely keep them under control. Steven thinks we should go public and force the government to help protect us."

"What did Robert have to say?"

"He can see both sides of the argument. He's not in favour of a register but he thinks we need a better way to keep track of our kind so we can offer assistance. He said Stella wouldn't have had to be on her own so long if we'd had proper records."

Étoile and Seren exchanged a glance. "Perhaps," said Seren, "but I can't be persuaded right now."

"I'm not trying to persuade you." Marc took his hand from my shoulder and put it over his heart in an oddly sincere gesture. My shoulder felt strangely bare again.

Seren picked up her crochet again and Étoile resumed the winding. I gathered the conversation was over. I made a mental note to think about the council's problems later. *After all, they might affect me. And I hadn't even been offered a vote!* I'd always been the independent type and I didn't want decisions to be made for me by people who had never met me.

"I quite agree," said Étoile, who seemed to have picked up what I was feeling.

Kitty was an even later riser than I but stuffed with energy as she bounded down the stairs. Marc made an excuse to leave and I wondered just what it was with him. I didn't get the impression he actively disliked Kitty – he was always polite to her – but he never seemed to want to be near her and he had been oddly nice to me after largely ignoring me all week. I was mildly cross that he hadn't called, especially since we had been spending so much time together recently.

As we had a free day, Kitty insisted on dragging me (quite willingly as it happened) to the nearest town so she could take me shopping. After a quick discussion between Étoile and Seren, it was decided that there were no objections provided we remained alert, though they didn't say for what.

Fortunately, Kitty had a car with her, a white compact that was as neat as she was. We went to lunch first at a little Italian restaurant and sat out in the garden under parasols. Afterwards, she insisted on taking me into shop after shop until I left with two pretty summer dresses, a two piece swim suit, some new tops (not a single tee, per Kitty's insistence) and shorts, a light jacket and enough underwear to see me through a fortnight.

I felt only a twinge of guilt as I dipped into my money. It was fun and a small part of me wished I had had a friend like her for years instead of only a few weeks.

"I am very, very glad you are here," admitted Kitty as she drove us home past neat townhouses and then out onto the freeway. "Don't breathe a word of this but while Christy and Clara are very nice, they are also slightly maddening."

I mimed that I was zipping my mouth.

"And Étoile and Seren are gone so much. And Jared is, well, you've met Jared. He's just a boy anyway. Marc and I hardly speak these days so I've been very much attention-starved until you came along."

"I thought you and Marc were friends since you

were kids?" I asked as I tried to remember if Marc had mentioned anything about his past with Kitty. I didn't think he had.

"Oh yes. A long time, since we were really little."

"I wouldn't have guessed."

Kitty rolled her eyes. "He does his utmost to avoid me."

I wasn't sure if I should ask why. *If they didn't like each other, that was their own business,* I decided. I didn't want to pry so I was relieved when Kitty changed the subject.

"You know Evan thinks he's worked out why I can do the stuff I can with the weather. He thinks it might actually be useful." Kitty snorted and for the first time, I wondered if she felt a bit peeved to possess such an obscure gift. "He thinks I'll be able to use it to influence events, maybe even create my own storms. Perhaps even a tsunami, though, frankly, what use that would be, I have no idea. I could create rainfall during a drought. That would be handy, don't you think?"

I nodded.

"But I prefer the spells." Kitty was obviously feeling particularly chatty today and, though we were careful not to mention magic in public, in the confines of her car, it was fine. "I want to specialise in spell casting. David is keen too. I think he's going to leave soon, he said he's bored of feeling cooped up."

"Cabin fever?" I asked, partly to myself.

"We all have a little cabin fever," Kitty laughed. "We're all used to being able to come and go and live our lives as we please but it's all so prescriptive now. We have to be on our guard because the worst isn't just a possibility for us; it's actually likely to happen."

"Do you think it will always be like this?"

"I hope not." Kitty slowed to turn the corner and accelerated again on the long stretch of road. We were running through the town near Meg's house and I watched the roadside buildings – a car rental place, a family restaurant, shops – flit past. "Maybe when we're more in control, we can be more ourselves but until then, we're stuck doing what the council thinks is best for us."

"Don't you think they're doing what's best?"

"Well, yeah. I mean we're all still alive, right? But what the council wants is not necessarily what everyone else wants. Maybe I want to head to New York or LA or London or Paris and just get on with my career; but the council, well, they say no and that's it."

"We still get a choice though, right? You could just leave if you didn't want to be here. It's not a prison." I thought for a moment and barely voiced, "Is it?"

"No, you're right. I could leave, but I would be leaving without protection and I could get picked up by anyone at any time. In fact, scrap London and Paris. Europe's where the Brotherhood is." Kitty shuddered. "I wouldn't want to be there."

I shook my head. "No, you wouldn't."

Kitty gasped and placed a hand on my knee. "God, Stella, I didn't think. I'm so sorry. I know they attacked you. I'm so dumb sometimes."

"Not at all, and I was agreeing with you, I would not want to be anywhere the Brotherhood is."

"Thank God they're not here, right?"

"Right." Watching the news wasn't a big deal in the house but every so often, a newscast would flick on the television or someone would bring in a paper or the radio would mention it. No one made a big thing about it, but the square-set shoulders and the thoughtful expressions made me sure that everyone was waiting to hear what the Brotherhood were doing. So far, they had stayed across the ocean. At least, there had been no reports of any suspicious activity here. I thought things would be a lot worse if they made that geographical leap. Right now, I could feel relatively safe here, with their threat thousands of miles away. If they were here, I was sure we would have known about it by now.

Kitty indicated to turn into the driveway and she parked next to Marc's car. It had moved from where it was parked when we left, so he must have been out somewhere, but if Kitty noticed, she didn't mention it, so neither did I.

We grabbed our bags from the back seat and went inside. It was late afternoon and the house was quiet.

"Hullo-o," Kitty called and David ducked his head around the library door. "Where is everyone?"

"Headed down to the beach," David answered, repositioning his glasses on his nose. "I might head over that way myself soon. Hey, bring a swimming costume!"

"You swim in the sea?" I asked Kitty as we went upstairs.

"Sure," Kitty was rummaging through her bags. "It's a good job we got you that bathing suit. I'm quite ready to sunbathe. It seems a good day for it."

In my room, I snapped the tags off my bathing suit, changed out of my clothes and slipped it on. It was white with belted bikini shorts and a halter neck top and I thought I looked pretty snazzy in it, plus the pure white didn't show up my pasty skin too badly. I pulled one of the dresses over the top. It buttoned up the front so it would be easy to get on and off at the beach. I swapped my flats for sandals that were better for the sand and went to knock on Kitty's door. She waved me in and I leant against the doorframe while she finished rummaging in her closet. At last, she sprang up, gold sandals dangling in her hand and slipped them on her feet.

"Let's go!"

We veritably skipped our way out of the house and across the lawn. I could hear laughter from the beach and we followed it. By the time we got there, blankets had been spread out and cool boxes sat to one side, anchoring the fabric to the sand. Christy and Clara had taken towels and were sunbathing on their fronts. Jared was talking to Seren and Étoile in his usual animated way; Evan was reading a book, pausing occasionally to add to the conversation. It was Étoile who spotted us first and waved us over.

"It's like Spring Break," said Kitty gleefully, skipping towards them.

"Where's Meg?" I asked as we crossed the beach, the sand sifting through the straps of my sandals.

"She won't be out 'til later, if at all," Kitty replied, waving to the group. "She has this, um, skin condition and the sun bothers her."

"Oh, I didn't know." I guessed it explained her preference for night time walks.

"She doesn't make a big thing out of it."

I settled down on the blanket with Kitty flopping in between me and Étoile. I looked wistfully at Evan's book and wished it had occurred to me to bring a book too. Reading on the beach would be pleasant.

Evan folded down the corner of the page and closed the book, setting in down. I gestured to it. "May I?"

"Of course." He handed it to me and I turned it over to read the back cover synopsis, my elbows propping me up as I lay on my stomach, before passing it back. "Have you read the other books already?"

"One of them and I'm half way through the second." It was a whodunit set in the thirties and the dialogue was very witty. I said as much. "I hardly ever see you without a book."

"I like reading and there isn't a whole lot of entertainment out here."

"What would you do if you weren't here? At home or...?" I couldn't think where else Evan would be.

"I'd go catch a movie or attend a sports game. Basketball preferably, but I'll take football or baseball, too."

"I have no concept of American sports," I confessed which led to Evan trying to give a lengthy explanation of the rules of baseball.

I couldn't remember what it was that Evan said that made me laugh so hard but it gave me the kind of ache in my ribs that I hadn't had in a long time. Marc was crouched beside me in an instant, his hand on my elbow as the laughter came to a spluttering stop in my throat.

"Hey." I smiled, a smile that faded as I realised Marc looked thunderous. I hadn't even realised he'd come to the beach.

"Come for a walk," he said, his face stern.

"Um, sure." I scrambled to my feet and looked back at our small group. Seren and Kitty were taking turns slathering on sun lotion, even though the sun wasn't really all that hot. Evan had turned his head and was unscrewing the cap from his soda bottle. I could tell he was listening. He wasn't making too much pretence not to.

Marc led me away from the little group and for a few minutes we walked, until we reached the part of the beach where it twisted back on itself and headed back inland before stretching out almost as far as I could see.

"What's going on?" Marc snarled the question.

"Huh?"

"Back there." Marc jerked his head back to the group.

"We were just joking around, having fun. Goodness knows we've needed it these past weeks."

Marc rolled his eyes. "C'mon! I've seen the way he looks at you."

"Who? Evan?" I involuntarily turned my head and caught Evan's eye as he looked over at us. He held my gaze steady for a moment before turning away and tossing a juice box over to Kitty who caught it in one hand.

"Who else? What's going on between you two?" Marc jutted his chin toward Evan.

"Nothing." I shrugged my shoulders and the breeze gently lifted my hair and fanned it across my back.

"I've seen the way he looks at you," Marc repeated, sounding for all the world like a jealous boyfriend.

I gaped at him. "He's my teacher," I hissed. "He's looking out for me. He's helping me."

"He wants to help himself to you."

"What do you mean by that?" I'd had enough of the scowling and the conversation was taking a turn for the worst. Plus I couldn't pretend I didn't feel something for Evan. It was there, all right, every day a bit stronger.

"You know what I mean. He's had his eye on you ever since I brought you here. He's interested in you and you sat there, flirting with him."

"I did not!" *Did I?*

"Well that's not how it looks from here. You're practically making out."

"Marc!" I was incensed. *What business was it of his who I was talking to?* He hadn't staked a claim and even if he had, it was still a free world. I could talk to whomever I liked. Besides, I could hardly ignore my teacher. Not that Evan being my teacher was the problem.

"How do you think that makes me feel?"

"I would have thought that me making friends here would be good." I didn't even think to add: for us. There hadn't been any hint of an "us". It was a topic that never arose and besides the kiss in New York, I had to remind myself that nothing had actually happened. Even though we'd spent plenty of time together since talking about everything and anything, which was what made Marc's behaviour all the more puzzling. He hadn't made any moves on me, and I hadn't encouraged any.

"It's like he's got a spell on you." Marc looked at me quizzically and I realised his allegation was serious. I was astonished he'd even had such a thought, never mind spoken it. Magic on others was absolutely forbidden as I already knew. Spell casting to make someone attracted to another was strictly punished as

David had mentioned when he was running though some rules during a class. Marc knew the rules better than I.

"Are you sleeping with him too?"

"That's out of order, Marc. You know I'm not."

Marc sighed and kicked the sand dune. A spray of sand shot into the air. He ran a hand through his thick blonde hair and his shoulders seemed tense. Before, I might have reached out and gently kneaded them, or given him a hug, but right now, I was furious at his accusations and didn't want to touch him, not as a friend or as anything else. Instead I folded my arms and waited.

Marc took a deep breath and inclined his head towards me. "I have to go away for a while," he said at last, abruptly changing the subject. "I'm needed in New York again. There have been some developments."

"Is it the council?"

Marc nodded and his face showed he was unhappy. "Kinda."

"How long will you be gone?"

"I don't know."

"How long have you known?"

"Since this morning, pretty much right after I got back. I should have just turned round and gone straight back."

"Well, good of you to tell me. I wouldn't have wanted to get up and find you gone again," I snipped. I could have pinched myself. He owed me nothing. He was just sent to deliver me here. That was it.

"I'm sure you would have found somebody to keep your bed warm," Marc spat like a spurned lover, his face clouding as he looked over at Evan. I didn't follow his gaze so I didn't know if anyone else could hear. I imagined not from this distance, *but who knew what superhuman talents I didn't know about with this crowd of weird and wonderful people?*

"Hold on!" I raised a hand to him in a stop sign, palm flat towards him. "What's that supposed to mean?"

"Oh hell, Stella." Marc was getting more agitated and his toe was digging at the sand again. "Evan, he's ... he's not like us. He shouldn't even be thinking about it. You should stay away from him."

"What do you mean by that?"

Marc sighed. "You're a free woman. Do what you want but don't say I didn't warn you. I'll see you when I get back." He turned on his heel and strode back along the beach to the steps that would lead him to the house.

I stood still, watching him retreat, the breeze gently caressing me as I tried to assess what had just occurred. Marc acted like a jealous boyfriend, or someone who wanted to be more than friends, not that he actually said that at all. *Or had he assumed there was something between us?* I hadn't even had a chance to ask what he meant but it seemed clear. I was a free woman, all right. If he'd been thinking about making a move, he seemed to have scrubbed the idea away. Whatever feelings could have been had ceased existing the moment he stomped away. I watched Marc finish climbing the steps and disappear into the garden. I hadn't even begun to address what he said about Evan.

It felt like I stood there forever when Kitty came over and slipped her arm around me. If she had been a bit taller, I would have rested my head on her shoulder. Instead, she put another arm around my front, linked her hands together and hugged me. I breathed deeply, more puzzled than ever.

CHAPTER EIGHT

Kitty unlinked her hands and turned me around so that she could take me by the shoulders and look at me with her beautiful almond eyes. "Are you okay?" she asked.

I nodded, mute.

"Marc can be an idiot. Rash and foolish and sometimes he really doesn't know what he wants. It's not a reflection on you." Kitty kept her hands on my shoulders but without pressure. "I'm going to tell you some things that you might not want to hear and some things that you don't know yet. You'll probably wonder why, but I have to tell you these things because I want to be your friend and I want you to be mine. If I don't tell you these things and we talk about Marc, and you find these things out later, you'll wonder if I've been malicious. I want you to know that I'm not like that and I don't want to interfere where I'm not wanted."

"Okay," I agreed, curious. She had been friendly to me since my arrival and I wondered what it was that was important enough to make her look so solemn.

Kitty smiled, nodded, and took her hands off my shoulders. She slipped her arm through mine, patted my hand and led me off down the beach, away from the party. The first thing she said should have shocked me.

"I know I said Marc and I grew up together, but what I didn't say was that we were once together-together too. It seems like a long time ago now. We were quite young and it lasted for several years. We were getting to grips with the things we, well, I could do and we naturally drifted towards each other. He was very handsome and charming even then." Kitty smiled to herself but didn't look at me. "I loved him very, very much and thought he loved me too. We broke up two, no, three years ago."

"Why did you break up?"

"He had a roving eye," Kitty said simply. "We both had to follow different paths. I had to learn to get my talents under control and Marc needed to learn other things, like how to defend our kind. I think he also had some problems dealing with his lack of magic. I thought faithfulness was implicit, even though we were so young. Perhaps we were too young. I don't think his parents ever thought I was quite good enough either. Anyway, regardless of the reasons, Marc slept with other women and I found out the hard way."

"I'm sorry. Did he break up with you?"

Kitty laughed and I was startled. "No. No. I broke it off with him. He was very upset and said he would change, but I'd had enough. I think he genuinely meant to change, but the damage was already done. I loved him for a long time and he tried to prove himself to me for a long time afterwards. I'll grant him that. It was very hard and so awful and, to be perfectly honest, we're still not too happy with each other."

I absorbed this information. It made sense. They were civil to each other but never alone together. "Why are you telling me?"

"So that you understand why Marc is how he is. So you can make your decisions wisely."

I nodded and understood that Kitty was implying that she didn't want me to get hurt as she had. I would have my eyes wide open if I wanted to pursue Marc. Thing is, I wasn't sure I wanted to in a romantic way. I wanted him to be my friend. As far as trees went, Kitty was barking up the wrong one. Clarity hit me like a ten tonne truck and I embraced it like an old friend.

"After we split up, and Marc gave up trying to win me back, he started seeing other people but never really dated. You're the first girl he's been interested in for a very long time and he told me that he cares for you a lot. Don't be startled, we don't discuss you. That would be too weird, but he mentioned one night how much he cares for you." Kitty squeezed my hand. "However, Marc is still Marc and can still be a dumbass. A jealous one, too. You get that, right?"

I nodded, feeling more confused than ever. "I think so."

"Marc isn't the easiest person when it comes to relationships. I don't know what he wants. I'm not entirely sure he knows what he wants." Kitty shrugged her shoulders. "But if you're hanging around wishing and waiting for him to sort himself out, and I'm not saying you are, well, that isn't right or fair to you or him. I don't want him to mess you about since you're a bright and beautiful girl who deserves honesty and love and faithfulness."

"We're not together," I blurted out. "I knew Marc liked me, I guess, and I like him too, but nothing's happened. Just now, he was acting like an ass and then he warned me off Evan."

We stopped walking and Kitty gave me a sympathetic look. We altered our course slightly and headed down to the water edge. Kitty tiptoed in the water and waited for me, the waves lapping over her feet. "It's warm," she said, and after a moment added, "sort of."

I slipped off my sandals one at a time and followed her in. The lukewarm sea felt delicious against my skin. We stood there for a while looking out at the horizon and I let the peacefulness of the scenery wash over me and calm my insides until I got to the point where I no longer harboured vaguely violent thoughts towards Marc anymore.

Kitty held my hand as we walked back towards our beach and I felt relaxed, strolling through the shallows with the girl that I knew was honestly my friend.

"That's Marc for you," she said. "He doesn't know what he wants, but he wants to make sure you'll still be around when he makes up his mind. I'm sorry if you're hurting."

"I'm confused. I thought we were friends and maybe there might have been something." It felt weird to be spilling about Marc to his ex; I just had to remind myself that Kitty was my friend too. "But he just snapped. He asked me why I was flirting with

Evan and got all cross; then told me I could do whatever I wanted and he would soon be gone for a while. I don't quite know what to make of it."

"Were you flirting with Evan?"

"No. I don't know. Maybe." I sighed. *Of course, I was flirting with him*, but there was no way I was going to tell Kitty that Evan made my heart flutter like a million butterflies awakening every time I saw him. "We've been spending a lot of time together. Well, we have to, he's my teacher, but I do like him. What did he mean about Evan not being like us? I keep getting hints and I don't know what it means. And if Marc is so interested, why doesn't he just make a move?"

"You could go ask Marc," Kitty suggested. "Go up to the house. Everyone else is down here."

Ahead of us, our patch of beach was back in view. Someone had strung up a volleyball net and a game was starting up. The ball sailed through the air and I saw Seren leap up to smack it back over the net. She hadn't struck me as the athletic type but I revised my opinion when I saw her long, lean limbs.

Kitty was right. I probably should talk to him. I didn't want Marc to leave with any bad blood between us but I wasn't sure what I was going to say.

"I think I'll do that." I paused to give Kitty a hug, which was part of the new making-friends me, and she reciprocated warmly before giving me a push towards the steps. It took me a few minutes to climb the steps and cross the garden.

I entered the house through the screened back door and called for Marc. He didn't answer so I went up to my room. In the weeks before he left, we'd spent quite a few evenings talking in here, curled up on the window seat, as it was a bit more quiet than in his room downstairs. He'd taken to leaving some things too; a sweater, a book or two. Everything was gone. I sat on the bed and looked around. Not one scrap of Marc was left, he may well have never been in my room.

I went back out to the hallway and walked down the stairs to Marc's room. He wasn't there either, but the things he had left in my room had been recklessly tossed onto the dresser, so I backtracked to the hall.

Opening the front door, I ducked around the side of the building where the cars were kept – Marc's Prius was gone. To have vanished so fast, he must have already been packed, ready to go, when he caught up with me on the beach. At least, that solved the problem of what I would say to him. Apparently, it would be nothing at all. It was probably a good thing considering the way I was feeling. At least, I wouldn't say something that I might regret later.

Back in the house, I shut the front door with a thud and rested against it for a moment. I took the stairs two at a time and went into my room to pick up a shawl. *I'd probably need it if the night turned cold later.* Then it occurred to me that the other girls might need something too so I gathered up an armful and tossed them into a straw bag that was lounging empty on the landing. *At least, I had an excuse for coming back to the house,* I thought as I left via the back door.

I puzzled the whole scenario over in my head again. *Sure, Marc and I had been getting close but neither one of us had made any move and he had no right to think that he had some kind of say over whom I spoke to.* I felt myself getting angrier as I ran down the steps.

"Hey!" Seren called as I stepped onto the beach. "Where'd ya go?"

I held up the bag. "I thought we might get cold later, so I went to fetch some shawls from the house."

"You are sweetness, personified," grinned Seren, making room for me on the big towel on which she lay spread-eagled. Kitty waved to me from the makeshift pitch and Étoile tossed the volleyball towards me. I dropped the bag and caught the ball without hesitation, to Étoile's delight.

Seren laughed, "I think you've just been conscripted which is a good thing because the girls are losing." She waved her scorecard at me.

I slipped out of my sandals again and tossed the ball back. "I'm in!"

The game went on for a couple of hours. Kitty, Étoile and I versus Evan, Jared and Clara – we were the stay hards. From time to time, David or Seren joined in and dropped out – mostly they seemed happy to stick with each other's company and I wondered if there weren't some budding romance there. I watched Kitty's lithe body leap through the air to smash the ball back and we hugged and high fived as she scored another point for the team.

When it came to Evan's turn to serve, he stretched his long, muscular body to whack the ball over to our side. I was sure I wasn't the only one admiring his thick biceps, broad shoulders, bare chest and strong legs. The ball had gone to Kitty's side so she hit it back to Evan. They parried until the ball fell on our side and Evan stretched again. As he caught my eye and held my gaze, I realised I hadn't looked at anyone else and wondered if his stretching was for my benefit. *Yum.*

"Close your mouth," whispered Étoile, bumping me gently and I laughed as I looked away. When I turned back, Evan grinned at me, then I had to race to bash the ball that was hurtling towards me and him and he laughed as he smashed it back with ease.

While we played, the sun started going down and the sky faded to dusky blue. David and Seren had been gathering driftwood for a little firepit Jared had dug where a newly ignited fire burned. He and David were poking it with sticks to the amusement of Seren who was singing "me man, make fire" until she was scooped up by Jared, who ran her around as though she were a victory prize. After a couple of rounds, she was tossed unceremoniously onto the pitch still clutching her scorecard. She scrambled to her feet and called time, waving her hands for us all to stop whilst we clamoured for the result.

"Much as it pains me to say this," she gasped, brushing the sand from her body. "The boys are the winners."

A whoop went up from the boys with "false" cries from the girls.

"I propose a swim, because I'm hot and sticky and the sea will cool us down before we eat." This was met with unanimous approval but Seren didn't wait to hear it as she grabbed Kitty's hand and they ran into the sea before you could say "go." Again, I admired Kitty's lithe, unselfconscious body in the red two-piece.

I was still wearing my sundress, so I carefully unbuttoned it from the top to the skirt and slipped it off. Fortunately, I'd already put on the white bikini and the straps had stayed taut. I went to hang it over the net so I would find it after the swim and discovered Evan still standing there.

I mistakenly thought he'd headed to the shoreline

already but he had, quite obviously, watched me as I slowly unbuttoned my dress in front of him.

"I didn't know you were there," I mumbled. I fought to keep my cool as I saw his chest heave while he scanned my almost naked body. He didn't say anything. "I've never swum in the sea before," I admitted to fill the silence and Evan held out his hand.

"I'll take care of you."

I hesitated, then laid my hand in his as he pulled me into the sea after him until we were up to our hips. It wasn't warm but not unbearably cold so far out so I pushed off and swam tentative strokes. Ahead of me, Evan swung his arms into more powerful strokes then his legs flipped into the air and he disappeared. I treaded water for a moment, moving myself in a circle to see where he was, then, as suddenly as he disappeared, he surfaced, just inches in front of me.

Sea water trickled down his face and he brushed it away with a hand. I was close enough that everyone else seemed to disappear, and it was just the two of us, treading water. I was glad he couldn't hear my heart quickening its pace. He reached out and brushed my damp hair behind my ears, his fingers grazing my cheeks and not moving. I was close enough to lean in and kiss him. In the mere second the idea crossed my mind, my lips parted in anticipation; he splashed me with water and I laughed before he slid back under the water.

He reappeared next to Jared and they jostled, trying to dunk each other and splashing water at Kitty, making her laugh, before racing each other through the waves.

Étoile had swum over and was treading water next to me, mouthing, "hot, hot, hot" which made me laugh and we swam together before heading to shore. Kitty was waiting for us with towels. Étoile grabbed one and another for Seren.

"Did you find him?" Kitty asked quietly, when the two of us were alone.

I shook my head and droplets of water shook out. "No, he's gone. He's just gone. No note. It seemed a very..." *I struggled for the right word.* "Final. It seemed a very final thing to do."

"I'm sorry."

"Don't be. It's okay. Besides, I'm really pissed off with him for acting like such a jerk when he's supposed to be my friend and I would have said that if he'd been there." I towelled off and stood by the raging bonfire, still in my two-piece.

Skewers of meat had been produced from a cool bag and were being threaded over a rack. The scent of barbecue pulled in the stragglers from the sea who patted their stomachs and busied themselves handing out drinks.

Jared pulled out a guitar (clearly a hidden talent) and started strumming it as the sun set in streaks of orange and pink over the ocean until the only light that was left was the bonfire. Stakes with torches had been set out and lit so that there was light around the blankets too. Our little crowd stretched out on towels and dozed while the meat cooked. The atmosphere was altogether relaxing and joyful. I couldn't have wished to be anywhere else and for the first time, I knew what it felt like to really be part of something. I didn't feel at all awkward in their company anymore.

My bikini had dried off so I walked over to the

remains of the volleyball pitch, my feet sinking in the cool sand. My dress was where I'd left it, still hanging over the pole so I shrugged it on and redid the buttons, leaving the last few of the skirt semi undone. As I turned back towards the bonfire, I scanned the people for the pair of eyes I could feel were watching me and smiled when I saw Evan. He raised his glass to me.

"What shall we do for entertainment?" Seren asked to a resounding "whoop". "I already know the decision, of course, but I'm sure you would rather come up with it by yourselves than for me to just tell you."

"Dancing," came a shout from the back. I thought it was Jared.

"Gentleman, please. This is not a beach of ill repute," snorted Kitty.

"Dance with us then?" came a low voice. David did a low bow in front of Seren and offered her his hand which she took with coy smile. *Yep, something definitely going on there.* His suggestion was met with approval from all sides, a CD player was produced from somewhere and music blared out across our enclave. There were some more "whoops" as Kitty and Clara immediately started jumping around, arms in the air. No one could fail to admire their enthusiastic dancing whilst still clad in bikinis. I laughed and turned as I felt a body close to mine.

Evan took my hand and pulled me to him. I had to stretch to put my hands around his neck as he slipped his hands about my waist. A single one of his hands almost covered the base of my back. We danced slowly, no more than a shuffle and every so often he spun me out and twirled me around before pulling me to him again. He had only pulled on jeans so I found myself – happily – very close to his bare chest. Dancing with Evan was pure pleasure but eventually I shivered as we drifted away from the gathering, confessed I felt a little cold, and we went back to the bonfire.

Evan gathered up one of the discarded shawls and wrapped it around my shoulders before swooping up his t-shirt and sweat jacket and pulling them over his head. He fell backwards onto a blanket and pulled me down with him, so that I was nestled between his legs, my back to his chest, using his powerful body to shield me from the breeze that had whipped up. It was strangely intimate, though at no time was he inappropriate and I felt comfortable snuggled into him. But even I had to admit that I wouldn't be snuggled quite so close if there weren't some serious attraction going on.

Whether it was because of his intense body heat, or because, frankly, just being near him was a turn-on, I didn't want to move away from Evan so we stayed there for the rest of the night. Food was passed round and people came and went, sitting and chatting and then moving on again. By the time the moon was hanging full and bright over the ocean, my eyelids were giving sleepy tugs down and I feared I might dose off right there in Evan's arms if I didn't move soon.

I stretched my arms and felt Evan shift behind me as he tightened his arms around me. He seemed to be half asleep himself. A glance at my watch's glowing hands told me it was past eleven.

"I think it's time I went to bed," I muttered and, in an instant, Evan was on his feet and helping me to mine.

"Seren looks like she's heading up to the house, why don't you walk up with her?" he suggested.

I looked over. Seren had gathered up her things and, I noticed gratefully, mine too. *She had probably already known that I would walk up with her.* "Yes, I think I will."

Evan bent his head towards mine and I felt his hands brush my lower back. I tilted my head and wondered if he might kiss me under the moonlit sky; I certainly wanted him to. Instead, he dipped and I felt his warm lips brush across my cheek. I took a step back and his hands released me as I stumbled a step away. I paused for breath but couldn't say anything. Evan nodded once, and smiled.

What was with the guys around here? I thought as I caught up with Seren and offered to carry her surplus bag. *Was I misinterpreting everything? God! I was going to be so embarrassed in the morning.* We walked up the steps together, calling goodnight to the straggling partiers. "What a lovely day," she said happily, David just a step behind her.

"The best," I muttered, glowing hotly with the embarrassment of misinterpreting Evan's intentions. In the next moment, I wondered how it was that so much of the world's awfulness could have been pushed from our thoughts for this single day. It was a sobering thought that I could do without.

Seren kissed me on the cheek when we got to the house and wandered off to her room while I was saying goodnight to Christy and Clara who were looking a little worse for wear. David nodded to me as he passed and followed Seren upstairs. *It was fortunate that this sprawling house could accommodate us all so well*, I thought. It was nice to have a room of my own, instead of bunking down with several other girls like I had to do in one of my foster homes. Still, I did allow myself a second of speculation about which room David was heading to and I couldn't help but smile to myself.

I took the stairs two at a time and dumped my bag on the chair. My discarded clothing went into the hamper and I went into the en suite bathroom, reaching into the shower to turn on the taps. I held my hand under the water until it turned warm, though, really, a cold shower would have probably been more appropriate given the way I was feeling right then.

I sluiced the sea water and sand from my body and hair, shampooed and conditioned, covering myself in the vanilla-scented body wash that I loved. I assumed Seren's abilities came in handy here too what with the coordinated basket of toiletries that appealed perfectly to me. I wondered how often people had arrived here with absolutely nothing, like I did.

Standing under the water as I reminisced about the day, I thought how nice it was that we had laughed and played like normal people. Playing volleyball and swimming in the sea, telling silly stories, eating until our bellies were full and dancing on the sand.

It occurred to me that not once had magic been used, not that I noticed anyway. No one had thought to click their fingers to light the fire, the volleyball had been hit by hands rather than minds manipulating its path, the sky had gone inky and studded with stars all by itself. Not once could I think of an occasion where magic had been used. It had been as normal as normal could be. We were just regular people enjoying ourselves.

We had managed without magic, and magic had managed without us. Everything we did was real. Everything we felt was real. And it dawned on me that the attraction I was feeling towards Evan was all of my own making. "Crap," I said to the tiles.

I wondered if the others had come to the same conclusion as I and what they made of it, if they even thought about it at all. *Probably not,* I decided, *they'd all been on the magic bus long before me.*

I rinsed and turned off the taps, wrapping myself up in a towel. I dried off, lotioned and put on a mauve silk dressing gown that contrasted prettily with my hair and pale skin. Before I could really think what I was doing, my hand was on the handle of my bedroom door and pulling the door open. I stepped outside at the very instant I heard another door open and froze.

Evan stood framed in the doorway of his room down the hall. He had changed from his jeans, tee and zip-up top into loose, linen, dark navy pants that hung the long, sumptuous length of his legs.

My heart thudded in my chest and I took one step forward, then another. Evan waited for me silently until I stood before him. He looked at me for a mere second before taking my hand and pulling me inside without a word, closing the door with a soft thud.

By now, I'd been inside most of the rooms in the house but not this one. Being the corner room, it was a little bigger than mine. Curtains on both walls were drawn already. His bed sat beneath the one that I guessed looked out over the ocean. It was made up in soft grey jersey sheets, masculine but not off-putting and the comforter was folded back like he'd just been about to climb in. On the bedside table, a lamp was switched on and a book lay open, face down.

A desk occupied one side of the long set of curtains; a small pile of books and a writing pad the only clutter. The walls were a much paler grey and everything was tidy. Two doors led off to what I assumed were his en suite and a closet. He smelled fresh and clean and I guessed he had showered as soon as he came in too.

"There was no magic today," I said, not sure if I was stating the obvious or asking a question.

Evan shook his head. "None."

"Everything was real." Again, not a statement or a question.

Evan nodded his head.

"Huh." I nodded, glad that he agreed.

"Kitty might have warmed the temperature up a little."

"Figures."

"Why are you here?" Evan asked softly. With a snap, I realised that I was standing in Evan's room with barely a robe covering entirely nothing underneath and he was barely inches from me, fairly close to nakedness himself. *What was I doing here?*

"I just got out of the shower and I was thinking about you, then ... I don't know, I went to the door and you were standing at yours." That seemed to surprise Evan. I wonder *if I'd stayed still, would he have come to me and would we be in my room now having the same soft conversation, but perhaps he would be doing the explaining?*

"You were thinking about me while you were in the shower?"

"Um, yeah." *And why was I admitting to that?*

"Stella, I think you know that I want you – I've tried not to, but I do – and now you are in my room, wearing very, very little." He stroked my neck above the collar of my gown, running my hair through his fingers. "Well, that suggests that you want me too, but I want to be sure that I'm not treading on any toes."

I nearly looked at my toes before I realised he was being metaphorical. I gulped. "If you're asking if Marc and I are together, then no, we are not. I'm a free woman and I can do as I please." I used the same words Marc had thrown at me, but not for revenge, because it was true. I wanted Evan very, very much. "Am I treading on any toes?"

"No. There isn't anyone," said Evan, his voice still gentle but his fingers caressing my skin, just barely under the gown now. "I don't want to be a rebound fuck." I was a little taken aback as he swore.

"I'm not entirely sure what a rebound fuck is, but I can assure you that that is not why I am here. Besides, I've never slept with Marc. Actually, I've never slept with anyone."

"And you are here because...?"

He seemed to really want me to spell it out. I looked up at him and held his eyes steady in my own, before I answered, "Because I want you."

He smiled at last, a broad, happy smile, and his hand circled the back my neck, keeping my head tilted up as he bent to kiss me at last, his lips warm and sensual against my own.

A gasp of joy escaped me as his tongue entered my mouth and found mine. As I responded, the kiss intensified and I pressed my body against his, my arms wrapping around him as far as I could reach. I could feel his mounting excitement push against me through my thin gown.

It was Evan who broke off. "I've been wondering what it would be like to kiss you since the day I met you," he said, his breathing ragged. His hands were tugging at the little knot of my robe and he slid it open, his touch light on my skin. Then his hands slid beneath the silk and travelled from my stomach, running across my breasts until he reached my shoulders. I stood there almost naked in the half light of his room. His gaze was admiring.

"I am much too tall for you." He grinned suddenly as he swooped me up and lay me across his bed. "You would get an awful pain in your neck if we stayed like that."

I laughed and forgot about being even slightly embarrassed at appearing at his room and being almost entirely unclothed in minutes. Evan lay down next to me and propped his head up on one arm. He used his other hand to trail across my body and I shivered at the pleasure of his touch. We kissed again and I wriggled so that I was on my side too, pressing against him once more. My hands caressed him and I could barely contain my glee at touching his muscular torso. I stayed the temptation to let my hands travel lower. I could feel how much he wanted me but... *oh hell.* I let my hands drift and slid my palm along his erection.

Evan groaned and kissed me harder and rolled so that he was on top of me, resting on his elbows either side of me. He was supporting his weight but not so much that I couldn't feel him press his whole body against me as I pulled him ever closer. We stayed like this for a long time as my legs wrapped around him, the desperation to be part of him taking over, my baser instincts eager to take control.

"You've really never done this before?" he asked, breaking off.

I locked eyes with him. "Yes, really. Not for lack of wanting to, but for lack of wanting anyone who offered. Not that there was a queue."

"I doubt there was any lack of offers," he groaned, nibbling my ear lobe. "I'm honoured, of course, but I don't want to do anything you're not ready for and I'm not a one-night-stand kind of guy. I'm more date-and-take-it-slow. Are you sure you want me? Right here? Right now?"

"Yes, I want you." My voice was raspy as he peeled himself from me and reached over to the side cabinet to pull open the top drawer, palming a small packet. I may not know the mechanics of sex but I was familiar with good practice in theory.

He kicked his pants off into a heap on the floor and well, being pressed against me, I had some indication of his size, but now I was truly impressed. I pushed myself up with my elbows and surveyed him in admiration. Clothed, he was every bit impressive and I wasn't the only girl in the house who had appreciated his strong torso and muscular arms. Unclothed, Evan was quite a revelation. It wasn't just that part of his anatomy but he was probably the most beautiful man I had ever seen.

He pulled me up and slid the gown from my shoulders so it pooled at my feet then dipped his head to kiss me, long and deep. Lowering me onto the bed, he slid on top of me and held my eyes steady. He kissed me again and again and the flare inside me reignited hot and urgent. I pushed upwards to him and his hand cupped my breast. He bent to kiss it, landing feather kisses on the way across my neck and collarbone, while his hand moved south, caressing and parting my legs and pushing his finger inside as his thumb rubbed me quite the right way.

I groaned and kissed him harder until he moved his finger in a determined pulsing rhythm that had me biting my lip in excitement. Evan murmured, "Ready?" not quite waiting for my answer before he slid inside me, not too deeply at first but rocking until the initial piercing pain had gone and I had enveloped him completely. His voice was as ragged as mine when a wave of pleasure rippled through me and I rocked against Evan. Finding our rhythm and letting myself be swept away by the joy of being so intensely entwined with him, I luxuriated in being so close to him, part of him, as his body rippled above me.

Heat spiralled from my centre and I cried out as I came, my mouth fixed on Evan's shoulder, not quite biting, not yet, so that I wouldn't yell out loud. My hands ran across his back and I barely registered the ridges and edges of his vertebrae and the working muscles, taught and hard, under my fingertips. Somewhere in the back of my mind, I wondered at his strange topography as his back flexed and undulated under my hands; then his mouth sought mine. He kissed me deeply as he came to his own shuddering conclusion, thrusting ever deeper until at last we untangled our limbs and lay side by side, panting, and my thoughts were all stars and fireworks.

We lay quietly for a while, alongside each other, until I turned and kissed him. Evan responded enthusiastically and pulled me closer to him, until our bodies were fully pressed against each other, his hands exploring mine in long, smooth strokes.

"I don't normally make a habit of this, you know," I said, wondering what Evan thought of me now. Part of me wanted to shriek "he really likes me!" but I stuffed that away. I traced my fingers across his cheek, cupping his chin in the palm of my hand. His irises had darkened to purple-black, so vibrant as they shone against the whites of his eyes.

"Habit of what? Turning up at men's rooms practically naked?" Evan was amused.

"Hmm, yes, most definitely not in the habit of doing that."

"I could get used to it." Evan kissed me again and when I opened my eyes, his were back to their normal deep brown.

"I don't want you to think I'm something that I'm not. I want you to know that I don't wander around the halls, looking for..." I didn't want Evan to think my purpose was to offer up sex to men here, there and everywhere as the fancy took me. Well, obviously, even if I had, I'd never been taken up on it. Until now...

"I never thought you did, but should you get into the habit, I will happily leave my door open so you don't have to go far."

I laughed and laid my head on his chest. I could feel his heart beating and it was reassuring. His hand rested on my hip. We couldn't have been more familiar and easy in each other's company than right now.

"I'm not massively experienced in these sort of things. I don't think I'd be the type to sleep around. I've never wanted to." *That probably sounded strange after what had just happened.*

"I wouldn't have assumed that you did."

I don't know why I felt compelled to tell him, but I did. "I've never even had a boyfriend before."

"Me neither," Evan replied, but curious all the same.

"Um, no," I admitted and he shifted next to me. I could tell the truth had dawned on him. It wasn't just a roll in the sheets for me; he was the only person I had ever wanted so strongly and I had given him part of myself that I could never offer out again. Sure, I could have had a fumble with a spotty youth during school but I didn't want to cast away something so important on someone so insignificant. This was a memory I wanted to keep.

"I'm the first person you've slept with and I am absolutely touched that you would want me that much," Evan said softly but without ego.

I shrugged. I was still a little surprised that I had found someone I wanted enough. I found myself kissing his chest, my finger massaging his nipple until it was hard. Evan groaned and pulled me up to kiss him again. When he released me, he kept me pulled to his side.

"I don't understand though, I thought you and Marc were having some kind of thing?"

"I thought we might," I admitted. "But it never felt right. We kissed once a few weeks ago when I first got here, and it was nice but there was never any," *I struggled for the right word while I thought about what I wanted to say and settled on* "'progression.' The one time we kissed, it was nice, but it was a bit like snogging a friend. There was nothing there."

Evan was a quiet for a bit then he repeated softly, "I'm honoured."

I hadn't expected that so I rolled onto my front and looked at him quizzically.

"Well," he said, choosing his words carefully. 'You're twenty-four and you're hot. Seriously hot. You could have been with who knows how many guys. I'm honoured, however, that you didn't and that you chose me, and, well, that feels special."

I smiled at his carefulness not to insult me, or my lack of experience, and that he viewed our intimacy as an honour. He kissed me and I responded with a great deal of enthusiasm which led to a very nice repeat of other things.

"I can't lie though, I've wanted you from the moment I laid eyes on you." Evan kissed me again, long and lingering, his hands caressing my torso with reverence. He stretched an arm to draw up the covers and pulled me close. "Stay here tonight?" It seemed more of a question than a suggestion so I nodded and said I'd like to, but I didn't add that it was because I couldn't bear to leave him now. Evan snuggled up next to me and we were still before I grinned and sat up, pulling the covers up to my chest, suddenly bashful. "Watch this."

I focused carefully, emptying my mind of everything but the task at hand. I ignored Evan watching me and after a moment, he followed the direction of my eyes. I concentrated and visualised what I would do. Slowly, the key turned in the lock with a little snap.

I turned to look at Evan and realised I'd been holding my breath. He grinned at me and I could tell he was at once impressed and amused that when I'd finally gotten my telekinesis under control to use at will, I used it to lock us into his bedroom. While I could admit that was funny, privately, it gave me hope that I'd learn to shimmer as I pleased, just like Étoile, or summon an object like Evan could.

Evan pulled me back under the covers, laughter rippling from him, and kissed me deeply, his arms wrapped around me as I sank into him.

I fell asleep in his arms, his body curled around mine as though this was the way it was meant to be. I wished with all my strength that nothing would change. If only wishing had the power to make it so.

CHAPTER NINE

Dawn crept through the slit in the curtains. I blinked through sleepy eyes and saw, not my wallpaper with the delicate pink roses and pale yellow stripes, but grey walls. Evan's arm was still around me and I didn't want to move, except to wriggle a little so that I was pressed into him, absorbing the warmth from his lissom body. After a few minutes of stillness, he hugged me and I climbed over him so that we were face to face. He kissed me gently and the little knot of anxiety that had formed in my stomach eased. *Sleeping with someone else was actually pretty nice. I could get used to it.*

"Hey," he murmured, his voice still thick with sleep.

"Hey yourself."

"You are a very welcome sight."

I couldn't help it, I smiled. *How nice to get a compliment first thing in the morning. From my teacher... whose bed I was in. Hmm. I would have to have a proper think about the ramifications of that when I was alone.*

Evan twisted his head to look at the clock on his nightstand. "There's a good half an hour before we have to get up. Do you need to conserve your energy or do you need a wake-up call?"

As far as lines went, at least it was a funny one. I pressed my lips to his and murmured that I would happily take a morning wake-up call which led to something rather eye-opening, indeed. When we finished, I lay back on the pillows, feeling a little dazed and breathless.

Evan traced a line down my torso. "We have a very busy day ahead of us; we should get up."

"Are you telling me to push off?" I wasn't offended; I just didn't want to get up.

Evan gripped my hips and pulled me so that I straddled him. My hair fell about my shoulders and I had the fleeting thought that I desperately hoped it didn't look like a knotty witch's mess. Ironic, really, seeing as my hair would still be witch's hair whether it was combed or uncombed.

"I think you're in the position of power here."

"Now isn't that a nice change?" I kissed him and resisted the urge to flatten myself against him before slipping off the bed and stooping to gather up the robe I'd discarded the night before. I pulled it around me and tied the ribbon securely. I turned back to Evan who was gazing at me, hands folded behind his head, like I was a full English breakfast. "Now, I have to get ready because I have a teacher who gets very grumpy when I'm late."

"Shall I have words with him?"

"You might mention that I fully appreciate his talents." I couldn't help but giggle at my cheesy line.

Evan swung his long legs out of bed and stood in front of me quite deliciously naked. *Oh boy, I was one lucky girl.* There wasn't an ounce of fat on his body and he was muscular in a way that said well-toned, but not crazy body builder. He was a stunning man and knew it, in a very modest sort of way. His whole torso rippled as he moved to pick up a dressing gown thrown over a chair and shrugged it on, but not before I noticed white lines crossing his back in a painful pattern.

"I have to make it down the hall without being seen," I grumbled, wondering if I should mention his scars. Getting back to my room would be no easy feat in a morning when students and teachers would be tumbling out of bed (*together?* A fleeting thought about Seren and David looking cosy crossed my mind... *maybe we weren't the only ones getting lucky last night)* and heading down to the morning room for breakfast.

"You don't necessarily have to walk," Evan suggested in all seriousness.

I shook my head knowing what he was suggesting. "I've only moved myself that far a couple of times before and there weren't any walls in between."

"Try it and see."

Truth be told, I was a little worried that I might shimmer and reappear in the middle of the wall or, even worse, with an arm and leg either side of one. *That would be so not fun to explain, not to mention the excruciating splinters.*

"You're more in control of yourself now, something's changed in you. Try and see."

I shut my eyes and exhaled. I visualised the roses, the big iron bed, even the cream lamp and little silver clock on my nightstand. I panned the room in my head and watched it slowly unfold. I visualised myself in the room and held myself still, the concentration setting a vein in my temple throbbing, as the air fizzled and crackled around me.

When I opened my eyes, I was in my room. I let out a triumphant squeal and punched the air. *My first successful shimmer!* I jumped up and down like an over-excited toddler and dashed to my door, where I stuck my head out. Evan was waiting at his door, the linen pants back on *(shame)* underneath his robe, concern etched on his face. I mouthed "Not. In. A. Wall!" and his face broke into the most glorious smile that made my heart ding with happiness.

Voices drifted to me from downstairs and I pulled my head inside just as a door on our floor creaked open. The clock's hands pointed to eight a.m. so breakfast must already be underway. I took a quick shower, brushed my teeth and pulled on denim shorts, cut to the knee, a white blouse and flat shoes. I drew my hair back into a ponytail, added little pearl studs to my ears and slipped my watch on my wrist, before scampering downstairs, the smell of bacon and eggs leading me like a moth to a flame.

The morning room was two thirds full. Seren and Étoile sat at one end of the table, their plates half eaten. David was reading the paper and munching toast. Meg stood at the stove, frying bacon and eggs. She put a friendly arm around me as I approached and gave me a little squeeze. Despite the warmth of the morning, she was still cold as ice. Perhaps she was ailing or something, I thought. Her body temp never seemed to get anywhere near warm.

Looking over at the table, I couldn't help thinking Meg was the grandmother, or favourite aunt, I never had. In a flash daydream, I could picture them all as sisters, brothers, cousins, people I never had in my life. My heart ached for the perfection of that moment.

"How would you like your eggs?" Meg asked me, letting me go so she could reach a plate from the cupboard.

"Let me get that." I was a little taller so it was fairer that I did the reaching. "And, over easy?" I hoped I got my order right – *who knew there were so many ways eggs could be cooked over here?* – and asked for my eggs runny, not that I would complain however they turned up. I was ready to eat Meg out of house and home.

"Coming right up. Did you have a good day yesterday, honey?"

"Yes, it was lovely."

"I am glad. It was a real nice day and so good to see all you young people having fun." Meg's voice was so quiet I almost missed her adding, "Without the weight of this strange world on your shoulders."

Meg shovelled eggs, bacon and sausages onto my plate and I picked up the funny little bread dumpling they called a biscuit from the basket next to the stove. It was still warm. Without hesitating, I leaned over and kissed Meg on the cheek and thanked her for the lovely breakfast. Meg was quite overcome and shooed me away but I saw her wipe her eye and knew that the impromptu affection had touched her, making me feel glad.

I sat next to Étoile and she bumped a knee against mine. "Ready for another day of busy, busy, don't stop?"

"I guess so." I forked a big slice of bacon into my mouth and chewed.

"If the big guy picks on you, you tell me and I'll zap him," said Seren, a wicked glint in her eye.

I smiled and it occurred to me to wonder just how

today's lessons would go; *would Evan still get stroppy with me if I couldn't move an object or shimmered myself flat on my ass? He knew I could do both now and at will if I put my mind to it.* Whether I could keep on doing stuff was a different matter altogether. Fortunately I didn't have to think about it for too long because Evan turned up and helped himself to a bowl of cereal before pouring a mug of coffee from the pot on the table. At least, he didn't have to think through the politics of where to sit, the only chair left was opposite me. He surveyed my plate and looked back at his healthy bowl with disappointment, before re-inspecting my laden plate.

"I'm hungry," I protested.

Evan raised his eyebrows and looked over to Meg. "That looks a helluva lot better than cereal this morning. Can I get some too, Meg?"

"Of course you can, my dear. You just wait right there now and I'll fix you a plate and bring it over."

"We've got a packed morning ahead," said Evan, to me. "We're going to test what you can do."

"I'm watching you," hissed Seren, only half joking as she waved her fingers at her eyes, then to his.

Evan looked at her, his eyes darkening a shade and I wondered if he was going to get mad at her but then he broke into a smile and rolled his eyes. Seren raised her eyebrows at me in surprise. I think she wondered where "serious Evan" was and I had no intention of telling her why he was in a cheerful mood, assuming that I was the reason. Meg slid a plate in front of him and he ate with enthusiasm whilst I snuck sly glances at him until Seren caught me. I shrugged my shoulders and pretended to be as curious as she.

Étoile and David busied themselves clearing away

the breakfast things and stacking the dishwasher. It never ceased to amuse me that with all the magic present in the house, they still needed a dishwasher. Evan twirled a pencil between his fingers, then stabbed at the notepad he produced from his pocket. "Okay, this morning we'll pair up to practice. Seren take Kitty, Étoile take Jared, David you take Christy and Clara too. Stella, you're with me. Warm up and consolidate what you've learned. Find somewhere quiet to study and we'll meet up in the living room later today and do a little show and tell. Now's the time to really show off your progress."

"Will you be having lunch together?" Meg inquired.

Evan shook his head. "If you'd be kind enough to leave out a cold lunch, people can come and go as they get hungry. There's no need for all of us to sit together today."

Chairs scraped against the floor and the household headed off two-by-two as they filtered through the house and into the garden. Then there were two.

"We'll go up to the balcony," said Evan, ticking off his list.

I frowned. I'd never been on the balcony though I caught glimpses of it from outside. It led off one of the upstairs rooms, though I wasn't sure which one and had never had cause to investigate.

"C'mon," Evan said as he scraped back his chair and led the way, a flick of his fingers summoning me to follow. I traipsed after him through the hallway and up the stairs. We walked down the hall past my room and to his. He opened the door and ushered me in, and just as I was wondering what was going on, he opened the floor to ceiling windows that had previously been covered by curtains and beckoned me outside. I followed.

The balcony was the same one I'd seen from below. On three sides it was framed by a half-height white trellis, over which trailed climbing flowers, which pretty much concealed it from view, at least, from below. The panoramic vista over the ocean was gorgeous. The balcony was set up like a little bistro with a seating area of two iron chairs along with a wooden bench that overlooked the other side.

"It's so pretty," I said, my eyes venturing over the edge. I spotted David and Étoile, with Jared, Christy and Clara sitting cross-legged in front of them, on the lawn below.

"I like it," said Evan simply as he ducked inside and came back out with a bag of tennis balls.

"No rackets?"

Evan snorted. "Not quite." He knelt on the tiles and spread the balls out on the floor in a ring before he stooped to go back inside. He returned with a couple of floor pillows and tossed one to me. "Take a seat."

I arranged myself on the pillow, facing the balls as I assumed I was meant to do. Evan sat opposite me and looked at me expectantly.

"What am I supposed to do?"

"Move them."

I poked one with a finger and it rolled out of formation.

"With your mind."

"I suspected as much." I concentrated but when one ball rolled across the balcony, I wasn't sure if it was me or a gust of wind.

"Try moving them up." Evan jabbed a finger towards the sky.

I shuffled on the pillow and refocused, visualising the ball, any ball, moving upwards.

Evan sighed. "Stella, you have to open your eyes."

I opened my eyes. None of the balls had moved. I groaned in annoyance.

"It may seem easier to move things with your eyes closed so that you can visualise objects, but when you are faced with... situations other than the classroom, you need your eyes open. When you're fighting, Stella, you need to see where you're going if you expect to manipulate things around you." Evan looked at the balls and slowly they began to rise, whipping around each other, then holding still again. Some began to rise while others rotated. It was like a little dance of tennis balls. One danced towards me until it was level with my nose then glided around my head before drifting back to the other balls. They rotated again and I wrenched my eyes from them to Evan. He was looking at me, not the balls, and his face did not seem at all strained in concentration.

The balls dropped to the floor and Evan swept them up into a neat circle, but this time he used his hands in the conventional way. "Your turn."

I concentrated with my eyes open and felt like I'd been sitting there for hours by the time I shrugged my shoulders. I hugged my knees and rested my chin on them as I stared at the balls some more. None of them moved, no matter how intensely I insisted they should.

"I almost think you're trying too much," said Evan, as he got to his feet and tossed his cushion behind me. I was wondering if he was cross when he sat behind me, spread his legs either side of me and pulled me into him. I relaxed against him, glad to feel the tension drain from my muscles and rested my head on his chest. "You are straining and it should be more natural, more of an organic action. The magic is part of you, not something you need to strive for. You just need to find it and channel it." He tickled me and I squirmed and giggled. "Nah, it isn't there." He wrapped his arms around me again and nuzzled at my neck. "Try again. Don't visualise the balls anymore, just feel what you want them to do."

I raised my head and studied the balls, thinking how nice it was to be sitting up here in the warm sun, completely alone and relaxed with the heat of Evan's body warming me. I thought vaguely about the air and the balls and how they were part of the ebb and flow of life. I thought about the climbing foliage, their green leaves and the budding pink flowers. Evan put his hands to my temples and I relaxed. Finally, the balls began to rise.

"Hold them," murmured Evan, his hands steady.

The balls held still. I thought about the balls moving higher and they did. Lower and they followed. I got cocky and had them move slowly in a circle.

Evan nuzzled at my neck. A ball dropped to the floor but I raised it back to the others and kept them still again mid-air. When Evan slipped his hand inside my top, the balls exploded upwards and shot in different directions. I heard a yelp from below as one of the balls hit someone and I had to stifle a laugh. "What are you doing?" I asked softly so that my voice would not be heard by my unfortunate target on the lawn below.

"You need to be able to continue to focus even when under attack."

"Will my attackers be nuzzling my neck and slipping their hands inside my top?"

Evan stopped and his hand rested on my stomach. "No," he sighed, his voice heavy. "When they come, it will be much, much worse."

"Shame," I muttered, not even wanting to fix on the certainty in his voice. "I could cope with a nuzzling attack."

"Apparently not. Try and gather up those balls. You don't know where they are but you need to retrieve them. I will continue to, um, distract you."

"Poor you," I huffed but I was amused more than anything and relaxed into his arms while I sent my mind out to retrieve the balls. When I concentrated, I realised that I could send slivery pulses from my mind to locate things I was looking for. I found and moved all but one ball back to rest at our feet.

"Pretty good," nodded Evan, whose hands were still inside my top, as the last ball whizzed over our heads to land in the middle of the little pile.

"How did you learn this stuff?" I asked, realising I knew very little about Evan.

"Trial and error mostly. Magic has always been part of me. I grew up with my mom and she had some power of her own. She died when I was a teenager, before I had really gotten to grips with what I could do."

"How did she die?"

"She was attacked one night. She couldn't defend herself. I was at school – I was on the track team and putting in some extra time – when I got home she was dead."

"I'm sorry." Evan didn't need to drive home the point about me being able to defend myself. I didn't want to end up dead too soon either. Nearly falling into the hands of the Brotherhood had given me a healthy respect for my life. I shivered. I did not need to be thinking about them.

Evan changed the subject quickly to bring us back to the lesson. "See if you can move just two balls around. I'm going to give you instructions and I want you to match them."

"When did you come here?" I asked, ignoring him briefly.

"The first time I was seventeen, after my mom died and I've come back a few times over the years. I come and go as I please. Concentrate. Pick up the balls."

I moved two into the air so they were parallel with my face. Evan kissed my neck and murmured instructions. Whilst he tried to distract me, I moved the balls left, right, up, down, circled them and moved them independently as he instructed. I could barely contain my glee that not only was I moving the balls at will, but I could see what they were doing too. It was far more interesting than shutting my eyes and visualising an object moving then opening my eyes to see that, yes, it had actually moved. This was way cooler even if the concentration was making my head throb a little.

"Okay, drop 'em."

"I beg your pardon?"

"The balls." Evan gave a little snort and I blushed. "Forget them for a while now. You did good. How far do you think you moved yourself this morning?"

Assuming he wasn't talking about our nocturnal

acrobatics, I calculated the distance between Evan's room and mine; it was a big house. "Twenty feet, maybe?"

"I guessed thirty. You said you've not shimmered that far before?"

"Ye-es," I said, struggling to think over my burgeoning headache. "Well, I've panicked and moved myself across the street, which was probably the same distance and I can get myself across a room, but through walls, that was a first." *Intentionally anyway*, I thought. "I thought I'd get stuck," I admitted, then added, "I've gone a lot further when Étoile held on to me. How far can she go?"

"Both she and Seren can go very far. When they were stronger, they could go even further."

"They've both said that but I don't know what they mean."

"They had a sister once. Three is a very potent number in magic and they were stronger," Evan replied at last.

"What happened to her sister?"

"That's a story for another time," said Evan, who seemed about as willing to be drawn as Seren and Étoile were. At least, I had a new little piece to their puzzle, even if I wasn't sure what it meant yet.

"That's what everyone else says," I huffed.

Evan looked at me and seemed to be puzzling something in his mind. "I'll tell you but only because it explains things about Étoile and Seren and they are your friends. Just the basics though. I don't know a huge amount and it's their story, not mine," he emphasised.

"Okay."

"Étoile is the oldest, then Seren and finally Astra.

They look so alike you would, and people do, mistake them for triplets. They are, indeed, very close in age. All three born in under three years. Their family is pure magic, barely of this world at times. Their mother more so and I think that made them stronger still but the sisters are better at integrating than most of their kind. They're like a super witch. Rare and powerful. Étoile and Seren have told you already that they can do similar things. That power is magnified when the three are together."

"Where is Astra?" I asked.

"I'm coming to that. Étoile used to work on Wall Street, did you know that?"

I shook my head. I was surprised but when I thought about it, it made sense that she was a financial whiz. She didn't seem to work but had a lot of money.

"She packed it in when Astra disappeared. Astra was the more flighty of the three. She was less concerned with the world, less concerned about protecting humans from us and not all that interested in concealing ourselves from them. She was getting reckless. She was starting to use magic openly and her sisters, as well as others, had to cover her mistakes. It got old very fast for them. Then one day, Astra left. Nobody was too bothered at first. She'd had an argument with her sisters and they thought she had just gone away in a huff. But she stayed away and they started getting concerned."

"How long has she been gone?"

"Two years."

"Can they find her?"

"They should be able to in theory; their bond is a strong one, but they can't and because of that, they're afraid for her. We've all put our feelers out but no one has seen or heard from Astra in these two years."

"What do they think happened?"

"They know she's alive because they would know if the bond had been severed. They think something has happened to her." Evan didn't have to spell out that he thought it was something terrible. "She's unstable as it is. It isn't good that no one can sense her anywhere. There's another theory."

"What's that?"

"She's gone stark raving mad," he said bluntly.

"I don't know what to say."

"Best to say nothing. Étoile and Seren are pretty sensitive about her, worried and also, I think, a little embarrassed. They'll find her and deal with her eventually." Evan shrugged his shoulders. "Or, she'll find them." Evan didn't sound too happy at the latter prospect.

"I hope they find her again." I knew what it was like to lose a family. I didn't envy them their pain.

Evan changed the topic swiftly, reminding me he was still here to teach. "So you shimmer further when you panic and when you're..." Evan struggled for the right word before settling on, "relaxed?"

"Or not wanting to get caught barely dressed. Definitely a first."

"Not wanting to get caught barely dressed?"

"Next to your room," I added to clarify, lest he get any funny ideas.

"Okay, so we need to work out a trigger for you. Something that you can control so you can actually move when you want to, not when you panic and need to." Evan thought for a moment. "What did you do when you wanted to leave this morning?"

It was only a couple of hours ago so it wasn't hard to remember. I had pictured my room very clearly. I felt the softness of the bed covers and the strong iron bed frame, imagined the light trickling through the curtains, the pink roses on the walls, and everything else as fully as I could until I had recreated the room in my head. I could feel the desire to be there reverberating through my bones.

"I made a picture in my head," I told him excitedly. I could feel my blood jump as the slightest traces of electricity coursed through me. "I could see exactly where I wanted to be and I moved. It's not like it was that far."

"Baby steps, honey." Evan ran his hands along my forearms and pulled me into the here and now.

"I don't know if I can do it again." I might have been saying one thing but my blood was telling me something else as little licks of power hit my pulse points.

"Try. Try now. Visualise my room." Evan stood up and took a few steps towards the doors before closing them.

I breathed deeply and closed my eyes to concentrate, allowing the little surges to well in my veins now that Evan wasn't touching me to ground me. I pictured the grey walls of his room and the big bed. I pictured the neat desk and the little stack of books. I breathed, once, twice exhaling and vanished.

The door was shut when I opened my eyes and seconds later, Evan was filling the door frame.

"It worked." I grinned.

"Do it again. Visualise the hallway."

I saw it clearly in my mind and poofed myself away in a burst of energy. Evan followed me through the door.

"So you need to visualise," Evan decided. "How much detail do you need?"

"A lot. I need to see a lot of the place I want to be." But when I reflected on it that didn't explain all the times I'd ended up in places I'd never even thought about.

Evan drew me back inside and for a moment, his eyes went from me to the bed; then he shook himself with a grunt and held my hand as he led me back outside. Truth be told, I was both elated that I could move myself again at will and disappointed that the bed wasn't figuring into the scenario. I sat opposite him and watched as he puzzled in thought, stroking my hands absently.

After a while, he said, "I don't think you'll always need as much detail but the visualisation can be your trigger for now. Right now when you're learning, you'll need to be certain of where you want to be. When you're more practiced at it, I think you'll just be able to get a general feeling of where you want to be. Maybe you'll even be able to get there just by seeing a picture or reading an address or even just thinking of a person to be able to find them."

"But what use is it? Other than I'll be able to get places quicker?" I paused. "So, maybe one day I can just think about being in Paris or Rome or LA and just magic myself there?" I'd always wanted to travel. *Now there was a chance I could be my own private jet. Cool!*

"Maybe, though it takes some strong magic to go those kinds of distances at will." He mulled it over. "Regardless, you will be able to get places quicker or get out of situations faster. People pay good money for fast, efficient service, especially in our world."

"Are you saying I have a future career as a supernatural Fed Ex?"

Evan laughed. "With your potential, you can pick and choose what you want to do."

"When Étoile came to me in London, she moved me just by holding me. I didn't do a thing. When I was thinking about how I could move before, I could feel it in my veins but when you touched me, I felt it fizzle out. Do you think I could move people too?"

"Maybe." He looked at me for a minute and, as if he could see what I was thinking, said. "You are not trying with me."

"Oh." I tried not to sound sullen.

"It's not exactly an exact science. You might move me, but not my clothes. Or forget my head."

"You're right." I sighed. "Can I try with something else?"

"Start small. Try the tennis ball." Evan picked one up and set it on the table between us. "It isn't like telekinesis this time. Think where you want it to be."

"Okay." I stared at it for a full five minutes but the damn thing never moved a millimetre.

"Relax a bit. You've used up some energy just moving yourself. Twice," Evan reminded me with obvious approval.

I stood up and walked over to the edge of the balcony, closing my eyes. I let the cool breeze wash over me, imagining it was cleansing my body of the energy I had spent. I knew I could do it. I just had to tap into the power, wherever my body held it, and use it to move that stupid tennis ball. I'd drop it on the lawn. I could visualise it now. I could see the yellow ball disappear from the balcony. I could see it drop at the foot of the tree.

"Stella," said Evan, his voice wary but pleased. "The ball has gone."

I swung round. I hadn't even been looking at it. It had gone, but it wasn't the only thing.

"Where's my table?" Evan asked, looking for all the world like he was trying not to burst out laughing. The corners of my mouth were twitching too.

"Oh... hell."

I looked over my shoulder and sure enough, the tennis ball, and the table, were under the tree just where I thought I would send it. Nearby, Étoile and David had interrupted their lesson to look in surprise from the new table and then up to the balcony. David gave me the thumbs up. Étoile cupped her hands to her mouth and called, "Perhaps some iced tea, too?"

Evan could barely constrain himself now, laughter escaping from his mouth.

"Jeez," I muttered, turning away from the gardens. "Now I've got a future as a cosmic waitress." And I rolled my eyes as Evan guffawed. Turning back to concentrate on the two objects on the lawn, this time, I didn't surprise myself when I brought both back to where they should be.

"Just be grateful it wasn't your pants," I muttered.

"Stella, you've cracked it," Evan said at last, rubbing his ribs as I watched him with my arms folded. "I'm not sure I'm ready for you to move me but I am awed at how fast you picked that up." He earnestly added, "Perhaps the key is just having faith in yourself."

"Can we take a break?" I kneaded my temples where the throbbing vein told me I was going to get a major headache if I didn't relax for a while. I closed my eyes for a second to take the throb away.

"Sure." Evan checked his watch. "It's after midday anyway. We need to eat."

"Already?"

I followed him into his room where I asked him. "You're not going to bind my powers are you? Not now that I've finally cracked them."

Evan looked shocked. "No, of course not. Whatever gave you that idea?"

"Marc told me that Seren had bound Jared."

"Ye-es," agreed Evan, "but only so that he'd stop breaking all the chairs and no more of the windows. It's not exactly convenient to get a glazier out here and there would be questions. Besides, Marc probably told you that Jared knows and was happy to ... actually. He asked. Why would you think I would want to bind yours?"

"So I don't accidentally zap you somewhere. Or your clothes." I ran my eyes over him. *Actually, that wasn't a bad idea.* I smiled to myself.

"Stella." Evan placed both hands on the tops of my arms and looked at me square in the eye. "I would never bind your powers and certainly not without your permission. I trust that you will be careful and you won't toss one of us out a window or into the ocean. And, I truly mean this, if you want to practice removing my clothes I am quite happy for you to do so in here. Alone. And you can use your hands." Evan winked and pulled me closer as I tipped my chin up, just about standing on my tiptoes so he could kiss me and let me melt into him. With the connection I felt between us, I never wanted this day to end.

We ate outside, a few of us on the grass in the shade of the tree while the sun was at its highest. I sat with Seren and Étoile and wished that I, too, had a sister. My surrogate sister, Kitty, as she appointed herself, was apparently running errands in town with Jared.

Evan sat with David, their heads bent together. They sounded like they were reminiscing about times long gone and I wondered if they had known each other prior to coming here. I wondered where they had been, and what they had done, in their other lives away from the safe house. The cut that marred David's face was less prominent now, more of a dark pink than an angry welt. I noticed his fingers sometimes trailed the length of it and I wondered what scars he carried inside. I also wondered if Seren was taking his mind off them. I thought back to the scars on Evan's back; *where had they come from?* I liked these people but there was so little that I knew about them.

"Evan seems to be a little less unhappy," observed Étoile softly as she chewed a sandwich.

"I hadn't realised he was unhappy," I replied. I picked up an apple from the basket Meg left for us and rubbed it against my jeans. Meg never seemed to join us outside and I wondered what she busied herself with during the day.

"Oh, I didn't mean to imply he was miserable." Étoile was picking her words carefully. "I just don't think he was overly enthusiastic about being here, but he seems quite cheerful now."

"He's grateful I didn't zap him into the ocean by accident in today's lesson," I deflected.

Seren chuckled. "We're all grateful for that."

"There's time yet." I laughed and Evan caught my eye and smiled.

"I rather thought it was because he had found something to interest him." Étoile was watching us from under her lashes. She had that air of amusement about her as if she were already fully aware. If I wasn't sure then, I was a moment later when she rested her fingers on Seren's wrist and Seren smiled and said, "Ahh."

So the cat was out of the bag.

"It wouldn't have taken her long to figure it out." Étoile seemed to be apologising for whatever had passed between them.

"I don't suppose I can ask what you saw?" *Was it much of a future?* I wanted to ask. *Or a future at all?*

"Snippets, but you'll find out soon enough. I wouldn't want to spoil the surprise."

~

I spent the rest of the day by myself, the headache still just tickling at my temples without quite hitting me. My eyes ached so I couldn't read or listen to music, and the idea of walking on the beach, each step jarring my body, put me off.

I stayed in Evan's room again that night. It was a humid night and after we'd made love – I was more than getting the hang of that – we kicked back the covers to lie there, his arm around me, my head on his shoulder with my hair fanned down my back. Our legs were entwined and our skin was sticky with exertion and heat. The last of the sunlight cast patterns on the floor and a storm cloud was already rolling in over the sea. I could hear raindrops pattering on the roof and hitting the table on the balcony. I kissed Evan's neck. After I complained about my threatening headache, he pressed his hands against my temples and the pain was gone in an instant. I had never felt more content as we dozed together.

The first clap of thunder woke me with a jolt and Evan tightened his arm around me, bringing the other over and caressing my side in smooth strokes as I snuggled into his embrace.

"I'm not frightened," I confessed, lest he think I was silly. "It was just loud and woke me. Didn't it wake you too?"

Evan shook his head gently. "I wasn't sleeping."

"Not tired?"

"A little, but frankly, you're very distracting. Even more so naked."

"Should I go?" I hated to sound hurt.

"Hell no." Evan twisted so that he had manoeuvred under me and I sat astride him, my thighs against his. His hands held my waist, his fingers almost touching in the middle of my stomach and back and once again, I marvelled at how big he was.

"How old are you?" I asked, curious, looking down at him.

"Older than you."

"Where are you from?"

"Nevada. Not Vegas, thank goodness."

"Do you have any other family?"

"I have a dad and a brother. I don't see either of them."

"Why's that?"

"My dad and my brother aren't the most stable and after my mom passed, I didn't need to be part of that anymore."

"I'm sorry."

"Don't be. I've accepted it." He ran his hands over my hair and traced the line of my spine, sending pleasurable shivers through me.

"Seems a good way of looking at it." I've never been entirely sure if I'd come to terms with losing my parents. I didn't even know if they had family. That would be something to investigate.

"Where do you normally live?"

"I have a house in Texas but I travel a lot. It's actually rare for me to be asked to take on work like this but I wanted a change and I was needed, so I felt duty-bound to oblige."

"You don't normally teach?"

"No. This is a very rare occurrence. Robert Bartholomew actually asked me and he's helped me out before so I owed him a favour. He made it clear I could have refused but he was insistent that he needed the help and I felt obliged."

I shuddered involuntarily at the sound of Robert's name.

"Cold?" Evan asked but I shook my head. He ran his ridiculously warm hands the length of my back and under my arms to caress my breasts. My body tingled from the inside out, though it didn't do anything to warm the fear in me. I tried to gulp it down.

"What is it that you do?"

He paused for a moment, as though thinking about what he should say. Finally, "I'm a tracker."

"Is that even a career option?"

"Not in regular schools."

"How come you don't have a girlfriend?" *Wow, I was nosy tonight.*

"I don't have a whole lot of time. Like I said, I travel a lot and I can never guarantee where I will be or how long the job will take. If I come home, I can be out again the next day or not for weeks. Women don't want to hang around waiting for a guy they won't see regularly."

That didn't sound promising. "Ever been in love?"

"Yes. It was a long time ago. She wasn't like us, but she knew about our way of life and understood. For a while, anyway."

"Do you date?"

"I am male," Evan pointed out, rather unnecessarily, seeing as a very male part of him was pressing quite heavily against me. He smirked. "So, yes, I date from time to time. I'm thinking I would quite like to not date for a while."

I frowned at him. *If this was going to be a brush off it was phenomenally bad timing.*

"I want to be with you, Stella, if you want to see where this leads. I can't offer any guarantees but I can offer me."

"Tempting," I said, a smile springing to my face. "Even if I don't see you for days, weeks or months?"

"I'll have to work on that. I am staying put while I'm wanted here."

"You're wanted rather a lot right now." And I could understand from the pressure digging into my leg that I wasn't the only one wanting and hoping right now. I moved to accommodate him and exhaled a deep long breath as he slipped inside me and slid his hands to my hips to guide me. I held onto his shoulders as he ground against me, until he pulled me up so that he could kiss me and hold me before rolling me onto my back and making me cry out with the ecstasy of it all. Later, we clung to each other, our skin sticking together with a soft sheen of perspiration.

"I have to shower. It's too hot tonight," Evan murmured after a while, extricating himself. He flashed me a broad smile. "You can come too."

Lightning flashed through the room as we slipped from the bed and padded to the bathroom. It was the same as mine except for a long, ladder towel rail and a cluster of men's toiletries on the shelf above the tub rim. Shaving gel and a razor stood next to the taps by a toothbrush and paste. Evan flipped the lever and the water whooshed out. He felt it for a moment with his hands before signalling that it was warm and pulling me under the jets. We stood under the water barely millimetres apart as he lathered soap in his hands and washed me, handing me shampoo from his own bottle (*I was grateful it seemed to be some unisex fruity scent)* and massaging it into my hair himself. When I was clean, I returned the favour, keeping my excitement in check as I savoured stroking his long limbs. *So freaking yummy.*

Bursting with cleanliness, Evan stepped out first, wrapping a towel around his waist as he held a towel for me so I could wrap myself in its toasty warmth.

Back in the bedroom, Evan drew the curtains against the inky blue sky and changed the sheets so that we could lie on fresh cotton. It was so oddly tropical (*Kitty's doing*, I wondered) that my hair was almost dry before I joined him in the bed again, sitting up so I could run my fingers through my hair to stop it getting all knotty. Evan patted his own short dark crop. "I'd offer you a comb but I don't have much need for one."

"No matter." I braided my hair so that it wouldn't tangle while I slept and snuggled against him, asleep again in minutes.

I was the first to wake the next morning so I slipped from Evan's bed as gently as I could. Our commingled bodies separated while asleep and he lay sprawled on his stomach, one hand under his head the other flung out towards me. I picked up my clothes and dressed quietly. I couldn't help my eyes flickering to the scars; there were a dozen or so, old and faded with time. As I was reaching for my socks, Evan's hand stretched out for me and drew me towards him.

"Running out on me already?" he asked, smiling sleepily at me as I wriggled in his strong arms.

I gave up and knelt beside the bed to kiss him. "Not in the slightest. I want to get changed before breakfast, before anyone else wakes up."

"Fair enough." He kissed me again, long and lingering and I thought twice about staying before I pulled away. I couldn't help lean in for one last kiss before I flipped the lock and sneaked out of his room. No one else was on the landing but I trod as quietly as I could until I got to my room, opening the door only as much as I had to and pressing it shut quietly.

I should have just been able to pull off my clothes but when I stepped into my room, shock rooted me to the floor.

The mattress was half-tipped off my bed; the pillows and covers scattered across the floor. The bathroom and closet doors hung open. Some of my clothes were on the floor and others only just on their hangers. The nightstand drawers hung open and the books had been swept onto the floor. My dresser had been rifled through. The drawers were only half closed; my t-shirts mussed up and the blue box with my parents' paperwork pulled out. Someone had searched through it and discarded it. Everything was in disarray. Tipped over, rifled, searched.

I couldn't help it. The scream shot from my throat before I even considered what a bad idea that was.

Seconds later, my door flew open. Étoile and Kitty reached me at the same time and were looking aghast at the mess and then to me.

"What's going on?" asked David, appearing behind them, rubbing his eyes and I was sorry that I had woken them all. Evan shoved past him and came to stand next to Kitty. He had paused to throw on jeans but otherwise his chest and feet were bare. If I hadn't been so frightened I'd have appreciated the picture a bit more. The sudden noise brought Seren sleepily to the door too and I heard feet bound up the stairs. *Oh, great. Marc.*

"Someone has been in my room," I said, somewhat obviously, in dismay, to my pyjama-clad crowd.

"Were they here?" asked Evan, his voice thunderous.

"No. No, they left before I found this."

"Where were you then?" asked Marc. He had pushed past David too and was standing in the door frame. Behind him, I could see David bobbing his head to try and see past. "If you weren't here when they did this?"

"I was. I was, uh..." I couldn't think past feeling so affronted that this was the only thing Marc could think to ask. *Shit, where could I say I had been?*

"She was with me." Kitty said, simply. "We were talking late and Stella fell asleep on the sofa in my room. I didn't have the heart to move her. We just woke up."

I smiled gratefully at her and she returned it with ease, but I noticed that she quickly cast a glance at Evan who was surveying the scene. No one questioned my alibi, thankfully.

"Did anyone hear anything?" Evan asked, looking round. Christy and Clara had stumbled into the hallway and hovered next to David, who was inching his way forwards. Like everyone else, they shook their heads.

"It was thundering for most of the night," said David, stifling a yawn. "You could have moved furniture and I wouldn't have noticed."

Étoile wrapped an arm around me. She was wearing the most elegant peach coloured pyjamas with her initials monogrammed on the pocket, though she had foregone her usual pristine makeup. "Is anything gone?" she asked.

"I don't think so." I didn't have much so it only took a minute or two to establish that nothing I'd immediately notice was gone. I wasn't sure whether to be thankful again for having so little. At least I could see everything I had, well, seeing as it was strewn across the floor. I couldn't imagine anything of mine that anyone could possibly want.

"Everyone out," said Evan, clapping his hands together to gain attention, and in full alpha male mode. "We'll get things straightened up, then try and figure out what's going on."

"If I'm not wanted, I'm heading back to bed," muttered David as he inched from the room. Evan was already shoving the mattress back into position and Kitty was helping him toss pillows back on the bed.

"Us too," said Christy as she and her sister both goggled at Evan's bare chest with unabashed admiration. Seren all but manhandled them from the room.

"I'll stay and look after Stella," said Marc stepping towards me. Kitty stood in his way. "I think we should make her a tea. Tea, right, Stella? Something warm for the nerves?"

"Yes, thanks, I'd appreciate that," I agreed, sensing that Kitty thought Marc should be out of the room. He looked thunderously at me but didn't object to Kitty giving him a gentle shove that left Étoile, Evan and I facing each other.

"Well," said Étoile. She looked from Evan to me with humour. "Well, hmmm."

"Do you see anything?" I asked.

"Not of the past, I'm sorry Stella, I don't know who would do this but I'm glad nothing seems to be missing." She gave me a gentle squeeze and whispered very delicately in my ear. "He's a good man. Always remember that. No matter what happens." She was gone before I could ask her to explain.

Evan was regarding me. He nodded at Étoile's fleeting back. "What did she say?"

"Oh, nothing," I waved it off. The door was still open as Evan helped me straighten up the room, pushing in drawers as I rehung my clothes in the closet. I didn't quite have the heart to admire his torso as he bent and stretched; the way I felt, it would have been a waste of a good ogle.

"Listen, will you stay with me a moment while I get dressed?" I knew I'd jump at the slightest sound and be more comfortable if he stuck around.

Evan grinned. "Absolutely." From across the room he closed the door with a sweep of his hand.

"I'm not giving you a thrill. I just want to change into something clean." I'd already pulled fresh jeans and a checkered shirt from the closet. I opened the just closed dresser drawer so I could pull out new underwear. *It felt kinda gross having to wear underwear that someone had searched through in the night but I didn't have a choice.* I changed quickly and when I fastened my last shirt button, Evan pulled me close, resting his chin on the top of my head. I relaxed against him, my muscles feeling like jelly with worry.

"I'm not leaving you. Try not to worry about this. We'll work it out."

"I know. I just don't get what whoever it was could have been looking for."

"Go downstairs. Meg will be making breakfast. Have that tea Kitty is getting you and try not to think about it. I'll be down in five. I promise."

"I don't want to be on my own." I felt like whimpering. *Pull yourself together,* I told myself. *You've survived all kinds of crap, you can survive a burglary.* But the other part of my mind whispered a warning.

"You're not. Go right downstairs. Everyone is awake now and you're safe." Evan kissed my hair and I was glad he couldn't see my lip tremble.

I wanted to tell Evan how glad I was that I spent the past night with him, instead of being here where maybe something awful could have happened. At once, I felt guilty. It wasn't like Evan was my guard when there was so much more, I hoped, between us; but instead I just nodded, grabbed my sweater, and followed him from the room. Downstairs, I could hear the sounds of breakfast being prepared in the kitchen. Meg was singing a show tune I recognised. It had been a big hit back when films were first in glorious Technicolor.

Evan left my room right behind me and, after a gentle push towards the stairs, he walked the few long strides back to his room. For the first time since I had been at the house, I turned back and locked the door before I went downstairs.

CHAPTER TEN

Breakfast was quiet with everyone critically appraising their cutlery or in a deep fug, rather than the usual morning chatter that mixed with the sounds of the coffee perking or the sizzle of Meg's pans on the stove. I sat in the centre of it all, feeling strangely uncomforted despite being surrounded by my brethren, my sisters and brothers in arms. Wands, even. I stifled a slightly hysterical snigger. Under the table, I felt Evan's hand press against my leg and I slipped my hand over his as David walked into the room. He rubbed his eyes and yawned widely before patting me on the head.

Meg hovered around the table like a confused butterfly, every once in a while exclaiming "in my own house" or "well, I never" and sighing heavily. She baked muffins in several flavours but there wasn't the usual vulture-like appetites that normally welcomed her sweet surprises; we picked at them morosely instead. Even the taste of warm chocolate chips melting on my tongue couldn't cheer me up and that was definitely one of my go-to happy places. I almost felt guilty for waking everyone up until I gave myself a little internal kick and a reminder that I hadn't asked to have my room rifled. *And just who the hell had gotten into the house?* It wasn't just a case of jimmying a window or a lock. Wards protected the house too. Judging by their faces, I could only imagine everyone else must have been thinking the same thing.

I stayed distracted all morning; my shimmering wouldn't come under control and my one and only bout of telekinesis brought every single book from the library shelves crashing in a heap on the floor. Eventually, Evan, with a sweep of his hand, restored the library to its perfection again in a few seconds. He told me to take a walk in the garden and that we would try again in the afternoon.

I didn't have the heart to be disappointed in my failure as I went outside. I was just glad to have a free moment to think. In the back of my mind, I was calculating my few possessions and where they had been in my room before it was ransacked. *My clothes were in the closet and the dresser, my little bits of jewellery on the top.* A few items of makeup and toiletries were in the bathroom and they couldn't possibly have been of significance so I discounted them immediately.

The only things that I had that could possibly have been of interest were the contents of the blue box with the papers and deed my parents left me. My new driver's license and bank card sat in the same drawer. But I checked the box and nothing seemed to be missing, not that I could remember an exact inventory.

No, whoever had gone into my room uninvited

had to have been looking for something else, something small that I might hide, but what? *What could have been hidden under a mattress or in a loose floorboard or behind a chair? Think,* I urged myself, *think!* It did no good; I just didn't have anything to hide. Whatever the burglars had thought I might have of interest didn't exist and I couldn't put a finger on what they might have wanted. The only thing I could conclude was that they thought I had something that I hadn't. *Or maybe they weren't looking for anything at all.* A new thought stream pinged into my head. *Maybe they just wanted to frighten me now as I'd begun to feel safe.*

Minutes later, another thought occurred to me. Perhaps they simply wanted me to know that they knew I hadn't slept in my room that night. That worried me more than the idea that someone had been there to steal.

Earlier, it had flickered through my head that if I had been there, perhaps I would have been dead by now,. *But if the intention had been to kill me, there would have been no need to muss up my room. They would have seen my smooth bed was unoccupied and could have closed the door and gone without my being any the wiser.*

So if the break-in wasn't to harm me, it left just three possibilities: They must have been searching for something they thought I had; or, they just wanted to let me know they had been there when I wasn't; or, finally, they just wanted to frighten me. The first was perplexing, the second and third were just creepy.

"I don't know what to think," I muttered, with only the flowers to hear me.

I hadn't really taken notice of where I was walking so when I ended up near the orchard that Meg was so proud of, I was a little surprised at my absentmindedness. All the same, I dropped onto the bench that overlooked the fruit trees so I could sit and ponder my unpalatable thoughts. The breeze was barely there but I could just smell the faintest hint of salty sea air. It seemed strange to find an orchard so close to the sea; *Kitty's weather magic must have a lot to do with the success of the fruit*, I decided.

Half an hour later, "You look lost in thought." Evan thudded onto the bench beside me and slipped his arm around my shoulders to pull me close. I'd been so lost in thought I hadn't even noticed his footsteps – but then, maybe he'd used magic to locate me. I rested my head against his chest and listened to his heart beating.

"I was trying to decide what ransacking my room would achieve."

"What did you come up with?" He was curious but I knew he was thinking about it too.

"Three theories." I repeated the two obvious ones to Evan and he nodded thoughtfully.

"Both sound possible. What's the third?"

"Someone wanted to make sure that I knew that they knew that I wasn't in my room that night. All night." I emphasised.

"You think someone knows about us?"

I shrugged. "Maybe."

"I'm not sure anyone would be that upset," Evan replied. "Except Marc. He hasn't decided whether he has a thing for you or not."

"I think not." His words on the beach had been pretty clear and he hadn't spoken to me much since he'd gotten back from New York. He hadn't been at breakfast this morning either. It occurred to me that I barely even spared a thought for him either; especially not since the night I'd gone to Evan and been welcomed so pleasurably.

"I wouldn't be so sure." Evan sounded cautious and when I looked up, I followed his line of sight and saw Marc striding towards us. Evan slipped his arm away and stood up.

"What do you..." but before he could finish, and before I could yelp, Marc had swung his arm back and brought his fist crashing into Evan's jaw. Evan staggered backwards, knocking into me as I jumped up behind him. When he steadied himself, and made sure I was still upright, he gingerly felt his split chin with his fingers. As he pulled them away, there was a trickle of blood on both his chin and fingertips. He looked at the blood curiously.

"What the hell, Marc!" I yelled, jumping forward. The energy surging in me suggested I knock him flat on his ass, or over the cliff edge.

"You fucking scumbag," snarled Marc, taking another swing, only to be glanced away like a fly as Evan casually raised his forearm to block the punch. Marc stood there, his fists curling and uncurling. "You couldn't keep your hands off her for a minute?"

"Hold on, kid." Evan tore his gaze away from the blood drops and huffed. If I didn't know better, I would have thought he was amused.

"Hold on, kid?" Marc mimicked with a sneer. "How long has this been going on?" He waved a hand towards me.

"Long enough that I don't have to answer to you," Evan deflected, before taunting, "Longer if you take a peek inside Étoile's head."

I looked up at him curiously and he gave me a tight smile. *So Étoile had seen how things would turn out before even I had known; maybe even from the day I had met him ... or before. But how had Evan known that? And when?*

"Marc, whatever has been going on between Evan and me has nothing to do with you." I stepped between them as if my body would be a barricade, not that it would matter if Evan decided to retaliate. He wouldn't need to throw a physical punch because I was sure a magical one would pack a whole lot more impact. Marc would have no chance against either. All the same, I was adamant. "Absolutely nothing."

"What about us?"

"There never was an "us". You told me that yourself. We're friends. Nothing more. We both know that."

"There sure as hell won't be now." Marc backed off a step but he was still shaking with adrenaline and his face was etched with anger and, I thought with a start, *disgust.*

"You already made the decision," I reminded him as gently as I could. I didn't play games; I didn't read minds. Marc had already told me very succinctly that any romantic ideas I might have had towards him were misplaced. And I found out very quickly that he was right. Yes, I had kissed him and I felt close to him but that was because I'd been uprooted to a place where I knew nobody. In my loneliness, it would have been easy for me to feel that there was more affection than friendship, until I thought about it properly. He could never make me feel the way I felt when I looked at Evan, not to mention when I was with him. Apparently Marc hadn't been quite so decided about his own feelings. "And I'm with Evan because I want to be with him. I'm happy."

"He's not like us," Marc hissed, his eyes flashing

from Evan to rest on me. "You shouldn't be with his sort."

"I don't know what you mean." I shook my head and followed that up with a shrug of my shoulders.

"He's not one of us. His kind is nothing but trouble. You should stay away from him."

"Marc, back off," Evan hissed his warning.

Marc dragged his eyes over Evan and he stared at him, his chin jutting upwards defiantly. He avoided looking at me as he faced Evan, scorn etched across his face. "You should know better. A witch and your kind? Since when has that ever worked?"

"I know what I'm doing," I said softly. I was still standing between them and I could feel Evan's hands lightly squeezing my shoulders. The merest touch from him was reassuring and kept my magic simmering at a level that it wouldn't erupt without my permission.

"I doubt that very much," Marc sneered as he stepped backwards before veering away from us to stomp towards the house without a second glance.

I pulled a tissue from my pocket and folded it in quarters as I turned to reach up and apply it to Evan's bleeding chin.

"He packs one hell of a punch," said Evan, his fingers closing over mine. "Thankfully, I heal fast."

"You should probably sit down for a minute all the same. That was a nasty gash. If you faint and land on me, I'm done for!"

"Might be quite fun though." Evan waggled his eyebrows at me.

"To be crushed by over six feet of muscle? Uh-uh." I shook my head.

Evan obediently sat back down. He took the

paper tissue from his chin and I watched in awe as the skin knitted itself back together, leaving nothing more than a thin line that paled and went away.

"Self-healing runs in the family," he said. "It comes in handy. You would not believe how accident prone I was when I was younger."

"You don't seem like the accident prone type." I looked at him sceptically, wondering *if that was how fast a minor cut healed, what caused those long scars that still remained?*

"I'm not anymore."

"What do you think all that was about?" Evan pulled me to him and rested his head against my stomach for a moment while I stood, gently stroking the top of his head.

"He might be pissed that you're with me, but I think there's something that runs deeper. He's angry about more than just you and me."

"You think?"

Evan nodded. "I also think he wants to protect you and can't, though I don't know why. He sees me as a threat or an obstacle. He would probably be a good friend to you though, if he could stop behaving like a jealous teenage boy." He thought for a moment. "So, you are happy with me." It was more a statement than a question.

"Very much so," I answered as I kissed him lightly on the lips, lingering until he pulled me into his lap and kissed me deeply. Losing ourselves in each other, neither one giving a damn who saw us now.

It was Evan who pulled away first. "We should get back to work before I become very distracted," he murmured, trailing kisses along my neck, his warm hands on my back just under my top. "I could feel you control your magic. Well done."

A thought popped into my head, one that overpowered the urges that were drawing my body to Evan's. I disentangled myself.

"Evan, I have to ask you something." Evan nodded, though not looking entirely thrilled at the interruption. "Last night you said Robert Bartholomew had personally asked you to come here."

"That's right."

"Why would he ask you to come here if you're not a regular teacher? You are only teaching me, but why not let David? Or Étoile?"

Evan pushed his chin out in thought and seemed almost embarrassed when he admitted, "I never thought to ask. He was calling in a favour."

"But why you? Of all people?"

"Complaining?"

"Of course not! But, Evan, there must be a whole bunch of people who can teach magic, why ask you to help me?"

"I think he wanted someone specifically to teach you. He wasn't pushy about it, but he made it clear that he wanted me to come."

"Yes, but why you? What made it so important that he had to come to you to ask you to teach me?"

Evan thought about this for a moment. "He must have wanted the skills I had, or known that they would be compatible with yours. He must have been aware of what you could do already or, at least, what you had the potential to do."

"Does that make any sense to you?" I still couldn't work out why Robert would call in a favour from Evan. *Sure, he had powerful magic. I could sense it in people, in my kind, now that I knew what to look for, but what made him so superior to the other witches?*

"Sort of. If you want someone to learn a specific lesson, you go to the person who can offer it."

"The teleporting and the telekinesis, a lot of our kind could help me with, right? What things would he want me to learn from you?"

"Those traits aren't widespread," he said to my surprise. "And they usually only run in certain family lines; but it's not just witches who have those talents."

"But you have the same traits. What else could Robert want from you in particular?" I was sure I was on to something; all those veiled comments that Evan wasn't the same as us. *What else could he be*, I puzzled: *warlock, wizard or sorcerer?*

"Maybe he wanted you to learn how to track people, things," Evan mused but he didn't seem entirely convinced. "Maybe he thought with your ability to move, to teleport, you might make a good tracker. They actually would be excellent traits for a tracker to have."

"What do you track?" He said that was what he was, but he never explained what it meant.

"People mostly."

"Like a bounty hunter?"

"Close, but not exactly within the law. I track people, people who've double-crossed or murdered or kidnapped. Not just people though. Other beings too. I find things that have been stolen or gone missing. Sometimes I escort people places."

"Like a bodyguard?"

"Sort of."

"Where to?"

"To justice, often," Evan said simply, which

wasn't quite the question I'd asked.

"Why would Robert want me to learn that?"

"Maybe to help you find work later, when things are quieter. You might not want to return to normal life, doing whatever it was that you did before you came here."

Evan might have been right about that but I still felt uneasy. "It just doesn't feel right."

We were silent for a while, my head resting against him as my mind raced.

"There is another possibility, of course." Evan mulled the idea and seemed reluctant to voice it as if it were ridiculous. "Maybe Robert just wanted me to protect you. I don't lose people and I can track them down, especially when I have a connection to them. I'm strong. Not many people would try attacking me. No harm would come to you with me here."

"Why would Robert go to so much trouble?"

"Why not? He was a friend of your parents, right?" I shrugged. I didn't know. I remembered that Steven, Robert's second in command said he was a friend but I didn't recall whether Robert himself was. Evan continued regardless. "He must have felt pretty bad that they disappeared and he couldn't find them. Then they found you just as the Brotherhood were torching whomever of your kind they could catch."

"Could be. Though I would never have had Robert down as my biggest fan."

"He's one of life's good guys, Stella." Evan's voice was warm and sincere, but it still surprised me. Apparently, a lot was catching me unawares today. "I've known Robert for a very long time and he is one of the most stand-up guys I've ever met."

It seemed strange to hear the man I cherished

speak so well of the man I inexplicably feared. From the moment I met Robert, I hadn't been able to shake off the feeling that something was not right. Either Evan had been duped for years or I had misplaced my instincts. I wasn't sure which was worse.

"Have you spoken about this to anyone else?"

I shook my head. "No, of course not."

"Let's keep it to ourselves for a while. I'll ask Étoile what she thinks later, if that's okay?"

I nodded.

Evan shuffled me off his lap onto my feet and, with a small groan of disappointment, stood too. We walked back to the house, passing no one and not in any hurry and then entering through the kitchen door. If we were sullen and thoughtful, then it was no surprise to find how subdued our housemates were. I wondered briefly if we could be considered a coven. When I asked Evan, he laughed.

"Not exactly hubble, bubble, toil and trouble, is it?"

I smiled. "Far from it. I clearly have to re-evaluate all my fairy stories."

"Don't just stop with the witches."

Which reminded me, *what exactly did Marc mean when he announced the differentiation between us?* A whisper on the corner of my mind reminded me that it wasn't the first time I'd heard it implied that Evan was something "other"." I'd assumed from the moment I met him that he was a witch too, or a warlock – *isn't that what they call boy witches?* – but when I thought about it closely, the magic I sensed from him was a different feeling than what I got when I was near Kitty or Étoile. Kitty hadn't been overly perturbed when I mentioned what Marc said to me once before.

It dawned on me that despite whatever everybody else saw and understood, I just wasn't getting it.

I wished I had had time to ask him but at that moment, we came to a dead stop in the living room.

Robert Bartholomew stood in the centre of the room. Seren sat to one side of him, ramrod straight with her hands in her lap. Her face was unreadable.

"We don't have much time." He dispensed with any greetings which was far from the genteel and courteous Robert I first met. He looked at Evan but nodded in my direction. "We have to get Stella out of here."

"Why?" I asked, aware that Evan was standing silently beside me.

"We've been infiltrated. It's not safe here."

"What makes you think Stella isn't safe here?" Evan bristled beside me, even though he was fully aware of my fears about someone intent on frightening me. Robert seemed to be implying that I would have to leave and Evan didn't seem one bit thrilled about only now being notified.

"I'm not going anywhere," I answered, even though my opinion hadn't been sought. *What was new here?* "I've already been forced to run from my home and then to here. When will I stop running, if not now?"

"She's got a point, Robert."

"Seren tells me your room was rifled this morning?" Robert solicited, *looking at me finally,* I thought sadly.

"Last night I think. But it wasn't someone from the outside." *I'd had the time to process it now. I was certain.* "It was someone here. No one else could have gotten in or out without being noticed. It had to have been someone here."

"Then things are worse than I thought." Robert paced the floor for a moment before turning to me when I asked,

"Do you know what were they looking for?"

"I don't know, Stella. Perhaps nothing. Do you know who it was?" He was looking at me strangely. I thought he had come to the same conclusion as I, that the whole aim was to frighten, not to steal. Perhaps it was to set me up to flee. "Did you sense a trace?"

"No." I wasn't sure what he meant but I hadn't felt anything but anger and then fear, and, come to think of it, nothing magical at all. "It could have been anyone here."

"Except me." Evan's voice was soft, so soft that only I could hear. I gave him a nod and Robert looked at him sharply.

"It wasn't me," said Seren. "And I will vouch for David too. He was with me all night."

"That leaves Étoile, Jared, Kitty, Christy and Clara," mused Robert. He added, "Marc too" as an afterthought, then signalled for us to sit, which we did. He perched on the sofa in front of us as he asked me, "What do you imagine they wanted?"

"Either to find something they thought I had or to frighten me."

"Which is most likely?" Robert pressed.

"To frighten me," I said. "I have nothing much of value and I don't think anything was taken." I thought again, *now I was certain which path I wanted to pursue*. "If someone wanted me to run again, they would want me frightened. They turned over my room to make me feel unsafe, to make me want to leave."

"Or," said Seren. "They wanted to make the council move you somewhere safer. Or, at least, somewhere other than here, maybe where you weren't among so many people. What do you think, Robert?"

"I think," he said, his face etched with concern, "I think that would ensure my coming to make sure you were all right." His fingers brushed his chin while he thought it over.

"If so," Evan chimed in, "Wouldn't that make this a trap?"

"Who would want to trap me?" Robert was perplexed but not without concern over his sudden predicament.

"Someone who has an interest in both of us. We both pose a threat to someone, though who, I couldn't say." I surprised myself by speaking up. I searched through my mind for all the people I had recently met, and those I was only aware of. *Could it be a Brotherhood trap? Maybe they were using me to get to Robert who was much further up the magical totem pole than I was.* I wasn't sure their reach stretched to America yet, or was so subtle that it could subvert an entire household of witches. *Besides how would they get through the wards that guarded the house?*

A cough sounded from the doorway and we turned to look at Marc waiting there hesitantly. "I can answer, at least partly." He scanned the room and was careful not to let his eyes linger on me as he said, "I went through Stella's room." He looked about as guilty as a man could be and I had to stifle a gasp. At least that explained why I hadn't felt any magical trace; Marc didn't have any to leave.

"Why would you do that?" Robert seemed relieved but cautious.

"I had to," Marc explained, taking a step back and holding up his hands as Evan stepped towards him, thunder marring his eyes. "Wait; hear me out. I was told to keep an eye on Stella, watch what she was doing and report back." *Whoa! News to me!* I gaped at him and wondered if it was distrust I saw mingled with the guilt?

Robert was similarly puzzled. "We have no reason to watch Stella, other than to make sure she's safe. What were you looking for?"

"Evidence," Marc said flatly.

"Of what?" It was my turn to question him and, shocked as I might be that he had rifled through my room, I wasn't going to miss my chance.

"Your parents' death," Marc answered.

"What kind of evidence could I have had?" I protested and Marc returned my look with a steely gaze. "I was five years old when they disappeared. Five years old!" I yelled. Marc at least had the grace to look ashamed.

"Mom told me I had to check. She wanted to be sure she's the real Stella. She asked me to find out what Stella knew about her parents' death and said I had to mess up her room to freak her out. I'm really sorry, Stella, I shouldn't have done it."

Boy, this conversation was getting weirder.

"Eleanor never said anything of this to me." Robert looked across at Seren who shook her head. "She was the one who was eager to bring Stella here. She wanted Stella where she could..." He trailed off.

I finished for him. "Watch me," I said, and it felt clearer now.

"Why the hell would Eleanor want to check up on Stella? Why should she suspect a kid of having something to do with her parents' death?" Evan stepped away from Marc and was addressing Robert now but Robert had sunk his head in his hands. When he finally came up for air, his face was chalky white as if he had endured a horrible shock.

"Oh no," he groaned, shaking his head. "Oh no. I should have realised. I should have known."

"I don't understand. Robert, what should you have known?" I might respect my elders but I was tempted to cross the carpet and shake the man. Seren was looking at him in utter bewilderment. I rather thought she might want to give him a shake too.

"There is only one reason why Eleanor would want to know as much as she could about what Stella remembered of Jonathan and Isadore's deaths." Robert scanned us all, his eyes landing on Marc last, his voice heavy with grief and disappointment.

I was sure he would have told us then, but instead, a bright explosion sent us flying from our feet.

CHAPTER ELEVEN

As it turned out it wasn't an explosion; I just assumed it was because that was what my brain rationalised. But it wasn't a bomb or a faulty electricity socket or even a gas line leak. It was a powerful surge of magic that smashed through the room like a tsunami.

The first, a bolt of magic with a purple haze, caught Robert squarely in the chest and he crumpled to the floor, his mouth half open in surprise as we were knocked backwards. I don't know if he even saw what hit him. I sure hoped not. He lay in a pool of his own blood, his torso ripped to pieces by the impact. His eyes glazed over and rolled into his skull as the last bit of life ebbed out of him in a whisper.

Seren vanished from her chair as Evan grabbed me and pushed me through the doorway to the hall while we half scrambled to our feet. Marc was nowhere to be seen and even though I was pissed off, I hoped he wasn't hurt. Seren reappeared in front of us and we almost collided as we skidded down the polished floor of the hallway to the kitchen. Evan pushed me into a corner of the kitchen as a flash of magic rushed past us, like a flame, the heat catching at our skin.

"Jared?" I whispered, wondering, hoping, somehow this magic was merely a horrible accident.

"Definitely. Not." Evan said slowly and decisively. He shook his head and I could see he was desperately worried.

The next flame was followed by Kitty, who had thrown herself through the doorway to the kitchen as shouts of fear and surprise followed her but I couldn't work out who they were from. She crouched near us. "We're being attacked," she whispered incredulously, fear evident in her voice, which rose a couple of octaves.

Seren was crouched on the other side of me and leaned in to whisper. "I'll warn the others."

"Get them out of here," ordered Evan as she flashed out of existence.

Someone screamed and I was just about to peek around the doorframe when Evan pulled me back. "Do you want your head blown off?" he hissed.

"Not really." I muttered. "I'm quite attached to it."

"What the hell is going on?" asked Kitty, keeping her voice to a whisper. "I was just walking down the stairs and got a flame ball thrown at me."

"We were talking to Robert in the living room," I answered, when it seemed Evan wasn't going to respond. "Seren was there but you've already seen she's okay. Marc was there too."

"Where is he? Is he hurt?" Kitty's eyes widened in concern.

I shrugged my shoulders. I wasn't ambivalent but

I certainly wasn't feeling like Marc's best friend right now. "I don't think so."

Evan was listening with more than his ears. The hallway was quiet again and I wondered if Marc had found somewhere to hide. I didn't want to think about the other possibility. "I think Robert's dead," he whispered after a moment and I nodded.

"Stella!" The voice was clearly female and most definitely calling me.

Evan put a hand on my arm, even before I started, and shook his head.

"Stella, I know you're there. We need to talk."

I looked to Evan and he slid his hand down to hold mine, the mere proximity of him giving me the strength I needed.

"I know you were going to tell, Stella." The voice crooned in such a pleasant, cajoling way that I had to remind myself of the inherent danger of answering the woman. "I couldn't let you do that. You would have ruined everything."

"Who the hell is that?" Kitty shuffled closer to me. I wasn't sure if she were trying to camouflage herself by me, or protect me. I wouldn't have blamed her if she started putting some distance between us. "Is it ..?" She looked green.

I paused before I spoke so I could look at Evan. He reflected the same heaviness on his face that I could feel in the pit of my stomach. He must have come to the same realisation as me. That wasn't good.

A tremendous roar disturbed our brief ceasefire. Magic splashed about the hallway, sparks trickling into the kitchen and I heard an agonized scream as feet rushed across the hallway, only to clash with the supernatural malice. It was silenced by the sound of a tremendous crash and a thud as something hit the living room wall.

Seren winked back into existence beside us. "Wasn't me," she whispered.

"Who would send a fool to be a foot soldier?" questioned the phantom voice. She laughed and it was the most unpleasant sound. "I would say 'goodbye, boy,' but he doesn't seem to be alive anymore."

I winced. *Boy? What the hell had Jared been thinking to barge in there?*

Seren's face crumpled as she fought back tears. "Magic is protecting the house, keeping us from getting out or anyone else from getting in. I can't break it," she whispered hurriedly. "I don't know where Étoile or David are. I don't know what she's done but trying to use magic here is like wading through mud. I'm finding it difficult to shimmer."

"Where are Christy and Clara?" Evan asked, keeping his voice low as I started to tremble beside him. Seren reached out to place her arm on me.

"Don't do that," I snapped in a hiss and she scuttled back. She and her sister had done this to me several times before but I'd only just allowed the thought to fully form. They could calm me down to the point of knocking me out when it suited them! "Every time you and Étoile want me to simmer down, you just touch me. I don't need to feel all Zen right now!"

"You could have stopped us any time," Seren shrugged. "We can only influence another witch's feelings as long as she allows it. Besides, your magic leaks when you get angry and it's distracting."

Evan said that to me once, the first time we met. I wasn't even going to go there right now but the sisters and I were going to have a chat later. I rolled my eyes. "Thanks for telling me that now."

"Um, no problem."

"Christy and Clara?" Evan prompted.

"I can't find them," Seren whispered, adding, "I have to look for my sister." She vanished as quickly as she had come.

"She's going to pick us off one by one," growled Evan.

"Why are you doing this?" It was Marc's voice and I tried to work out where it was coming from. He was closer to the living room than the rest of us so perhaps the library, or his room, which opened off the hallway. Next to me, Kitty sighed in relief.

"I just want to talk to Stella," trilled the singsong voice.

"We need to get closer," I said. "I'll move myself through there."

"I'm coming with you," said Kitty as she gripped my wrist. I could probably have disappeared without her but I didn't want to risk losing my arm. Or her's.

Evan started to shake his head, then paused. "Much as I hate to say it, you're right. She's just going to come after us anyway. I'd rather have some chance to do some damage than none at all. Seren is right about the magic. We need to be closer."

"You don't have to come." It tore me to say it; *of course, I wanted him with me... and I didn't.*

"You shouldn't go at all," said Evan, glaring at me like I was about to obey him. I couldn't hide, he knew that. His hand still held mine and I gave it a little squeeze. At last he said, "We'll go together. Moving another person is more difficult than moving yourself and there's a spell weakening all of us. You can draw power from me, if you need to."

"Can I do that?"

"Of course, but not often, and only because I volunteered." I clearly had a lot to learn. "Concentrate."

Evan whispered the location to me and I nodded as I pictured the living room. I envisioned, very precisely, the square of carpet behind the sofa to which he thought we should shimmer. It seemed to be the furthest spot from the door where the voice was coming. I hoped she was occupied with Marc who was unwittingly providing us with some cover. I took a breath, wished and felt the electricity sing through my veins, though I didn't dare close my eyes for even the briefest moment.

We landed, crouched in the same position, with our backs to the sofa instead of the cool kitchen wall. I hoped our magic would somehow be obscured by the recent activity and that we hadn't just announced our presence as loudly as ringing a doorbell. I felt inexplicably exhausted with the effort of moving through space and when I glanced at Evan, he was drawing in the same shallow breaths.

"It's the magic working against us," explained Evan when I looked questioningly at him. "It's going to be rough." He shuffled closer to me and his hand wrapped tighter round mine. "I can see Jared," he murmured in my ear, his voice barely louder than a whisper. Kitty released her grip on me a fraction and I leaned forward to follow Evan's line of sight. Jared lay at an angle, face down. One arm was flung towards us and I strained to see his face.

"Not moving," I whispered back. "But I don't know if he's dead or just hurt."

"I won't let you do this," Marc was saying. I doubted very much that he expected the reply he got as a red-hot flash erupted in the room like a lethal firecracker. There was no noise, except for Kitty's laboured breathing. I felt intense fear coiling within me for the first time in weeks. I couldn't hear a thing in the still room but I sensed the hum of power seeping all around us. It was cloying and terrible; it trailed over my skin, raising the hairs on my arms like static shock.

Evan had taken the opportunity to lean across us and sneak a look around the other side of the sofa. "Robert's definitely dead," he said to us after a long moment.

"Stella, I don't have all day. We need to talk and I know you're in here." There was no cajoling now, the woman just sounded impatient.

"How do I know you won't kill me?" I asked, my voice curiously strong and even, although my hands betrayed me by shaking uncontrollably.

"You have my word."

Somehow, I didn't think that counted for much as I sadly thought of Robert, whom I misjudged so badly, now dead while Jared wasn't moving. I didn't want her to work her way through the rest of my housemates before she got to me. Besides, I wanted to know why she was doing this.

"I'm going to talk to her," I said decisively as Kitty gripped my arm again, frantically shaking her head.

"It's a bad idea, Stella," agreed Evan. "We can come up with a better plan."

I rolled my eyes. "Like waiting here while she picks us off one by one is a good idea? I don't think so. I can't let that happen."

"Then I'm standing up with you. You'll need me."

"No," I shook my head. The thought of Evan getting hurt made my heart contract. "She came for me."

Cautiously, I swivelled on the balls of my feet and raised my head until I could peep above the sofa. After I was sure she had seen me and I wasn't about to get my head blown off, I stood to my full height, my shoulders square and stiff disguising the fear that nearly paralysed me. I kept my shaking hands behind my back.

Eleanor Bartholomew looked back at me and smiled a crazy smile that didn't quite reach her dull eyes. She was dressed like she was about to go to a country club in a pastel twinset and cream pants, as well as a string of pearls around her neck. There was a streak of blood across her top but I don't think she knew it yet. Her hair was impeccable, of course. It was probably de rigueur for society psychopaths to get coiffed first.

She wasn't alone. A woman stood behind her, limp brown hair straggled around her ears. She had a handsome face with sharp cheekbones. At least, she had been striking once. Now her skin was dull, her cheeks sunken and grey with glassy eyes that scanned the room but didn't seem to be registering anything. There was something disconcertingly familiar about her.

"You told Marc to search my room," I said. It wasn't a question; I was just stating a fact.

"Yes."

"It was you who attacked us at your apartment." Again, a statement, but I was curious. "How did you do it?"

"Astra did it." Eleanor reached to her side, her eyes barely leaving my face and stroked the woman's cheek with the back of her hand as I watched. Astra, the sister Étoile and Seren had been searching for, nuzzled against it like an affection-starved puppy. "I had to get you away from them all."

"Which is why you sent me here so Marc could watch me. What was he supposed to find?"

"Evidence." Eleanor shrugged. "I told him to seduce you if he had too. Did he?"

"No." *Sheesh. What kind of mother asks that?*

Eleanor shrugged again. "Spineless, just like his father."

"What did you think I was hiding?"

Eleanor laughed but it wasn't a pretty, happy sound. "Not what you were hiding, dear Stella, but evidence of what I was hiding."

Of course, it was so simple. She had never, for a moment, thought that a five-year-old child could be responsible for killing her parents, despite what she told Marc. She never doubted who I was either.

Eleanor had been the one to kill my parents and she thought I knew. It hit me like a cannon discharged into my chest. She had probably been waiting all this time for her world to crumble.

With fury rising through my bones to bubble in my chest, I sure intended for her to pay for it.

Of course, when you're not thinking straight, you're not thinking tactically and I wasn't thinking at all when I summoned the large plant pot from the hallway and brought it smashing down on her head, yucca, soil, and all. In the split second it took for Eleanor to register what was about to happen, she thrust forth her hands and sent a bolt of magic hurtling towards me.

I froze.

Kitty grabbed my legs and tackled me to the floor, where I sprawled on my back for a moment as Evan leapt up to cover me, completely unshielded, sending forth his own pulse of energy. Power crackled overhead. Evan met Eleanor's force with equal strength and, though not eradicating it entirely, certainly held it at bay and prevented it from reaching us. He stepped around the sofa so that he could pounce forwards, forcing Eleanor to stumble over herself. Beads of perspiration popped and trickled across his forehead and I saw the veins bulge in his forearms as he tapped into the very core of his being to defy her.

He hadn't reckoned for Astra issuing her own blast. I assumed it was she; her magic had a purple tinge to it, unlike the green flashes from Eleanor and the brilliant white of Evan's. I saw the violet-tinged flash of lightning stream towards him and only had a millisecond to yelp a warning. Astra hadn't sent a deadly pulse, but enough to distract him, allowing the green lightning to slash at him before exploding into shards all around us. As I watched in horror from behind the sofa, Evan was lifted from the floor, his face and body contorted as he hung weightlessly in mid-air before being smashed to the ground.

I was rooted to the floor as agony ripped through me, shredding any remote feeling of calm. I had never known pain like this. As I searched for any sign that Evan was alive, I vowed that this battle wouldn't end until one of us was dead; it would be Eleanor or me; that much was clear.

And like hell was it going to be me.

CHAPTER TWELVE

"I loved him," Eleanor whined, her chin trembling with anger. I could barely hear her as I stared at Evan's body, feeling that my whole world was falling apart. "I loved Jonathan. We could have had such a wonderful life together. We would have been happy together, but he wouldn't leave her. He wouldn't leave Isadore." Eleanor spat my mother's name into the air as if it disgusted her. It probably did. Inside my head, the puzzle pieces clicked into place; *the unhappy woman in the wedding photos had been Eleanor, which is why she was gazing at my father. My parents had hidden me with humans where she was never supposed to find me.* My mother had been the love of my father's life, though Eleanor saw her as nothing but an obstacle to her happiness with my father.

"No, you wouldn't, he would never have left my mother!" I was certain of it. I crept upwards, slowly at first, not sure if she would lash out at me. Robert lay dead at Astra's feet and she seemed to be nudging him with her toe. It almost appeared that she wasn't quite certain and thought he might get up with some encouragement. Violet flecks danced on her fingertips.

Eleanor's face tightened and she glared at me as if I had just uttered the most stupid thing. "That's why I killed her. I simply waited until he went out and left her at home. She was with you. I watched you both through the window playing happy family, talking about Daddy coming home. All I had to do was knock at the door and she answered it. It was so easy," Eleanor's eyes took on a faraway look and I edged backwards. "Don't move," she hissed, snapping her attention back to me, her lips twitching upwards at the edges into a strange semblance of a cruel smile. "She was dead before she could even say hello. I snapped her neck. I didn't have to check if she was dead but I did anyway. When I bent down to touch her neck and feel for life, I didn't know Jonathan had come back. He shouldn't have come back!"

I could see the scene in my mind but I didn't know if I was imagining it or remembering something I once witnessed. I could envision Eleanor, a much younger Eleanor, stooped over my mother's inert body in the little porch of our home. I could also see myself, tiny and afraid. The magic hanging about us, cloying and raw, was palpable.

"He saw you with Isadore dead?" I urged her to continue but my heart didn't want to hear what she had to say. I wanted to clamp my hands over my ears and block it all out. Instead, I waited.

"He shouldn't have come back. He shouldn't have come back for hours and by then, I would have been there to comfort him. I would have helped him get over her. There was nothing to stop him loving me once she was gone." Eleanor was hysterical with what she saw as the injustice meted out to her.

"He would never have loved you." *The voice of reason and I were going to have to sit down some day so I could tell it to shut up during life or death moments.*

"Of course, he would have! I would have left Robert and given myself to him. Jonathan would see the sacrifice I made and would have loved me all the more. He always saw the good in others."

"You would have left your own child?" I couldn't imagine how a parent could abandon their own blood. I consoled myself that at least I knew, for certain now, that my parents never turned their backs on me, even though I never really believed that they had. It was strangely comforting to know that I was loved and hidden from harm all these years until I could defend myself.

"Marc would have been fine with Robert. They didn't need me, not like I needed Jonathan." I scanned the room for Marc, then what I could see of the hallway. I couldn't see a body so I assumed he was alive, at least, and within earshot; and my heart pined for him. I wondered if Robert had ever known or suspected what Eleanor had done. I concluded that a part of him had to or he wouldn't have come to warn us; the puzzle pieces clicked just a bit too late for him. He tried to warn me, even hide me again, just as my parents did, in plain sight with people who would protect me, but he was too late and fell into his wife's trap. It was almost too horrible to be true. Eleanor intended to kill us all.

"Why didn't you kill me?" *Did she think she would become my mother or had she planned to get rid of me, the last obstacle between Jonathan and her?*

"The moment I realised Jonathan had seen me, he disappeared. I could smell his magic in the air as he snatched you from inside the house and disappeared. He was back within minutes. He tried to get to Isadore but I pleaded with him. She was gone; I could take her place. I could love him more than she ever did." Eleanor paused and, if I hadn't seen her murder her own husband, then refer to my mother's death with such indifference, I might have pitied her psychosis.

"I tried to show him. I tried to take him inside so I could give myself to him, show him what a wonderful wife I would be to him, but he was furious. I could see the disgust in his eyes. He hated me and I couldn't bear it. I stabbed him and I stabbed and I stabbed; and eventually he died too, leaving me covered in his blood. It shouldn't have happened. He should have been free the moment Isadore was dead. He should have been free to love me. She was the only problem; she always got everything she wanted."

"He would never have loved you," I whispered again. "Never. You are pathetic, sad, deluded and evil. How could anyone love someone like you?"

Eleanor screamed and the veins in her forehead heaved as she shook. She locked her eyes on me and I saw her mouth barely moving as she started murmuring. Behind me, there was a tremendous hiss and rush of air so I could barely hear her. But before I could begin to puzzle what she was voicing, I fell to the side as my arm was roughly yanked down. Just seconds later, the bolt whistled through the airspace my head had occupied only moments earlier. Continually ducking my head was getting to be a very nasty, albeit necessary, habit.

Newly crouched on the floor, I could see Evan lying on his back, his shoulder at a strange angle to the rest of his body. He was bleeding from a jagged cut on his cheek and more blood oozed from wounds across his body. Even in his unconscious state, I could see his face contorted in pain. It was all I could do not to lurch towards him and cover his body with mine.

Kitty caught my eye and shook her head. "You would be totally exposed," she warned. "Stay down. He's not going anywhere and I can see him breathing."

I nodded obediently, heaving with relief. I could just make out his chest rising and falling in shallow breaths. Kitty was right anyway. Unconscious, Evan was hardly a target. Eleanor might even assume he was dead from across the room. If I threw myself out there, she would have me in her line of sight and I didn't know if I could defend myself against her superior strength. Even worse, Evan was definitely no longer a participant in the fight.

I sank from my crouch to the carpet and took a moment to catch my breath, but when I saw Meg lying on the rug a few feet away, sprawled on the floor, it was all I could do to stifle a scream. I hadn't even realised she had snuck into the room. The bolt meant for me had hit her squarely in the chest and, judging by the hole it left behind, Meg was quite clearly dead.

Kitty gripped my hand. "She would have wanted it this way." Before I could twist my neck to glance at her in bewilderment, Meg's corpse began to shrivel and disintegrate, her body sinking into itself. Her pretty, aged features collapsed and became nothing more than ash, enveloped in her cardigan and long floral skirt.

"What the fuck?" I didn't usually curse but after seeing an old lady's bones crumble to dust in front of my eyes, it seemed to be the appropriate comment.

"Well, she was a vampire," muttered Kitty. "That's how they, you know, go."

"She was a vampire?" I repeated incredulously. *Sweet old Meg?* It would have been hard for me to believe if I hadn't seen her ashes still smouldering slightly in front of me. *What else didn't I know?*

"Yes, not particularly by choice, but out of necessity." Kitty was huddled up next to me now as the air crackled over our heads. I wondered where the rest of our household was. I hoped they had the good sense to hide or find a way to break the hold Eleanor had over the house.

"Why would anyone consider it necessary to be a vampire?" I asked.

Kitty hurriedly explained. "Well, her only daughter was really sick and had two little children of her own; then Meg got sick too. Cancer, I think, though they couldn't diagnose it back then. The daughter died and Meg knew her poor health would jeopardise her being able to raise the little ones. So one night, a vampire was passing through and Meg asked to be turned so she wouldn't die and could survive to look after her grandchildren until they were grown. It was an awfully brave thing to do, losing her life just to bring up those kids. What would have happened to them otherwise? They might have starved or been put to work."

"Wouldn't social services have looked after

them?"

"Not a hundred years ago, honey."

"Where are the grandchildren now?"

"Oh, dead a long time I think. Lived until they were old and had grandchildren of their own, thanks to Meg."

"And she still kept on living?"

"She wasn't sure how to end it, but she sure was fed up of it. Especially when Dynasty finished."

"You're kidding?"

"Meg did not joke about Dynasty. Whoa... incoming!"

Kitty and I hit the floor at the same time as the sofa exploded in a heap of foam and ticking fluff. We scrambled to hide behind the last intact sofa, my hands nudging Kitty along until she squawked at me.

"Stella." Eleanor's voice boomed over the melee in a curious mix of venom and cajoling. "Stella, I know where you are. There's no point in hiding. There's no time for hide and seek. Let's end this, Stella. Let's end it now. This should have happened years ago. You're on borrowed time."

I surveyed what I could see. Evan, bleeding, and totally out of it, Meg's ashes, Kitty trembling next to me but whether from fear or anger now, I couldn't tell. The part of the house I could see from the side window was in flames and I could hear shouting. I hoped no one was inside that wing. I pressed myself down and sent out a pulse into the room. Just like before, the strength of Eleanor and Astra's magic made it like walking through jelly, slow and awkward; but I found traces of other beings in the room. We weren't alone. Quickly, I drew back into myself. After a moment, I craned my neck slightly to the left and could just make out Marc and someone else. Yes, the Chinese print jacket sleeve I could just see told me Étoile had returned with Seren and was standing next to him.

"Étoile and Marc are on the other side of the room," I whispered, my voice barely audible, but Kitty nodded.

"Come out Stella and they can all go," coaxed Eleanor.

My eyes connected with Marc and I could just see him give a single shake of his head and my heart went out to him. *How appalling it must be to see your mother, the person who raised you, murder your father, attack your friends as well as her own son, and worse, not be able to do anything about it.* For the first time, I felt lucky that my powers were already part of me and only needed to be tamed to do my bidding.

"The hell you will," I yelled back. "You won't leave any of them alive." I didn't add, not even your own son. It seemed too cruel and I hardly wanted to rub Marc's face in it.

Eleanor laughed and strangely there was a note of joy in it. I had to catch myself from gasping. She was actually enjoying the murder and mayhem and if I wasn't certain before, I was now. I had to end this. Eleanor couldn't be left to destroy any more lives.

I stood and faced the devil.

She grinned at me, the sardonic smile dancing on her lips, her eyes steady but somehow not there. The Eleanor that I had first met in New York was the same twinset and pearls Eleanor here now, but all shreds of humanity had vanished. This one was sinister and destructive and hell-bent on annihilating me. My heart clamoured in fear.

"Come here, Stella."

"Not a chance."

"We should be friends, my dear."

"I refer you to my last answer," I replied caustically.

"We could change the world. Your power and mine. Imagine! There is nothing we couldn't do."

I nodded at Astra who was rocking on the balls of her feet. "Look how your last experiment turned out. No thanks."

Eleanor didn't even spare a glance for Astra. My friends' sister stood behind the older woman, shifting so that she was swaying slightly instead of rocking, but otherwise not doing anything. She wasn't even eyeing up the opposition. Instead, she looked faintly bewildered, like a puppet whose strings had fallen now that the puppet master was looking for a new toy. I struggled to pity her after what she had done to Evan.

Eleanor's smile fell and her face took on the ghoulish air of someone utterly possessed. I couldn't understand why she was bargaining with me; perhaps she was under the same delusion that caused her to think my father would love her after she disposed of my mother. Perhaps, in her deranged mind, she really thought I might consider joining her.

"Last chance," she crooned.

"The answer will always be no."

"Oh Stella, what a mistake you have made. You will have to watch your friends die. One by one, each and every one of them. I'll let you determine the order, if you like?" The words slipped out like she was offering me something delicious.

"You won't hurt anyone anymore." My voice was

firm. *I think*. Inexplicably, I noticed a mist was rolling through the room, rising from the carpet. I glanced over my shoulder and saw Kitty sitting with her eyes closed, muttering a spell. She said she could control the weather and now she was trying to blind Eleanor with it. *Smart.*

"Is that a question, dear Stella?" Eleanor laughed and behind her, Astra shrieked in echo until Eleanor swatted her and she recoiled in silence, a tear rolling down her pallid, mask-like face. Eleanor looked at the mist coiling about her feet with amusement. "Let's start with Kitty, the little weather witch, shall we?" She extended a hand towards our hiding place and began to mutter an incantation. Kitty was drawn into the air, her chin pointing to the ceiling as her legs flailed. She clawed at her throat, her spell shattered, as an invisible hand squeezed and held her mid-air.

"Shall I tear her limb from limb? Or strangle her? Maybe, I should turn her inside out." Eleanor let the various tortures drip from her tongue like she was reeling off the specials of the day. "Or shall I save that for last?"

Kitty screamed. The pitiful shriek drew Astra's attention and she smiled wanly at her as Kitty's left arm stretched above her and cracked. Her legs jerked in the air.

"One down, three to go," Eleanor warbled in a sing-song voice, wagging her finger at Kitty.

Kitty whimpered and her face lost all colour as her right leg bent at an unnatural angle.

"No. No!" I cried. I could feel the electricity coursing through my veins as my fury rose. "You. Will. Not. Do. This!"

I focused the way Evan taught me. I obliterated

the room from my consciousness, taking no note of the pain and fear in the room. I shut out Eleanor's mocking laughter and Kitty's terror. I found Astra's madness and pushed her back. I vaguely registered her shout as I hurled her into the television, knocking DVDs off the shelves to clobber her one by one. The flames and ripped furniture, the glass, the ash and Kitty's mist retreated to the edges of my peripheral vision. I locked my gaze on Eleanor and reached out with my hand to summon my essence. I called with my mind, my heart, my body and my soul. I had never felt more connected to my magic as it rushed through me, light shooting from my fingertips and burning through every pore. I felt the air hot and heavy around me as I glanced off the blows Eleanor aimed at me like they were nothing more than static electricity.

I thrust my hand further forward and yelled. The magic streamed from me into the open and after a moment of horrified silence, the screaming started.

It could have been seconds or eternity for all I could tell of the time passing. I felt the last of the magic fade around me and recede from my fingers. I blinked and when I refocused, Eleanor was kneeling, her head thrown back and her face ashen and lifeless. She began to slide down until she crumpled on the floor, with her head coming to rest at Robert's feet. Astra hadn't moved from where she landed, her legs splayed under her. Her mask was slipping and she looked more perplexed than frightened as if she didn't quite know how she had come to be here. Slowly, she started to move her lips. It took me a moment to realise she wasn't reciting a spell but instead, singing a nursery rhyme. "Twinkle, twinkle, little star..." she whispered in her soprano tone.

I barely registered the flash of blue as Étoile darted across the room from her hiding place and threw her arms around her sister, crushing her arms at her sides. It was more like a straightjacket than an embrace. She nodded at me and they vanished.

"Stella. Stella," Kitty moaned. She had fallen from the invisible grasp of Eleanor's incantation, now that the magic had died with its issuer, and was slumped against the armrest of the sofa. Her skin had taken on a puce green hue and her whole body was convulsing with shock. Marc rose from his hiding place, visibly shaken and scrambling towards her. I wondered if he could feel the magic simmering around him. *No, not around him,* I corrected myself, *coming from him.*

He wouldn't look at me as he dashed past and when I finally turned my eyes from the devastation and rested them on my outstretched hand I could see why.

There sat Eleanor's heart, the red pulpy mass of muscle in my palm, the arterial tendrils draping over as blood dripped to the floor in a staccato rhythm.

It beat for a few moments more, then, very decisively, gave one last shudder and stopped.

Finally, Eleanor's sadistic, vindictive heart was just as dead as the rest of her.

CHAPTER THIRTEEN

I let Eleanor's lifeless heart slip from my hand and fall to the floor with a dull thump.

With bile rising in my throat, I forced myself to look at my outstretched hands. They were stained with her blood. My stomach turned over and I hastily wiped my hands on my jeans as I stepped away from the organ. I reached for Kitty just as Marc vaulted over the sofa. He caught her before she collapsed.

"She needs help," he said, his face was agonised and at last, I understood something else; how much he truly loved Kitty. The pain he must have suffered was terrible. He saw his father die and then the one person he adored being tortured by his mother. His world had collapsed in less than an hour, even if the events that brought us here had been put in motion almost twenty years ago.

Marc eased Kitty into his arms and lowered her to the floor. His hands groped over her sweater and found the mess of her shoulder and arm through the thin jersey, before running down to her leg. Her face was beaded with sweat and pain, her skin ghostly pale. "I think her collarbone and shoulder are broken, her leg too."

I nodded, mute and horrified. "Where did Étoile go?" I breathed finally as I stepped further away, stumbling and almost falling over a broken lampshade. They didn't need me anymore and now that I knew Kitty was safe, I had a more pressing urge. I edged through the debris to Evan and sank to my knees beside him.

"She said she'd take Astra somewhere safe. Somewhere where she couldn't hurt anyone else again, or herself." Marc was cradling Kitty in his arms, her face lolling against his shoulder. Any other time they would have looked serenely content but not now, with their faces torn and scorched. I felt fleetingly glad that I was not envious of the comfort they found in each other's arms. It seemed somehow fitting that they might gain something when so much had been lost.

Evan still hadn't moved. I brushed hair away from my face where it had broken free of its ponytail and shrugged off my sweater so I could press it against him to stem the bleeding from his head wound. I laid my ear on his chest and his heart seemed faint and uncertain as I willed myself not to cry. Of all the people I had come to love and like over these past few weeks, he was the one I couldn't bear to lose and now, he was slipping away at my fingertips. I couldn't understand why he wasn't healing. A salty tear coursed over my smudged face and dripped on him. I felt a little burst of energy echo from me. It was like wearing nylon and getting an electric shock that tickles at the skin, creating sparks.

My back was against the door into the hallway and I could hear other people stumbling through. Whatever magic Eleanor had spun to set up barricades to enclose us in the house had fallen when she did and I breathed a sigh of relief. The air was whispering to me. Help was coming.

I compressed my bare hands harder against Evan's wound, my fear of losing him turning to desperation and felt the current again, but this wasn't the white hot anger I felt when facing Eleanor. I reached inside myself for the last ebb of energy and poured myself into him, not understanding what I was doing but knowing that if I didn't try to fix the internal damage, in some small way, Evan would die with me by his side, never knowing that he saved my life and we won the battle.

He told me I could take power from him and now I was giving it back. Light flickered from me and seeped around my frame and his. It seemed to stream from me to him and, for a few fleeting moments, I felt we were one and the same. I cried with the pain of the work I didn't understand and the pain losing him would cause me. When I could not send any more of my energy to him, I crouched over him and rested my head on his chest, my silent sobs shaking me. I could feel him; not just his skin or his fading warmth but the magic welling in him. I could see it. It was like a light cord had been yanked thrusting me into the sun after a lifetime of darkness. The magic trickling through him was white hot but it was fading too. My heart thumped. He was so weak.

It was Étoile who lifted me off him, then pulled me to her and let me finish weeping dirty tears on her favourite jacket. I didn't even realise she had returned and I briefly wondered where Astra was.

"He's alive," said Étoile, pushing me away gently so she could rest her long fingers against the pulse on Evan's neck. A haze of pink seemed to trip languidly over her. "But we need to move him now. Eleanor's magic has interfered with ours and he can't heal here."

"Stella, darling, we're going to get Evan some help." Seren delicately pried my fingers from where they were coiled around his shirt's placket.

"I'll come too."

Seren shook her head. "We aren't strong enough. It will take both Étoile and I to move him and we can't manage another. We'll come back for you, I promise."

Before I could say anything, she and Seren were holding Evan with one hand while clasping each other's hand. They locked eyes and vanished, leaving the air charged with magic for a few plaintive moments. I could see, feel and smell magic everywhere around me. I felt like I was drowning in it.

Exhausted, I stayed on my knees where Evan had fallen, the debris forming a makeshift marker around the place where he lay. Choking back the last of my tears, I wiped the few escapees from my smudged face with my sleeve. I tried to feel relief that Evan would soon get help, but all I could feel was a desperate sadness. My throat felt raw from the sobbing as well as the acrid taste of burning and Kitty's mist. My body was shattered. I knew I couldn't do this anymore. I never expected to have to fight for my life. I never expected that I would have to kill. *In self defence,* a weary part of my mind reminded me. *I never wanted to kill. Or be a killer. It was self defence.*

I fully expected to die in this room, I suddenly realised and the panic started to rise in me.

Kitty groaned behind me and the noise brought me rushing back to the present. When I turned to them, I saw a faint sheen surrounding both her and Marc. Marc was brushing his fingertips at the colour around his coat in wonder.

"What is it?" he whispered.

"Your magic," I said simply.

A thought had been niggling at me for a while, never quite becoming a fully formed idea but now I knew what had held Marc back. Eleanor had spellbound her own child so that his magic could never come to fruition. It was illegal among witches, so her reasons for doing it to her own child were beyond me. I could never be sure, but I suspected jealousy and bitterness had a lot to do with it. She resented Robert's lack of intuitive power, considering him weaker than she, and I wondered if she might've been frightened of Marc's potential, just as she had been frightened of mine.

Instead of nurturing her son, she caged him in a life which had no value in her world. She continued to resent him, and taunt him, because she planned to leave him behind. Perhaps there was no rhyme or reason to it. Perhaps it was just another act of her cruelty.

"It has a colour?"

"I think because it's suddenly come back after so long. It's more intense." It was a guess but it sounded right, though I faltered when I thought about it. I had never seen a colour surround anyone else until moments ago; but Evan had seen mine the first time we met. I wondered if everyone with magic could see auras like Marc's pulsing, shimmering emerald – so much more vibrant than his mother's pallid hue – and I wondered what he would be able to do now. I hoped the return of his magic made him happy and gave him a place in the world that both accepted and excluded him. I hoped he wouldn't be too hard on Étoile for teasing him all this time.

"You need to get Kitty out of here."

Kitty was lying unconscious in his arms but every so often she would let out a low groan. I suspected her physical recuperation would be lengthy once the bones were realigned. I hoped she would recover mentally too. Apparently, I was hoping for a lot at that moment. *Maybe if I spread the hope around like a splatter gun something would stick.*

Marc nodded. "Where should I take her?"

"You know better than I. There must be someone you can call?"

David was scrambling towards us. His glasses had been knocked from his face and his hair stood up in tufts. He looked downright shell-shocked.

"We need to find Christy and Clara. They must be terrified," he said, his voice unsteady. He looked around the room and groaned. I followed his gaze to Jared's body. He wasn't moving and I could see the whites of his eyes. We scuttled towards him.

"He had such promise," David muttered, staring down at him. "With time, he would have been really good. I shouldn't have unbound him, but I couldn't leave him unprotected. The idiot. The brave idiot."

I took David's hand in mine and he patted my hand with his free one. We looked at Jared for a moment, then David leaned forward very slowly and used his fingertips to draw Jared's eyelids down.

"He didn't deserve this," I said and David inclined his head in the briefest of nods.

Behind us, I heard Marc dialling on his phone before speaking urgently into it. After a few moments, someone else teleported into the room: a young woman in jeans and a cropped jacket. She knelt beside Kitty and felt for her pulse, timing it against her watch.

"We got your call just as Étoile and Seren arrived," she explained hurriedly as if Marc was about to admonish her for being tardy. She sniffed the air and grimaced. "Is anyone else injured?"

Marc shook his head. "No. I don't know. I don't think so."

"Let's go." The woman put her hands on Kitty and Marc. They were gone before I could ask after Evan, or where they were going, or even who she was.

"Someone will be here soon," said David, who lingered in the doorway. "If they weren't alerted at the hospital, someone else will sound the alarm. No surge of magic like this goes unnoticed."

"How would they notice?"

"They just do. The council notices everything."

"They didn't notice Eleanor," I said, still unable to look at her. I had a right to be sceptical. The head of their organisation was a maniacal murderer who escaped their notice for years.

It was David's turn to be cynical. "I wouldn't be so sure of that." He was stroking his scar again, in that absent-minded way of his.

I looked at him with curiosity. *Would they really have let Eleanor get away with murder?* I wasn't sure of anything, except that I didn't trust the council as far as I could throw them. The corpses surrounding me – those of Robert, Eleanor, Jared, and what was left of Meg – were testimony to their neglect and ignorance without even counting the injured. The council were at best indifferent, at worst, incompetent, in my opinion.

David returned my gaze with a cool look of his own and I wondered if I should reassess the geeky teacher. Perhaps he knew more than he was letting on, but my chance to ask him was foiled as something heaved against the front door. It splintered and twisted off its hinges. I braced myself for attack as a small group of men charged in, dressed to the nines in SWAT gear with the most enormous weapons. I would have reacted on instinct if David hadn't immediately lurched between them and me as he greeted them, running a shaky hand through his dusty hair.

"We're here," said one man, somewhat obviously, as he stepped forward. He shook David's hand as if they were at a business meeting rather than a crime scene. "Is the problem contained?"

"The problem is dead," I muttered from behind David. I could feel the shadows of Evan's power behind me; it seemed to hang in the space. I didn't want to look at the imprint he left behind in the debris, lest I unleash the uncried tears bubbling inside me.

The man who appeared to be the leader looked past David to me and then around the scene. He surveyed the damaged room and the results of Kitty's mist and the conflicting incantations from Eleanor. I realised that Robert never had a chance to spin a spell of his own before he met his fate. Residual magic seemed to hum in the thick air, like a stagnant heat wave.

"We'll remove the bodies," said the team leader, nodding at his men who were waiting for instruction. "And we'll put everything to rights."

"The council knows about this?" David asked.

"The order came from Steven," confirmed the leader, removing his mask to show an unremarkable middle-aged face. "Killed a vampire, huh?" He looked vaguely pleased and full of admiration as I remembered Meg. Her ashes still smouldered in a heap a few feet away from me. I didn't think there was anything to celebrate about her losing her life. As far as I knew, she was a sweet old lady who offered room and board to people she didn't have to give a damn about. I didn't want to get my head around the bit about her being a vampire just yet. Now that I had witches and vampires checked on my list, I didn't even want to think about what else might be out there. I still wasn't even certain what Evan was.

"She was a good person," I muttered, too weak to argue. I was almost grateful that the SWAT guy let it pass without comment.

The crew ignored me. "Anyone else we should know about?"

David took the lead again. "There's just me and Stella here. Christy and Clara somewhere too; I guess they're hiding. Everyone else has gone." He looked around for his students, like it just dawned on him that he had no idea where they were.

The man nodded and turned his back to issue directions to his team. Some of them fanned out through the house, weapons at the ready. When they returned a few minutes later, they whispered to their team leader and he turned to us impassively. "They found two more bodies upstairs. Two girls."

David nodded, his head bowed. He sighed. "Christy and Clara. What happened to them?"

"According to my team, they were hit by a pulse of magic that took them straight out. They wouldn't have felt a thing."

It was strange to hear a magical SWAT team use the same platitudes that a regular cop would use. I was too exhausted to comment; too worn out to even cry. I didn't know if I should feel relief or anguish as the crew retreated outside. Presently, they came back, minus their helmets and protective vests, carting cases loaded up with chemicals and mops. They were like a domestic cleaning crew, but on steroids.

I couldn't take anymore. I'd have to leave the questions and any supervision to David who, thankfully, had been spared most of the fighting. For me, the idea of talking calmly and logically about what happened was just too much.

Stumbling past them, I lurched out of the room and aimed for the stairs. If I'd been in my right mind, or even a little less tired, I could have zapped myself to my room but I had to salvage what little energy I had left.

The upstairs landing was just about intact and no one had been fighting in the bedrooms. My room was exactly as I left it.

I headed straight for the bathroom and scrubbed my face and hands until they were pink and clean. I wanted to throw up as I pulled off my bloody clothes, dumping them on the bathroom floor. *Maybe the cleanup crew would take them* I hoped as I pulled on clean jeans, a tee and zip-up sweatshirt. I didn't want to see a single stitch of those clothes ever again.

When I stepped into my bedroom, still slightly rumpled from Marc's rifling, the weight of what happened hit me. All the adrenaline that had kept me upright and talking dissolved and I dropped to my knees in the centre of the room, my chest heaving as the sobs wrenched my heart.

CHAPTER FOURTEEN

I waited for three days and no one came.

That night, my world fell apart again and I spent it sitting at the top of the staircase, my knees huddled to my chest with one of Evan's sweaters wrapped around me. It was the only place I could perch to watch the supernatural clean-up crew as they put the house to rights without getting in their way.

Four of them stayed, each in navy jackets and caps so dark they were almost black, speaking quietly to each other while they worked. Though they didn't use any magic, there was something "other-worldly" about them and I knew they weren't the type of workmen you would find in a regular phonebook. I didn't know how to call them, or how Steven was tipped off to our plight, but I felt glad someone had sent them to clean up the mess that had been left behind. I was sure they would send a full report back to the council and it wouldn't be pretty.

They took Eleanor and Robert's bodies first, zipping their corpses in body bags and moving them to a waiting van. I heard what I thought was the foreman, who doubled as supernatural SWAT leader, and another workmen discussing the "accident" they would stage to cover up the deaths so no questions would arise from the regular authorities. Apparently, they would "die" in a fireball of a car accident on their way home to the city from a short distance away. Their brand new Mercedes would be driven down from their apartment to complete the picture. It was plausible and a good way to ensure their estate wouldn't be wrapped up in probate for years on account of their disappearance or any autopsy investigating why Eleanor's heart was missing with no visible wound. Marc would be able to grieve publicly. No one would know Eleanor was a murdering maniac. No one would ask questions. People would eventually move on.

They took Jared next. As I looked at his frozen face before they zipped him up, I thought it was such a waste that he had been killed for nothing. I wondered if he had family and who would mourn him. I hoped someone would. I didn't see them take Christy and Clara and I felt grateful I didn't have to see their once vibrant bodies now lifeless. I'd never thought of them separately – they were always Christy and Clara, never one or the other – and it reassured me a little to think they were eternally together now.

The bodies gone, the remainder of the team started the cleaning process and I was surprised that they had regular cleaning chemicals among their kit. I don't know what I expected them to use. The living room and hallway had taken the worst of the violence. The team soaked the blood from the floor and removed rugs, stacking debris in the hallway.

Curtains were pulled down and the sofas were "ummed" and "ahhed" over before being finally removed. They were totalled.

I watched from the stairs as they swept up Meg's ashes. I could hardly believe that she had lived for decades only to be murdered in her own house. I wondered if she was relieved her long life was, at last, over. I hoped she was at peace. I also hoped to hell she was the only vampire I'd ever meet because I was sure she wasn't indicative of her kind.

David sat with me for a while but we didn't speak. Having him next to me, however, was a small comfort and stopped me having a melt-down.

When the workmen came to the area where Evan's wound still stained the floor, the wood inexplicably started to bubble. At first, I thought magic had charred it.

"Fucking daemons," one of the men spat in a cockney accent, his face filled with disgust as he poured solution from a jar he'd uncapped. I wondered how he came to be so far from London but I'd never ask. "Can't live with 'em, can't clean up after 'em." The wooden floor began to fizz against the chemicals and the smell coiled towards me. I couldn't watch anymore. My stomach heaved and I made it to the bathroom with only seconds to spare before I hurled into the bowl.

I stayed away from the cleaning crew after that. I didn't want to think about what they meant by daemon. I didn't get the impression the cockney man felt it was some kind of racial slur, but rather a statement of fact and that worried me. I knew Evan was something else but I assumed it was something more akin to me. I had no frame of reference for daemons.

"They're like us, but not like us," David told me. I sat on my bed with my head bent over my knees to stop the dizziness from making me pass out. My cranium was throbbing again; the pain that began during the fight had edged up to my temples. "Daemons are magic, like us, but it's a different kind of magic. Our magic can be divided into two; witchcraft and pure magic. They're just pure magic." He made them sound like a cereal choice.

"Demons are evil," I said, my voice squeaking through my arms.

"Daemons," David emphasised. I felt the bed indent as he sat down next to me. "They look like us, some of them, and gradually, you'll be able to tell them apart from humans, witches and well ... everything else." I didn't even want to think about what he meant by that as he continued. "They share magic with us but they are faster and stronger, among other assets, and they can shift between planes. Just because Evan is a daemon doesn't mean you have to think any differently of him."

"Why didn't he say anything?" I was pitifully aware my voice had become a thin whine.

"I guess because so many witches hate his kind. It's kind of a mutual thing."

"You all don't hate him," I protested.

David shook his head. "No, but we're not all entirely comfortable with him either."

"How can you say that?" I raised my head to glare at him. "You lived under the same roof as he. He took a blast for me!" I didn't bother to add that we still didn't even know if he had lived through it.

"If you ever have the misfortune to meet other

daemons, the kind you don't want to meet, you'll see." David gulped as if he had unpleasant memories to swallow. "Evan is very, very powerful and we're lucky he's not against us, but other daemons are. Plus, he's my friend and he might freak me out at times, but I can deal with that." Fatigued, I collapsed and let David wrap his arms around me as I cried on his shoulder.

Still, no one came for me.

On the third day, I woke alone in the house. I couldn't find David, though his car hadn't moved. I had no way to contact Étoile or Seren. They promised to come back for me once Evan was safe. The clean-up crew had finally gone and the house was looking perfect again even though the living room was missing its array of comfortable furniture. My head still hurt and the panic was rising in me as I gasped for breath.

With a knot in my chest, the ragged sobs ripped from me as soon as I went back to my room after searching through the house. I hunched forward on my bed, my balled fists pressed against my streaming eyes. When the tears finally subsided, I wiped my eyes with the backs of my hands and dried them on the blanket. Only one thought echoed through me. *Since they hadn't come back, Evan's injuries must have been more severe than we thought.*

He might even be dead.

Perhaps they didn't want to come back for me.

The unpalatable thoughts swirled in my head and I cried again for my lot before I managed to stagger off to my bed. I fell asleep in my clothes and felt musty and unkempt. On auto-pilot, I brushed my teeth and hair, splashed water on my tear-streaked face and pulled on fresh jeans and a button-down shirt. After a moment, I shucked them again, showered quickly and pulled my clothes back on when I was properly clean.

From the bathroom doorway, I looked around my room. *I loved it here,* I realised with a pang of sadness that cut deep into me. I felt safe, mostly, and amongst friends. For a while, I felt that a future with Evan might be on the cards.

I couldn't help remembering the last time I'd packed so fast. My grimy hovel in London was a distant memory and I'd acquired so much more since then. Not material things but friendship, someone I loved and who, I thought, might have loved me. It hurt to acknowledge that I had lost my new life even faster than my old one.

Evan might die – might have died – because he tried to protect me with the speed and strength David said daemons possessed, against a malevolent, vengeful witch at the top of her game. The anxiety gripped me like a fracture spreading through my being and I clutched my head. Kitty had been tortured because of me. I attacked Astra, the sister Étoile and Seren had tried to find and save. Even Meg's unnaturally long life had come to a swift end. Not to mention extracting Eleanor's heart from her body while her son watched. *I was probably quite unlikely to win Friend of the Year.*

It was the oldest story in the book, of course. Unrequited love devastated not just one family's lives, not just robbed me of a mother and father but also of the love they would have given me. They would have been my guides through this strange life but they lost me, and I them, in the minutes it took to snatch their lives from them. I could only fleetingly be glad that my father had made the snap decision, in his terror, to hide me before returning to my mother's side and dying. I had no doubt Eleanor would have snuffed me too, even though I was just a child.

Eleanor was mad. I could never be sure if it was due to the grief of not being loved back, the grief of having to remain with a husband she considered her inferior, or a son she didn't care for, or because she was already on the precipice of insanity.

She spent years subverting herself in her misery, pretending to be the perfect wife; and then I stumbled into her home, on the run from witch hunters. Yet, she couldn't even let me go then. It was all too clear. She had glimpsed me in the house that night almost two decades ago and never lost her fear that I would remember she killed my parents. She thought I would avenge their deaths and tried to kill me first. By that point, she didn't care who she took down with her.

The sad thing was that I didn't remember ever seeing her. If Eleanor had left me alone, I might never have known the reason for my parents' death or her role in it. I would have stayed entirely oblivious. There was some sort of cruel irony in that.

It didn't take me long to pack again. I tucked my blue box of keepsakes and papers in the top of my bag and zipped it shut, rearranging the contents so the one thing I would need first was right at the top. As I took one last look around the room in the house of happiness and heartbreak, at the pretty yellow walls and the window that offered me a last glimpse of the waves breaking against the beach if I craned my head just far enough, I felt a great upsurge of sadness wash over me again.

I breathed in the house for the last time, then closed my eyes, picturing the place I wanted to be and with all the strength that I had left in me, ported myself out of there.

When I opened my eyes again, I was facing the bridge as I intended. I hoisted my bag up on my shoulder and curled the strap of it around my hand. I turned towards the town. Though I was too far to see the house, I didn't dare look back in case I broke down. Everyone was now safe, and whatever help that had been offered had come and gone. They didn't need me now. I caused them so much anguish and they all defended me until they couldn't. The threat was gone and I hoped one day they would forgive me too.

It took me twenty minutes of walking to locate the car rental building that I glimpsed once before, on the day I drove past with Kitty. It was a small building, quite uninspiring but serviceable with a big placard on the front proclaiming "Jackson's Nationwide Car Rental". Inside, a pasty-faced clerk sat behind a desk that spanned the length of the office. He was chewing gum, his hair tipping forward over his forehead and brushing his collar at the back as he pored over a car magazine. He'd slung on a tie but the knot was too tight so the tails trailed limply on the desk.

I showed him my new license and asked for a small car, whatever he had. He tapped on his computer keyboard and told me there was a Toyota available, just filled up, quite new, but unremarkable and available all week I was to drop it off at any of their partner agencies. I agreed and as he went to the little room behind the desk to get me the keys, I muttered a little spell. As soon as I left, the computer would "lose" the information entered by the young clerk and when anyone thought to inquire, it would seem like a computer malfunction.

No one would be blamed. I paid for the car in cash for the whole week, even if I wasn't sure I'd need it that long, and the car would be dropped off in exactly the same condition it was when I hired it. The spells I wove would ensure the clerk couldn't quite give a description other than I was a "nice local gal". If I was going to make a clean break of things, I had to start right now on my way out of town.

The clerk showed me out around the side of the building where the car was waiting in a small parking lot. He unlocked it for me and showed me the button to press on the keypad. I thanked him and threw my bag on the passenger side. He watched me with mild amusement as I assessed the automatic gears and worked out if my feet were hitting the right pedals before I fired up the engine and cautiously drove off the forecourt. Turning south, towards the highway that would take me out of town, I saw him give a half hearted wave from my rear view mirror. He would forget my face within minutes.

After a few miles, it occurred to me that I should have probably bought a map and some food while I was still in town so I pulled off at the next exit and found a gas station within a few blocks. I pulled into a parking bay, out of the way of the pumps, and locked the car. I bought a map, a big one covering the country and a smaller, local one for the state, along with a six pack of soft drinks, a chicken sandwich and some snacks to keep me going. Again, I paid cash, and again, the cashier would not recognise me if anyone happened to inquire about an English girl passing through.

I ate the tasteless sandwich in the car, with the engine off, and spread the map out across the wheel, marking off my route by pen. I wished I had thought to hire a navigation system that would just tell me where to aim the car. It probably would have signalled motels too, but *hasty exits don't always come with the best laid plans* I reminded myself. I folded the map on the seat next to me on top of the blue box, which I patted absently with one hand, like it was a pet. After I ate my sandwich, I got out of the car to toss the wrapper in the trash can. Minutes later, I started up the engine and turned back onto the road, putting my pedal to the metal, as they say.

I knew where I was headed and felt glad that I had, at last, a home to go to. One that was truly my own and where I would, I hoped, be safe. It wasn't the home I once dreamt about, where Evan and I would be cuddled on a porch together. Hell, I didn't even know if it had four walls and roof but I did know that it had some significance to my parents once and there had been a lot of love between them, love that kept them together even in their last moments of life.

If anything was a recipe for starting over, that was it. It would, of course, be an absolute bonus if the house I was driving towards had walls and a roof because I wasn't planning on adding "builder" to the list of things I could do. I also doubted my magic had any power when it came to a hammer and nails.

The thought of Evan set the waterworks going again and this time, barely forty miles out of town. I had to pull over to let the gasping, wracking sobs heave from me as I gripped the steering wheel like it was a life belt. I snivelled into my sleeves and wiped my eyes with the backs of my wrists as I wondered where the hell Étoile and Seren had taken him and whether he was still alive. I wondered if the pain in my body would ever lessen and since the pain was the last connection I'd had to him, would I even want it to? I forced my tears back down. If I let the great chasm of grief inside me – all that desperation and sadness and that awful aching need to have Evan with me – open up now, I would surely fall apart.

"Pull yourself together," I sniffed, trying to make my voice stern and pep talk myself into business. "Put on the radio. Get back on the road."

I twizzled the dial until I found a radio station that was playing something upbeat and fired the engine back up. I turned on my indicator, edging back onto what I still considered the wrong side of the road. I didn't think I had any tears left in me which was just as well because with the mileage I was going to put in over the next few days, I wanted to be wide awake and alert.

I drove all day until I was tired enough to pull into a motel and sleep for a few hours. After a vending machine breakfast the next morning, I was back on the road and drove for several hours until I spotted the next large town. I circled until I could find another of the chain rental places. This one was next to a car dealership. I didn't stop, but noted the location and drove on a little further.

My next objective was a bank. I withdrew a chunk of the cash in my account. It was no small sum and the teller was awkward about giving it to me, but she did so nevertheless and I stuffed it into my bag. I would work out what to do with it later, but right now all I could remember was Étoile's warning that it was possible to track people electronically. I couldn't afford to leave a trail for myself by using my bank cards.

I wasn't sure I wanted to be found. I wanted a life. And until then I would be paying for everything by cash.

I drove back to the rental chain building, parked and took my bags out, one now loaded with cash. I went inside to return the keys and was quick to place my hand on the computer when the clerk wasn't looking. He was surprised when the machine seemed to combust, little sparks exiting the monitor. I heard the computer fizzle angrily under the desk.

"Good job you paid already," he said, giving the monitor a pointless slap, perplexed at the computer's sudden demise.

"Absolutely," I agreed, forcing a perky smile onto my face as I watched a news item run across the screen. "Three women have been found burned in New England towns with sinister messages left at the scenes" said the recap rolling across the screen. I felt my breath catch as a shiver spread through me and my smile faded. *The Brotherhood had made it to America, and the prognosis was surely not good.* Aware that the clerk was watching me, I thanked him for his time and hurried out.

I took a Greyhound bus for the next few hundred miles, partly doubling back on myself to confuse any potential followers, my bags safely stowed next to me in the seat. I slipped off at a large town and took a cab from the bus station to the nearest reputable car dealership, according to the cabbie.

I took an hour to circle the cars, asking a few questions from an eager middle-aged salesman and eventually bought a small car with some of the cash. It wasn't new but it had low mileage and a good service history. I took the keys and paid them extra to fill the tank.

I drove for the rest of that day, the cash tucked away in my bag. By the evening, I was familiar with the new car, had tuned the radio, and adjusted the seat until it felt comfortable to me. It had a CD player and I reminded myself to get some CDs to stash in the glove box. It was the first time I'd ever owned a car and it seemed exciting that I could just point and go as I desired. Even driving on "the wrong side" was starting to feel natural with practice.

It took me a day longer than I estimated to get to my destination. That was partly my fault for missing a couple of exit signs and driving further than I had to only to double back. I slept in little motels in towns that were only names on a map. They were comfortable, unremarkable but safe and I could shower and rest. I ate from service stations and fast food places. By the third day, my body started to hate junk. I craved fruit and had to circle around to find a market to buy a bag of apples. I stopped off to eat one in the pretty town square with an immaculate lawn and flower beds, flanked by shops painted every shade of pastel. There was a gazebo in the middle and they seemed to be holding some sort of fete. It was pretty and genteel and I hoped the residents were happy there before I slid back into the driver's seat and left as quickly as I had arrived. As per usual, no one remembered me as soon as I was gone and that was how I wanted it to be.

I knew I hit the small town of Wilding before I had consulted the map or spotted a sign. There was something about the town that enveloped me the instant I drove into the town limits.

I had to pull over a couple of times and try and guess where I was and eventually, with the lack of landmarks, I just gave up and drove into town. I parked outside a diner on what seemed to be the main street of the attractive town. It had an old world feel to it with its hand-painted shop signs and storefronts. It was past the lunch hour inside and the waitress was hovering by the counter, chewing on a pencil, while she watched the last of the straggling diners. She took one look at me and the address I had scrawled on a piece of notepaper and pursed her lips in thought for a moment before writing down some directions on a napkin.

"Not many people head out that way, honey," she drawled, tucking a piece of bleached blonde hair behind her ear. Her embroidered name plate read "Darla." "It's not a big residential area."

"But this house is there?" I replied, checking the address again and Darla's directions.

"Well sure it is, honey, or I couldn't have told you where it was, and real pretty it is too. And there's another one right across the street, but that's all." Darla flicked a finger at my notepaper. "What you doing, going out there?"

"I might be living there."

"There's a lot more nicer places in town, you know. With bars and shops and stuff a pretty girl like you needs. You bought that place? You could probably get a good price for it. I hear it comes with some land."

I smiled at her. "I best check it out first."

"Sure, honey, you do that. You come on back soon and tell me how you like it."

I nodded and stuffed a couple of small bills in the tips jar Darla had sitting on the counter, seeing as I hadn't ordered anything and she hadn't insisted on forcing a menu on me. When I got back to the car I almost regretted not taking a seat at the counter and getting something to eat, but I was hungrier to see the house. I drove away from the route I'd taken in and followed Darla's directions back out of town.

Being on the smaller side of towns, it wasn't complicated to follow her directions and I was on the right road in minutes. I passed through town and followed the tree-lined street past the occasional house and a building that I guessed was a bar with several cars parked outside. The boarding spread across the building read "Loup Garou". I would have to look that up, I thought, storing the unfamiliar words away in my mind as I turned my eyes back to the road.

My parents' house was exactly where Darla said it would be and was, as she said, real pretty too. With no cars in the vicinity, I didn't bother with the turn signal, but drove off the tarmac onto the dirt drive that curved towards the house.

The house was set at a right angle to the road with a carport off to one side but I parked right in front. It was a ranch house with white clapboard, just one storey high and a wide porch with spindle rails and four steps leading up to it. The front door and windows either side looked out over a large, neatly kept lawn and the porch seemed to have been swept recently. The only tyre prints on the drive came from my own newly purchased car. I wondered what it would be like to marry, or raise a family there, and the pain cut through me like a knife as I shoved the memories of Evan firmly into a corner of my mind. *If he lived, I would find him one day.* I clung to the idea like a security blanket.

I unclipped my seatbelt and rummaged in the blue box for the small envelope that held the key, then, leaving everything else inside, I stepped out to look around.

The afternoon sun was high in the sky and I held a hand like a visor over my face. I breathed in the fresh air, which carried with it the scent of grass and pine. Something in the atmosphere tugged at my psyche.

About a hundred yards away, and across the road, stood another house. It was similar to this but with a second storey and situated so as to face the road. There were a couple of chairs parked on the porch, one rocking slightly in the breeze and some tubs of greenery. A wind chime hung from the porch rafters that tinkled in the gentle breeze and the sound made me smile. Parked furthest from the house was a truck, a small blue car next to it and then, a little way back, the shiniest motorcycle I had ever seen. That house was clearly occupied and I wondered if it had been they who swept this porch and kept the lawn tidy. As I watched, a man sat up in one of the chairs. He looked at me for a long moment before raising a hand. I waved back.

I turned from the neighbouring house, walked around the car and skipped up the steps and paused. *I could feel the magic.* I could sense it more decisively here, but just as I began to wonder about it, I felt the magic flitter around, recognise me then recede and fade until it had gone. Instinctively, I understood.

David mentioned such a thing in a lesson once. Wards had been spun about this place, wards that would ensure it would be left alone until such a time that it was reclaimed by someone it recognised. I wondered if it had been my parents doing and if they knew they would never return. I was glad that they had the foresight to protect their house but maybe it was something they always did. I didn't have the good fortune of growing up with my people, my birthright, so I could hardly distinguish between fortuitous planning and everyday business.

I crossed the porch to look in the windows. The curtains were open and I could see that the place was clean and free from the cobwebs and rodents, which I might have expected after enduring more than twenty years unoccupied. I wondered if this was thanks to the wards, but maybe it was courtesy of whoever had kept the lawn trimmed. *I would have to find out about that.*

Slipping the key into the lock, I expected it to be stiff after years of disuse, but it sprang open as if it had been newly oiled. I breathed a sigh of relief, the weight of my new life slipping casually about my shoulders like a favourite shawl.

There were groceries to buy, of course, utilities to connect, if necessary. A new town to explore. Regular, mundane things to bring me into my new life, the life I might have had if my path hadn't been maliciously diverted. But I could lay my parents to rest now and I knew when I found Evan, I would find my peace. I touched my fingers to my temples; my headache was finally gone.

I smiled, stepped over the threshold and shut the door on my past.

Continue the Stella Mayweather series with Unruly Magic, out now in ebook and paperback!

A witch on the run.

A quiet little town where everything is far from normal.

A fractured witch council threatening to tear the supernatural world apart.

Life hasn't been easy for novice witch Stella but small town life seems to be agreeing with her. When a seemingly innocent girl begs for her protection, Stella is pulled into a dangerous game of unruly magic.

With bewitching friends and two super-sexy and mysterious men by her side, Stella is plunged into a mystery where she must uncover dangerous secrets before she ends up paying the ultimate price.

www.ingramcontent.com/pod-product-compliance
Lightning Source LLC
La Vergne TN
LVHW091023080826
845145LV00002B/333